PRAISE FOR
The Summer Before

"*The Summer Before* is a gripping and emotionally charged exploration of trauma, guilt, and the unyielding strength of friendship. With the intensity of Kate Elizabeth Russell's My Dark Vanessa and a haunting complexity that lingers long after the last page, this novel offers a profoundly empathetic and thought-provoking examination of the aftermath of a harrowing experience and its far-reaching consequences."

—Anna David, New York Times bestselling author and CEO, Legacy Launch Pad Publishing

"Emotionally resonant and brimming with hope, *The Summer Before* is a pulse-pounding recounting of how tragedy twists and shapes family, friendship, and life as we know it."

—Taylor Higgins, international bestselling author of *Between the Stitching*

"Masterfully crafted, *The Summer Before* is a poignant exploration into the repercussions of evil, even for those on the periphery of a crime. Part love story, part coming-of-age story, part legal thriller, Braley weaves a meaningful story of love, healing, and ultimately hope. An emotional page-turner I couldn't put down."

—Suzanne Redfearn, Amazon bestselling author of *In an Instant*

"*The Summer Before* gives readers a shocking and raw look at the devastation that is left in the wake of childhood trauma and abuse. When one woman takes a closer look at the complex details that caused her relationships to implode, she can finally face her existence built on a lifetime of lies and shame. With powerful writing, Braley gets everything right, from the smallest detail of the Jaws Bridge in Martha's Vineyard to exactly how guilt can bring you to your knees and not let you back up until you are ready to face the truth. A unique point of view on a gut-wrenching topic makes this book hard to put down and will stay with you long after you have read the last page."

—Addison McKnight, author of *An Imperfect Plan* and *The Vineyard Remains*

"Propulsive and emotional, *The Summer Before* is a powerful story about the evolution of a formative friendship layered with years of secret trauma. I devoured Braley's sharp and vivid prose, and I rooted for her complex, authentic characters from beginning to end."

—Julia Spiro, bestselling author of *Someone Else's Secret* and *Full*

The Summer Before

by Dianne C. Braley

© Copyright 2024 Dianne C. Braley

ISBN 979-8-88824-484-5

All rights reserved. No part of this publication may be reproduced, stored in a retrieval system, or transmitted in any form or by any means—electronic, mechanical, photocopy, recording, or any other—except for brief quotations in printed reviews, without the prior written permission of the author.

This is a work of fiction. The characters are both actual and fictitious. With the exception of verified historical events and persons, all incidents, descriptions, dialogue and opinions expressed are the products of the author's imagination and are not to be construed as real.

Published by

◢ köehlerbooks™

3705 Shore Drive
Virginia Beach, VA 23455
800-435-4811
www.koehlerbooks.com

the Summer Before

Dianne C. Braley

VIRGINIA BEACH
CAPE CHARLES

*To the victims, both loud and silent:
You are not broken. May you find solace, healing,
and the support you rightfully deserve.*

"She was powerful, not because she wasn't scared but because she went on so strongly despite the fear."
—Atticus

Chapter 1

The wind picked up, sending leaves dancing down the sidewalks and piling them on the brownstone steps leading to basement shops and apartments. I figured I'd walk before the snow fell, and it was too cold for the half-hour it took to my Kenmore Square apartment. The Green Line would be jammed with the rush-hour work crowd, and I enjoyed the time alone to think. Jay had been hovering over me since I came home from the hospital, even though I'd ended it. I only did it to save him because he loved me too much to save himself from me, which I couldn't understand. It seemed we were back together, but nothing was discussed. I loved him. He was everything I'd ever wanted when I used to think about those things as a girl, but he deserved more than picking up my pieces. He said he'd come by tonight, and I needed my game face on to let him think I was fine and normal, the way he wanted me to be, and that took some time, especially now, after my once again infantile display at Doctor Harpers. I thought of myself curled up in a ball ten minutes ago, defiant and demonic, realizing I'd never be what Jay wanted or what I thought I should be, who I used to be, or who I thought I was.

Fall is the perfect season in Boston. The crisp air sweeps away the stagnant stink of summer in the city. Scarves and jackets offer protection, and red wine warms the soul and blurs memories. It's exactly what I needed after a long, hot season of trying to convince everyone at the magazine, along with Jay, my mother, and myself, that I was okay. Darkness had arrived earlier, and the sun was nearly set over the Charles River. I hurried along Storrow Drive, guided by the giant Citgo sign illuminating the sky. I tried to think of a fresh angle for an article about the sign, something different from the mountain of others. It was a Boston landmark slated to be taken down in the eighties, but people were up in arms in typical Bostonian fashion, screaming about its value. The artists said it was irreplaceable pop art, popular in the '60s, but the Red Sox fans were the most incensed. The sign overlooked Fenway Park, and not being there might mean lousy juju for the beloved team, so it stayed.

"Inspired by Citgo. Is that a good title?"

I could interview some local artists and get their take on the sign.

"Nah, crap! I'm sure it's been done."

I had to get something to turn in to Jerry, or I was a goner. The magazine had already put up with me on leave while I was in the nuthouse, and I promised at least an idea for my next piece by this week.

"Fuck."

Jay's shoes sat neatly outside the door. I took a breath, tucking my hair behind my ears, pausing nervously before going in.

The door opened, startling me, and I stumbled, tripping over his size twelves.

"I thought I heard you." He stood there, towering over me. I'd always loved how tall he was, how small I felt next to his six-foot-two frame, but that had changed, just like everything else.

"You scared the shit out of me, Jay. Jesus." I righted myself, brushing past him and avoiding his eyes.

He shut the door and followed behind me as I dumped my bag and coat on the table, seeing it knock over a glass. The smell of onions made my eyes water. He had set the table. I noticed as I picked up the glass. I wasn't hungry but figured I'd have to eat or I'd hear about it.

"Oh, sorry. I didn't realize you were cooking . . ."

"It's okay," he interrupted, picking up my coat and kissing my forehead as he walked past me to the closet.

"I guess that goes in there, huh?"

He closed the door and turned to me, smiling, his right dimple on display. "So, dinner is on. Tell me about your day. Are you feeling better?"

I plopped down on the sofa, brushing off the coffee table to seem like I cared about things, although I didn't. I cared about Jay and wanted to care about everything regular people did. I hoped that if I pretended and kept up the act, it would finally connect, and the want would become real.

"I'd like to think my life is more than Doctor Harper and the 'incident.' Let's not talk about it, can we?"

I looked up at him, leaning against the kitchen island. His eyes looked through me, and I hated it. I wanted to look through him, but he was solid, and I was anything but.

"I wanted to bring something up to you and don't want you to get mad." He stirred whatever was in the pan, banging the wooden spoon against the side.

"Oh, God, Jay. I'm okay. Let's be okay." I moaned, laying down, tucking my legs under me, careful my shoes didn't touch the couch, knowing he would cringe.

"I ran into someone today, my friend Ron." He walked over and sat next to me. I closed my eyes, not caring. My head sunk into the pillow, and I felt my foot move. I looked, watching him take off my boots.

"Ron, the drunk lawyer? The guy who hit on me at your office?" I stared ahead, wishing the TV was on to distract one of us from the conversation.

"He's sober now, and yes, that Ron." He got up, put my shoes by the door, and returned to the kitchen, stirring.

"What about him?"

"He lives on the Vineyard now and works there too."

"Not the best place for a sober person." I rolled my eyes, hoping he didn't see.

"Well, he told me something about trials; I guess I asked him, but—"

"Jay." I sat up quickly, twisting toward him. "Stop worrying about me. Let's leave it alone."

"Leave it alone. Are you serious, Maddie?" He raised the spoon, letting sauce drip to the floor. "You tried to fucking kill yourself, and you want me to leave it alone?"

I got up, glaring at him as I passed, and headed into the bathroom. I wanted to lock the door but didn't because I knew he'd worry, which infuriated me.

I can't lock the fucking bathroom door in my own fucking apartment.

I turned the water on as hot as I could tolerate and enjoyed the burn on my skin. Sometimes, the shower felt like my only escape, where I could be alone when he was there.

"Mads," he said, cracking the door. The steam dissipated like a clearing fog. I wiped off the small mirror he had hung for shaving, seeing a blurred image of my face. My skin was lobster red, making my eyes green like a dragon's. I felt like a dragon, angry and destructive. I could make out the three freckles on my nose and remembered Summer naming them that day after school. "Venus, Saturn, and Jupiter. The largest is Jupiter." She giggled, tapping on my nose. We were in third grade and had just learned about the solar system. Now I tapped Jupiter as she did, staring at someone I didn't recognize.

"Mads, listen," Jay went on. "I want us to be okay, back together and okay. I want you to be okay, Maddie. Isn't that what you want?"

I traced Jupiter over and over, connecting the freckles like dots until the fog returned and I couldn't see.

"Yes, Jay," I groaned robotically, unsure what I was agreeing to.

I heard him move closer, just outside the shower curtain. He was so close, and I'd never felt farther away from him.

"I know you want to hear her voice, to understand what really happened—Summer's own words. You never got that chance, not being allowed in the courtroom while you testified. I know it's tearing you apart, Mads." His voice softened, almost breaking, and he cleared his throat. "You believe her now, just from the sentencing, but that only happened when you stopped believing him. I know you need to hear her side, Maddie."

I wanted to scream or run, and I wasn't sure which. He was right about it, and I hated that he was. I hated that he knew me so well when I didn't because everything I knew was a lie. I shut the water off and stood behind the curtain, covering my breasts, shivering as the water dripped rhythmically down to the tub.

"Maddie." He paused, letting out a long breath. "Ron said you can listen to the trial; every trial's recorded. I looked it up, and it's there. I got it."

The wind raced from me as if someone had punched me in the gut. I tore the curtain back. Jay moved back, and we stared silently at each other, and I cried, shaking and nodding. He grabbed my robe from the door hook and covered me, taking my hand. I stepped over the tub, my feet feeling like weighted blocks.

"Jay," I whispered, putting my head on his chest. It was the closest I'd felt to him in forever. "Thank you."

Chapter 2

The chair reclined back as I pulled the side handle and placed the headphones on my ears. I paused, staring at the triangle play button on my phone, and held my breath as I pressed it while forcefully closing my eyes.

"All rise, the honorable Judge Tabatha Stone presiding," the bailiff said loud and crisp. I recalled his fiery-red hair and clean-shaven face coming in and out of the courtroom to the hallway. He was boyish-looking and wore large, shiny shoes that appeared too big and didn't match his stature. I fixated on shoes whenever I couldn't look up. Whenever the door opened and shut to the courtroom while I sat outside, I could never be sure who it was. If it were Cat or Summer, I thought I might internally combust, so I kept my eyes on the ground, making everyone's footwear another thing about them permanently stained to memory. The day I testified, I couldn't look down much. Instead, I centered on the brass handle of the large wooden door. I wouldn't even look at my father, and I could never look at Summer. I was thankful she wasn't there, but it consumed me why she wasn't, although I felt sure I knew or thought I did back then. I figured she couldn't look at me and still live with all her lies. But had she been there, I was sure I'd have gone mute, feeling unconfident in my beliefs, seeing her face, and hearing her voice.

The shuffling sound of papers, then a request by Fire Hair to stay standing for the jury. I remembered their faces, especially the lead juror, as if it were yesterday. Her thin silver bun, two large wisps of hair clinging to each side of her face, and the freshwater pearl chain connected to her glasses that she fiddled with incessantly—I remembered. It was just over six years ago, and I was only in the courtroom to testify for two days. I still saw the door and shoes in my sleep . . . and their faces when they read the verdict. A mixture of sad and disapproving eyes gawking at us all on the wrong side and at my mother and me with pity, as if we were pathetic fools. I know now that we were. However, I thought they were the monsters.

The lawyers introduced themselves and exchanged pleasantries with the judge and jury. Sarah Martin introduced herself as the prosecution with the other man by her, whose name I couldn't pronounce. Sarah was young, in her early thirties, it seemed. She had the kindest voice I'd ever heard. Although she was the enemy trying to destroy our lives, I was more comfortable speaking to her than my own mother when she deposed me before the trial, and it was the same on the stand. I wasn't sure if it was a tactic or if she genuinely cared about the situation, even though I wasn't on her side. I tried my best to hate her for coming after my father and trying to destroy us, but it was hard. She wore her hair down in a sharp-angled bob I was envious of. It was bone-straight, unlike mine, so large and wavy. She was pretty in a plain-Jane way and spoke with the tiniest hint of a lisp that made her seem even more genuine and sweet.

Gabe Heinz piped up for the defense and was the opposite of Sarah. Older, almost near retirement, he'd told us numerous times in the few meetings we'd had with him. He spoke fast and garbled and seemed to masterfully double-talk as if to overcompensate for his lack of knowledge or not putting the effort in. He was always running out in the hallway, rifling through his briefcase, or coming in late with disheveled hair and a wrinkled suit. Judge Stone reprimanded him more than once. I heard it in the hallway and figured then we were in trouble. Oddly, he was supposed to be the best on the South Shore for this sort of thing, and I figured there weren't many to choose from, understandably. I thought the whole thing odd because it wouldn't have been hard for my father, Bill Plympton, the founder and, at the time, CEO of Cytrix, the largest cybersecurity firm in New England, to get one of the better Boston or New York lawyers to fly out to the island where we were living. He had a team of lawyers and the means and money to pay for anyone, but he had wanted to keep things discreet—more secrets.

"This is all one big mistake," my father repeatedly said. My mother would nod, silent and unwavering. The dutiful wife is who she is or who she'd become. I often wondered if she had ever been her own woman. I would try to imagine what she was like when she was young. Years after Nonie died, I found a picture in a drawer at her cottage on the island when Mom and I cleaned it out. It was grainy, but I could make my mother out, Missy Plympton's face—or Missy Steel as she was then. She wore a floral scarf loosely wrapped around her neck, and her long auburn hair hung mid-flight, blending in with the scarf trailing behind her. My mother's smile was large and bright, and her lips a dark cranberry color, something she'd never wear now. Lips that dark aren't proper, not subtle enough to blend into the backdrop of your husband's shining star without being noticed. She sat on the top of an open convertible with one leg thrown over a young man's lap whose face was blurred from a stain on the image. Her arm dangled on the shoulders of a woman beside her who had her head back in laughter. She looked happy and free in a way I'd never seen. I didn't know this woman, and I wanted to.

"I don't want my contacts in the city to get wind of any of this if I can help it," Dad had told my mother and me right after they had charged him, making us swear to secrecy. No one on the island, not friends or family, could know about this. He had even got his arrest kept out of the local papers. Usually, everyone knows everything on the island, but somehow, he had managed to keep his "accusation," as he called it, hush-hush.

"Jesus!" I gasped, spinning around, feeling the headphones slide from my ears. Jay held them, looking at me disapprovingly as I scrambled to press stop on my phone, not to lose my place. "What the hell, Jay? You scared me!" I got up, brushing nothing off my pants, feeling caught and trying not to act it.

"You promised to talk to Doctor Harper about listening to this alone, Maddie. What happened to all that we talked about yesterday? What happened to that?" He rested the headphones on the kitchen island and grabbed the broom, doing his daily sweep: how he unwinds at the end of the day.

"I will tomorrow, at my next appointment." I walked toward him and grabbed the broom mid-sweep, being playful, hoping he'd lay off. He kissed my forehead, pulled his comfort stick back from me, and continued.

He'd been at the apartment an awful lot lately. He had done so initially after I got out of the hospital, and although we'd been officially broken up for a while, we never really stopped seeing each other. I ended it by saying the words only because he wouldn't. I knew he was miserable, and life with me, obsessing over the past, self-loathing, and depression, was something he'd never signed up for. When my drinking turned from a good-time escape to a necessity to get by, and I became an angry, manipulative beast, I knew I'd rather be that way alone, disgusted with myself, than have another person disgusted with me.

I chose my words carefully. "Hey," I started, breaking his trance. "So, what are we here? You're here a lot, and I, I, like that." I stumbled, losing my train of thought. "I mean, are you back? Are we?" I breathed, feeling suddenly exhausted. He leaned down, sweeping the three crumbs in the dustpan and emptying them into the bucket. He took his time responding, which both annoyed and excited me. I've always liked a chase. I was sincerely asking, though; I wanted to be with him. I wanted to be with him more than anything, but I didn't want to need him, and I didn't want him to feel he had to take care of me. When did we become so codependent? I also wanted to be alone and listen to the trial and needed to know if I ever would be unchaperoned—God, it's like I have an ulterior motive for everything.

He took my hand, leading me over to the couch. He was always so dramatic, unnecessarily sometimes, so I didn't know if this was just that or if he was struggling.

"Listen," he said, brushing the hair from my shoulders and touching my cheek. "I've never left," he went on, almost surprised as if he didn't realize this. "I mean, things were shit, Mad." He looked into my eyes, and I fixated on the small lines at his temples. I'd never noticed them before, how they moved as he spoke. I'd always thought he was handsome with his jet-black wavy hair, that one piece that always fell on his face, and the right dimple that only came out when he was sincere, which was always. The man was the most honest I'd ever known—the only one. I had suspicions about even Jerry, who was like my father's replacement.

Jay's ice-blue eyes darkened like the sea, so I knew he was serious. They always changed color whenever he was serious or excited, mainly when discussing work. He loved being a journalist and having sources and secrets. I was envious of it all. I, too, loved writing, but about culture and art. I wished I had his enthusiasm, yet nothing excited me anymore. I felt like the walking dead most days.

"I know things were shit, and I was shit," I said, chewing my inner lip, fidgeting my hands, regretting I'd said anything. Not everything needs a title, especially in my life—I'm still shit.

"I'm here. I am." He rested his hand on my leg, staring at me intensely. I felt like I was under a microscope, like some fragile bird; I guess I was, but I hated it. I pushed my body hard to the back of the couch and crossed my arms like a child, just like at Doctor Harper's.

"You're talking to me like Doctor Harper, Jay," I said, lowering my voice and trying to gain composure. Glancing left, I eyed the large sliding door to the balcony and envisioned myself running toward it and throwing myself over the side, wondering how Jay would respond. If they want a crazy bird, I'll give them one.

"Sorry." He pulled his hand back, seeming guarded.

"Just don't treat me like I'm—" I couldn't think of what I wanted to say, so I stood, pacing before him.

"Like you're what?" he asked, watching me.

I brought my hands up under my hair, squeezing my head and massaging my brain with my fingers. "Like I'm fucking nuts! That's it, Jay. I said it." I threw my hands down to my side. "Like I'm crazy. Okay?"

His face changed to a look of concern.

"I know you're not crazy. You're not." He got up and moved close to me, opening his arms. "Come here."

I walked into his arms, and he closed them around me. I laid my head on his chest, thinking if I should protest. Maybe I was crazy. Perhaps I am and have always been. I wasn't sure, but I didn't want to be treated with kid gloves. I pushed back from him and smiled as sweetly as possible, remembering the other reason why I brought all this up in the first place.

"Jay," I said in my most feminine voice, pushing my bottom lip out ever so slightly to where it couldn't be considered a pout but still made me look vulnerable and in need of him. He liked that.

"What, babe?" He kissed my nose.

"Would you mind if I went to the hotel for a few days?" I made sure to say it quickly before the coming mood shift.

"What? Why?" he asked, stepping back, confused.

"Well, tomorrow, I thought I'd talk to Doctor Harper and tell him about the trial." I grabbed onto his finger and moved our hands back and forth. "And then Jerry needed an article from me, like yesterday, and I need to buckle down and write. We need the money, Jay," I said softly, shifting my eyes away.

He pulled his hand from mine and walked to the kitchen.

"Where are you going?" I followed behind him.

He opened the fridge, surveying inside.

"Jay?"

"Do you not want me here, Maddie? Is that it?" He turned sharply, shutting the door.

"What? No. What do you mean?"

"We're together more, and now you're running away? What the hell, Mad, the hotel?" He squinted, confused. "Are you serious? I thought you never wanted to see that place again."

I hadn't been to the Park Plaza since New Year's Eve before everything happened. I still wasn't sure why Cytrix kept paying for the suite, which was still in my father's name. He remained listed as the founder and owner of Cytrix, with my mother the interim replacement for him on the board. I only found out when the hotel called the last time I saw my mother, asking if she'd be attending the New Year's ball they always held. Her face sobered, and she said nothing, putting the phone down on the table, leaving it off the hook, and walking over to the window overlooking the water below the cliffs.

It was one of her moments where she died inside a little more. I've seen so many.

When the *Martha's Vineyard Times* called for a comment on her husband's conviction, when the Vineyard ladies who lunched told her they were "restructuring the group" and looking for fresh faces, canceling her membership, and when Annie Brokaw and Sissy Martin kept canceling their tennis plans until Mom finally gave up—these were just the ones I'd known or heard about. With each, my mother's already dim light dimmed further. I never understood why she chose to stay on the island, and every time I asked her, she'd only say, "It's our home." I didn't get it because she wasn't even from there. She had moved to the Vineyard full-time with Dad when Cytrix was nothing more than an idea. They purchased a summer cottage near her parents. Missy summered there as a kid, as Nonie, her mother, spent a lot of time there. The cottage had been in the family for a while, but no one ever lived there full-time. My dad fell in love with the island, and while his work was in the city, he wanted to be on the Vineyard more. Growing up in the plains of Kansas, he'd never seen anything like it. He never grew tired of exploring the sandy bluffs and hidden lagoons. He'd take me most of the time, and later, Summer and me. For as long as I can remember, we'd cruise around in the Wagoneer, the three of us. I loved it when he was home, and Mom didn't have him tied up speaking at some charity or hosting an event. We'd fish out on Chappaquiddick until the sun went down, taking lunch from the Edgartown Diner. Sally always put in molasses cookies, although we didn't order them. "Heaven isn't better than this," Dad would say, casting our rods, then lighting a cigar, and we'd sit waiting for a nibble.

They met in Boston when they were in college, Bill and Missy. She, the rich, quiet girl everyone knew and loved, and him, the outspoken tough guy from Kansas, smart enough to get a full ride to Boston College after serving in the Air Force special forces. He was older and didn't know the area well, but being an American history buff, he'd say he had a calling to go to Boston. She grew up in the city, in affluence. Big George, her father, was a real estate developer and owned a chain of women's clothing stores that he eventually sold. She grew up groomed for exactly what she'd become: the wife of a rich and powerful man. But he wasn't when they fell in love, although she'd always said she knew there were big things to come from him the moment they met on campus that fall in the city.

She was entranced by Jane Eyre, reading on a bench in the quad, trying to catch the last remnants of summer. Dad saw her. He'd seen her before, he'd said, around campus, but he'd been nervous about talking to her, and nothing made him nervous, so he knew that she was special. He walked by, unsure what he'd do, trying to muster up the courage, captivated by her thick, coppery mane glistening in the sun. Just about there, he lost his nerve and decided to continue past her. She looked at her watch and leaped up from the bench, realizing she was late for class, banging smack into him and dropping her book on the ground. He, of course, picked it up, and the rest, as they say, was history. They took things incredibly slow; he'd always joked that she was a strict Catholic. Big George was protective, but eventually, they married. They had one of the largest weddings in the city at the Cathedral of the Holy Cross, New England's most prominent Catholic church. She made a beautiful home and was a philanthropist, carving out a name for them, being well known for giving back, especially on the Cape and islands. There wasn't a charity Missy Plympton wasn't involved with: animals, children, the elderly, conservation, the Land Bank, and affordable housing. You name it, and she was either running it or highly involved. She loved it, but she was also good at it. And he ruined it all for her. But she was still writing him, my father, with ferocious dedication. She also visited him at Concord prison every other Thursday, making the long haul, taking the ferry, and then the one-and-a-half-hour drive. She hung on his every word; she always had. As much as I grew disgusted with her belief in his lies, I rarely pressed her. But I stopped listening when I could. I told her gently, but sometimes she'd forget and ramble. He's not eating well; he looks tired; I think he's depressed, she'd say, and I'd let her. It was easier to deal with a mother in denial and dead inside than a mother entirely dead, one who took her own life because, if his crimes were true, nothing about her life was ever real. And what, then, was her part? Even in my suicide attempt, she never believed the real reason, blaming it instead on depression. "Life changes," she said. I would have screamed the truth in her face and put it up in lights if I thought it would have helped, but it wouldn't have. And while I didn't respect her choice "not to go there," I also knew she didn't have a choice. At least not now, but deep down, it's there in a place she couldn't visit. She knows the truth.

◆ ◆ ◆

"Jay, I want nothing more than for us to be together. It's what I want. I just need to get through this, close this up, and get my life together." I leaned on the kitchen island, trying to catch his eyes. "And the hotel, well, I'd been thinking of all the good memories there. All the New Year's Eves there with Summer. And let's be honest; I don't have many options. I can't afford to go anywhere on my own, so . . ." I rambled, pleading my case.

There was no dimple in sight. He was scowling, furrowing his brows.

"I can leave. Just say the word, and I'll go back to my place."

"Jay, this was our place, is our place. You don't have a place." I laughed.

Seeing me laugh made him smile, and I realized again how much this man loved me. The air lightened, and I was glad.

"Well, Kevin lets me think that I do."

"You can only use the college-buddy card for so long, sweetie. Plus, he has a family now, and you have hardly been there. It was nice that he let you stay for a bit, but come home permanently." I moved in front of him. "I want you here when I get back, and the hotel might be good for me. Maybe I'll conquer a demon or two."

With one arm, he pulled me to him again. "Promise me you'll talk to Doctor Harper first—not just about the trial but going to the hotel."

"Jay, I," I started. He interrupted, touching my nose with his finger.

"Promise me, Maddie."

"Okay, I promise. It's just a few days."

He kissed me, softly at first, and something that seemed long forgotten ignited. It was a feeling you had, but you didn't remember until you felt it again. It surprised us both, and we paused, looking at each other, confirming it. He took my hand and led me to the bedroom. I followed, both surprised and thankful that I was feeling at all. I'd become so accustomed to being numb: a pinprick, a stubbed toe, or a bumped elbow, I welcomed. It was pain that assured me I was still alive, and pleasure seemed like something I'd only read about now or noticed in the actions of others. Maybe it was all helping: the medication, Doctor Harper, and McLean's Hospital. Jay's breath tickled my neck, and he moved behind my ear—maybe I'm alive.

Chapter 3

On the day of his sentencing, her face became forever tattooed in my mind. Whenever I'd blink, it's all that I'd see. I hadn't seen her since that night on the island, our island—when we rode the flying horses, which we did every summer, and it didn't matter that we were older now. We swore we'd always ride it again, at least once, somehow trying to recreate that night when we were small, both getting the brass ring simultaneously. The night our sisterhood was sealed, or so we thought. If I'd known it would be our last ride, I'd have studied her face more, her movements, and everything she'd said. I'd have clung to it . . . to her, but I didn't know our world was about to implode. I wondered if she knew it would happen the next day. Her world had already turned on its head, and she had kept it a secret. I'll never know how she did. But maybe I couldn't or wouldn't see. I know that now, but by then, I hated her. With every ounce of my being, I despised her. Her corn-colored hair, turned-up nose, smirky smile, and how she pulled on her lip when thinking. The things I had always liked about her, I then hated the most.

I tried my hardest not to look when the judge called for her to read her statement, feeling I'd burst into flames if I did. Everything about her sickened me, and I could not understand why she'd do this to him, to us, to everything. Still, I couldn't stop loving and missing her, loving us, and longing for before. Even that day, the truth was there in all my hate and rage. I loved her, and I knew she'd never lie. Not about this. It was true—all of it.

Here's the thing about evil: fear fuels it—giving it life and allowing it to linger, seeping into everything around you, ruining everything good and normal. And once evil has possessed your life in the way it has mine, there is no escape hatch except one. At least, that's how it seemed. My years of blindness and flat-out refusal to believe only increased its strength. Slowly, it killed everything around me and everything in me, unhurried and smothering. Strangely, I still couldn't see, and I wouldn't until I let go of my belief in the past and all that I had ever known to be real. The devil was so close, and he had been all along, and I never even knew, but how could I when he was God to me? The accusation hit like a bullet, one echoing shot that triggered a rockslide, crushing us all when it came out. Summer, he destroyed once and then again. But my hate and denial, I fear, killed her the most. I was convinced of it now . . . now that it was too late. When her eyes met mine that day in the courtroom, I saw the tiniest glimmer of life in hers. The way we used to be was there, but only for a second, and I crushed it. It was soon destroying me, too, over the years—the evil, leaving me a shell of nothing—and I figured I'd finish the job for her and me. It was the least that I could do.

◆ ◆ ◆

The trees moved in a rhythmic pattern, back and forth, then pausing, and then back and forth again. Their pauses were perfectly timed, like they'd practiced the dance. I imagined the rustling sound as they swung together and wished I were there with them instead of in here. I didn't want to be here, but I guess no one did because, if you were, that meant you were nuts, fucked, or both. It didn't matter because I had lost my say when Mrs. Janson entered my unlocked apartment and found me, reporting she had heard a noise. She had described it as a screaming moan to the police, but I don't remember. Now I'm stuck coming here three times a week, the deal I made with Doctor Harper and Jay that allowed me to be discharged from McLean's Hospital, someplace I never thought I'd be.

"So, it's evil." Doctor Harper paused, shifting in his seat. "Do you think that's the cause of this? The reason this happened?" He tapped my journal with his pen. "The reason for your father's actions?" He furrowed his brow.

I sighed, tilting my head back and staring at the ceiling.

"Aren't journals supposed to be private?" I asked, twirling my hair, glancing down at the dead ashen ends, then over to him.

He crossed his legs tightly as a woman does, unlike a man, where an ankle rests easily across a knee, leaving a gap.

"Usually, but you know this is different, and you agreed to keep track of your feelings for our sessions here that I could read." He attempted a smile.

I breathed, reaching my hands behind my head, talking slowly and methodically. "That's what Sister Margaret said." I enjoyed being difficult. "It's evil—the devil."

"Sister? You're Catholic? You hadn't mentioned that before," he said curiously.

I slumped down, still looking at him, then above at his diploma on the wall: Harvard Medical School Psychiatry 2002.

"Catholic?" I laughed, smoothing my hair back. "Raised, I guess. Not an active participant."

He put my journal on the side table, tucking the pen inside the cover. He was meticulous with everything he did and took his time. I knew it was a strategy but needed to determine its purpose.

"Madeline, you brought up evil in that entry. Why?"

"Why?" I stiffened. "Are you seriously asking me this?" I said, shaking my head. "You know why. The devil is evil. He's the keeper of it all, and I guess it's his fault." I looked out again at the trees.

"Do you believe that?"

I refused to make eye contact. "So Sister is a liar?" I whispered loudly, screwing with him now.

He said nothing, and neither did I, letting him linger. I didn't believe it at all, at least not today. But sometimes I did because I couldn't believe the alternative, that it was just him who did it. Thinking that made me want to be on the bathroom floor again, except I'd lock the door this time, ensuring to keep Mrs. Janson out.

"Madeline?" He leaned toward me.

I turned, meeting his eyes. "I don't know what I believe."

"Tell me about your thoughts on evil. When did you first learn about it?"

I swept my sleeve across my face, wiping a developing tear.

"Indulge me, Madeline." He smiled.

I stood and walked to the window, turning my back to him, pausing, and letting out a long sigh before I spoke. "Satan, Lucifer, the devil—this religious entity is supposedly around to entice humans to sin," I said, touching one fingertip to the glass and then going on. "Red-faced with black eyes and horns, scary as hell," I emphasized, half glancing back. "And he is hell—the devil, right?" I turned back to the window again. "So they say anyway, or he's in charge of it," I whispered. "You know the guy, Doctor Harper." I glanced back again. "Maybe you've met him. I have."

I often wondered if he was real growing up—the devil—or just a figure we humans made up not to take responsibility for the horror we are capable of, making evil something other than us—something that takes over because we want to see ourselves as inherently good. To make it seem like this "thing" took charge, causing us to lose ourselves. But even at a young age, I knew we weren't good, at least not all of us. I'm unsure how I knew because my world was good, and the people in it seemed perfect—too perfect. Maybe that's how I knew.

"So, when did you learn about it—evil?" he asked again, his voice calm and smooth.

"I don't know." I sighed, pulling my hair in front of my face.

"Everyone learns this at some point in life. I guess the lucky ones are those who get to believe we are good for as long as they can. Even when we realize there's evil, it's usually not close enough to affect us."

"What do you mean?" he asked.

He knew what I meant but just wanted me to keep talking. I knew the game, and I had to play.

I clamped onto my bangs, moving them back and forth like windshield wipers, pulling the ends and covering my eyes. Whenever I came to a session, I immediately turned defiant and childlike. I'd often leave feeling embarrassed and wondering why I did it, but I didn't care enough to change it. It was freeing somehow, and I thrived on the rebellion.

"Like the evil in houses, cities, and countries that don't touch our own are tragic, but someone must have known somehow. Someone must have looked the other way, or something caused the person to do the unspeakable act, the evil. But then it's in your life; it's there, it's been there all along, lurking and hiding in the shadows. It's all around you, and you don't even know it." I shrugged. "You can't see it, feel it, anything," I emphasized, tossing my head and throwing my hands up.

I heard him scribbling on his notepad but didn't turn around. It was easier to talk to the trees.

"Madeline, tell me, are you upset that you never knew? Should you have?"

My face felt on fire as I held back from crying. It was more tears of frustration from being here than the mess of what had become my life. I lifted my head to the ceiling, encouraging gravity to stop the dam from breaking.

"And what if you love him?" I blew out after holding my breath. "The evil one. This person that the devil has infected. And what if there isn't any devil to blame, and it's just your person, connected to you, who is the devil himself? Who then?" I breathed, feeling my lip quiver. "Who then are you?"

I watched the trees again, suddenly feeling peaceful, and it stunned me because I hadn't felt that in forever. Then Sister Margaret's virile voice spoke as clearly in my head as it had that day, what seemed like a million years ago, in confirmation class.

◆ ◆ ◆

"The devil's only power is the power we give him," she snarled, glaring at me. Her pupils widened as she waited for a reaction. We had just finished learning about temptation, and then, of course, the story of Adam and Eve came up. It came up a lot with Sister. She reminded us how Eve was so awful and weak that she ate the apple in the Garden of Eden, even after God told them both not to. I wasn't sure Sister realized she was a woman because she disdained them—at least the biblical ones. Even Mary, Jesus's mother, she wasn't impressed with. She once said the innocent virgin was just a vessel for Jesus's birth, making her seem like she could have been anyone, or it could have been any womb. And maybe she could have; what did I know? Most of Catholicism didn't sit right with me anyway.

"Eve could eat anything she wanted—except the fruit from that tree, and if she or Adam did, God told them they would die." She slapped the desk with her masculine hand, startling us.

I stared at her knuckles, thick and leathery; they reminded me of Big George's, my grandfather's hands. I put my head down, seeing where this was going. She'd be on a tirade about Eve and how she ruined everything. The whole story was nonsense anyway. Eve was made from Adams's rib, girls were inferior, and I wasn't biting. Then she, of course, wants to eat the apple. Adam is so innocent in all of it. At least, that's what Our Lady of the Sea Parish wanted us to think, with Sister Margaret leading the charge.

All the women's fault.

"Okay, time for some questions. I need to see if you're listening." Her eyes squinted, and she darted them around the room, searching for a victim. "Father Francis may want to quiz you before allowing you to receive the sacrament." She made a noise, which was her attempt to laugh, but it sounded like she was choking.

Immediately, I put my head down, hoping she wouldn't call on me. Her cracked brown loafers squeaked against the linoleum as she shuffled over to us, stopping directly before me.

She cleared her throat, prompting me to look up. I didn't. "Tell me about the devil, Madeline Plympton." Her fat fingers moved toward my face, touching just under my chin. They smelled like chalk and cigarettes. We all knew she smoked. Sometimes, we'd see her on the side of the rectory. She'd see us coming for class after church and scurry behind the bushes.

She lifted my chin so my eyes met hers—cold, dirty icicles. I shifted in my seat, looking away.

"Is the devil in your life, Madeline? Do you allow him in?" She breathed, and her hot, stale coffee breath stung my eyes.

She shuffled the length of the room slowly in front of us, squeaking with each step, making sure not to speak, creating fear in our bellies as we anticipated what she might say. I looked up at the clock, relieved there were only minutes left of class. She quickly shuffled back toward me and leaned over, putting her meaty hand on my shoulder, looking left and right for her next victim . . . but just then, the bell chimed.

Everyone jumped up and ran toward the door, except me, still pinned under the weight of her hand.

She put her face to mine again, and I pleaded with God for this to end. "Remember, Madeline. The devil not only exists in you but also in people around you," she whispered. Lifting her hand, I sprung from my seat and pushed past her to the door.

"Do you have any devils around you, Madeline?" she called after me.

"Thank you, Sister. I'll think about that tonight," I shouted, heading out of the room, hurrying to the stairs, and pulling open the metal door. I felt the rush of cold air on my face.

◆ ◆ ◆

The trees were still, except for one leaf spinning its way to the ground, and I jealously watched its descent.

Doctor Harper cleared his throat and then spoke. "So, who are you, Madeline? Are you different because your father is not who he seemed?"

I ignored him, still feeling that day in the rectory, the sunlight and frigid air bursting into the dark staircase when I escaped, feeling free. *Maybe Sister sensed something then*, I thought.

I walked back to the chair, circling it, running my hands over the smooth red leather, wondering how many people like me—who tried to off themselves—sat here. Or was it mainly just people moaning about their relationship or mother? A large picture of Brant Point Lighthouse on Nantucket hung above his head, and I caught a glimpse of myself in the glass, wondering when my hair had gotten so long and when I'd lost my shape. I'd gotten so thin. I looked down at my ends again, resting just over my chest, feeling the dry brown strands.

"I was just a Vineyard kid with a mom and dad, who I loved, just like everyone else, or so I thought. I don't know that person anymore. I don't think I ever did, and nothing is simple," I said, collapsing into the chair. Tucking my legs under me, I stared at the lighthouse. "Can I ask you something?" I said, resting my chin in my palm.

"Of course." He raised his right eyebrow, intrigued.

"Why do I see a shrink with a picture of Nantucket in his office? I mean, this doesn't seem right."

His eyes widened as I kept my composure, having him believe I was serious. I partly was because Martha's Vineyard and Nantucket are rivals of sorts, but regarding mental health, I figured it didn't matter where my doctor had a summer house.

My face cracked, and I laughed, letting him off the hook. He let out a noise I assumed was a laugh, but it seemed forced and uncomfortable. I figured that took a lot for this stolid man, and I appreciated the effort.

Regaining my composure, I exhaled, letting out a long breath. Something felt odd. I had an empty sensation, not a lost or lonely empty one but a good and freeing kind as if I were new and fresh. The tightness in my neck and shoulders eased, and I felt weightless for a few seconds.

"I think I needed that." I shrugged.

He adjusted his glasses. "Laughter is the best medicine, they say."

"Yeah, maybe." I stared out the window again. It was the first time in forever that I cared about what I needed. Tears filled my eyes again, and I suddenly felt sorry for myself. Then the guilt came, predictable and lugging behind like a ball and chain. I had no business feeling sorry for anyone except for Summer, only ever sorry for her.

"I forgot what that felt like—laughter." I turned back to him, noticing his bushy brows.

He cleared his throat and took a sip of water. "Do you plan on going back to the island?"

I'd thought about the island a million times. My mother asked me whenever we spoke, which was rare nowadays. I could no longer be on board with the denials and la-la land mentality she used to save herself. In that, she's culpable now. It's been too long, and I can't see her the same way. But I was guilty too, and I couldn't let myself off the hook because my opinion changed, and I realized what had been true all along. I wasn't even sure I entirely accepted that he did it, which made me sick. I never looked for the truth, believing in him blindly, just like my mother, until somehow, I woke from my pathetic slumber far too late for it to matter.

He never once said he was innocent, and I never assumed he couldn't be. He'd say everything but that to anyone who would listen. Of course, his lawyer said he didn't do it, but he never took the stand to say it either. He never tried to defend himself, and we never asked, Mom or I, because we were monsters now. Or maybe we had always been. I didn't know. We were coconspirators, unknowingly blinded by our history, me by my blood. If he was guilty, we might be too. For so long, I wouldn't allow the thought of anything but his innocence and Summer's betrayal to enter my head. It was never possible until I couldn't not see it years later in college when the Me Too movement exploded, and the dreams came. Women everywhere dug up ancient burial spots and old keys they'd long tossed, unlocking all the secrets, and opening Pandora's box. I didn't realize I had a key until the dreams.

I'm a fucking fraud.

"I'm not sure. I hadn't returned for anything more than a quick visit since college. I've been here in the city for a while, only visiting sparingly. Maybe Jay and I . . ." My voice trailed off, unable to finish the thought. Thinking about Jay was second in line to the guilt of Summer, and he deserved so much more than the mess who was me.

"It's clear you love it there," he went on. "You spoke about it often in the hospital and wrote about it in your journal," he continued softly as if I needed soothing. It annoyed me, but I liked it because I did.

I crossed my legs, circling my ankle around like my father when frustrated. As soon as I realized it, I stopped, feeling sick that I had any trace of him.

"I'm not sure I can go back anymore; I haven't been in a while." I grabbed my ankle, holding it still.

"What are you sure of, Madeline?"

"It's Maddie. Please call me Maddie," I said, cutting him off.

"Does your name bother you?"

I let go of my leg, spinning my ankle wildly and purposefully, feeling myself spiraling.

"What's with all the questions? You know the answers. Most of them, anyway. It all stems back to him. Everything is fucking him, and I want that to stop." I tapped my other foot, losing any remnant of composure I held. "Can you make that happen? Can anyone?" I launched, bursting from my seat. "Fuck." I clutched my head and moved toward the window. "He called me Madeline. He was never anything but perfect. I was perfect—fucking Mom in her perfect pants with the iron crease like fucking 1955. He and his fucking fancy car without a speck of dirt to be seen anywhere." I spun around, holding up my finger and pointing. "Not even a crumb!" I yelled, seething, pacing back and forth. "Church, degrees, volunteering. The whole island thought we were saints. We were so fucking perfect, all of us." I turned to the window, pressing my hands to the glass. Staring down, feeling dizzy, I closed my eyes, wishing I could peel the glass open, jump right in front of Doctor Harper, and splatter on the ground. Maybe then he'd get it.

"So, you're saying it was all pretend?" His voice came from behind me, close, out of his chair. I touched my nose to the glass. An overwhelming sense of thirst overcame me, and I licked my lips, then the glass, seeing how it tasted, and I had no idea why.

"Maddie?"

"What?" I sucked my tongue back in.

"You're okay, Maddie."

"The window. It tastes like snow, newly fallen snow," I said, turning to him.

"Maddie," he said, coming close and touching my shoulder. I pulled away as if it burned.

"Tell me more about that day. The day of his sentencing that you wrote about. It seemed you stopped writing abruptly. Why?"

Breathing in deeply, I turned to face the window again. Just five stories down, I could be free. If only the window would open. I framed my hands around my saliva spot, enjoying the mess.

I hesitated to answer and closed my eyes, thinking it might help. "I never expected Summer to speak." It was all I could muster.

He said nothing—one of his long, awful pauses. The silence between us was maddening.

I wasn't sure why I didn't expect her to speak because it's common for victims to do so during the sentencing of their perpetrator. But what did I know then, being seventeen and in the bowels of hell? I looked at her once, only once, and saw it. Our eyes met as she stumbled on her words, talking of nightmares, then shifting her gaze to him. She spoke to him as tears spilled down her cheeks, the same as me as I said this. He looked ahead, my father, not acknowledging her existence as if it was all somehow beneath him. I remembered Cat grabbing Summer's hand and squeezing it supportively while looking at me with the heartbreak of a mother whose child had been violated. It was then I turned away. He didn't move, not a shift in his seat or a tilt of the head, nothing, and I wasn't sure I recognized him. I didn't know it yet, but I believed her. After one look, one sentence, I knew she was telling the truth, and the truth and my refusal to allow it in began smothering everything around me: relationships, jobs, and, finally, my sanity. Until eventually, I felt nothing, not even pain, and the only thing I could think about was that day when the light went out of her eyes when I turned my head from her forever like she never existed—like we never did.

"And what did she say?" he uttered, breaking the quiet, stifling us. I clasped my hands behind my back, resting my forehead on the window.

"She asked him a question," I answered, closing my eyes tight and wishing it all away.

"Okay, what was the question?"

I felt him close again. I envisioned myself falling backward to see if he'd catch me. I wondered if anyone could catch me.

I didn't think I could say it, but the words came from my mouth as if, somehow, she was inside me, saying it herself. I'd never been closer to anyone in my life than to her. She was my life; I felt her in me every day and still do. They say friendships when you are young are the truest kind, and we were more than friends. We were sisters, not by blood but in every sense of the word. I was happy she didn't have my blood, but she might have been spared if she did.

I gritted my teeth and clenched my fist, hissing out the words. "She asked him, why her?" I said, pressing my face, wet with tears, against the window, watching the fog spread from my breath, trying to get her from my mind, but I never could. I thought of Jay's words—"Not that day, Mads; think of all the good ones. The you and Summer before days."

Years passed, but I stood stuck forever in that day, no matter how far I moved. I left the island, sickened by the house, my mother, and the perfection, but I missed the Vineyard's peace and beauty. It was my home, the only one I'd ever known. I'd never planned on leaving, at least for long. I left for Boston and went to college as expected, attempting to be normal. To defy my father somehow, I chose Boston University, not Boston College, his alma mater. To those on the outside, I looked fine. Jay seemed impressed. We met in creative writing class. He hated it, liking nothing but the facts, as he was studying to be a journalist and was all about nonfiction. But he couldn't escape the class.

I worked as an intern then at the magazine and loved assisting with its weekly exposés of art in the city. Jerry, whose name couldn't have been more perfect, looked like Jerry Garcia but acted the opposite of the free-spirited musician. He was more a disgruntled postman type, about to blow at any moment. He took me under his wing, seeing potential. I was glad someone did. Jay took notice, starting up a conversation after class. He said he liked my "whimsy" in the short story I'd written—having read it to the class for a project. I wasn't sure what he meant because there was nothing whimsical about it, but his smile accented his right dimple when he said it, and I liked that. We got through an assigned essay on Byron, then drank and danced the night away at McGinty's, the local college haunt. It all seemed like an act. Life hadn't felt real in forever until that night with Jay. He felt real, he was real, but my darkness smothered that just like everything else. He couldn't fix it, and he tried, but nothing could. Nothing could fix any of it unless someone could erase what had happened—or at least make me see the truth so that I could have been there for Summer then, so we could still exist despite him. Jay couldn't, and I left him, setting him free once I realized the way out.

"Maddie, what are you thinking?" Doctor Harper asked. I ignored him, thinking of how I got here and that day in the bathroom, scared of who I had been and terrified of who I was.

By then, I so loathed being in my skin that I felt excited to get my father gone, no matter the consequences. As far as I could see, purging him from my veins was the only way out, and I was okay with the choice because it was mine. Something was finally mine, and I'd never felt freer. Then I did it or tried, but neighbors can be nosy. Mrs. Janson was the worst offender. I'd sometimes see her at the mailbox, and she'd smile. It was the only nice thing in my life anymore: her smile. It reminded me of Summer's—half turned up at the corner, almost smirking, but you could tell the difference by the crinkles near her eyes.

"Come sit, Maddie," Doctor Harper said, touching my shoulder again.

I didn't want to be touched and suddenly felt rabid, like a dog. I wanted to bite. Spinning around, my eyes locked sternly with his.

"I'm not sitting, Doctor Harper. I don't want to." I fumed. "I'm unsure what to do, but I don't want to sit."

"Maddie, why are you upset? Did I upset you?" he asked in his serene way.

I sidestepped away from him, sliding along the glass, moving my feet. "You don't seem to get it, Doctor Harper, what he did, do you?" I felt myself becoming unhinged. "And you know what else she said?" I raised my voice, feeling my knees weaken. I looked up, attempting to blink back more tears. Snot fell from my nose, and I wiped my face forcefully with my sleeve.

"Maddie, calm down. I do get it. I do. What did Summer say that day?" He leaned against the bookshelf, keeping his distance.

The words made me sick, her words; my father didn't deserve them, and he never did from any of us—especially her.

I shielded my face with my hand as I spoke. "She said she loved him." I repeated it twice and let the tears tumble to my chest. "I'm not sure of anything anymore. Nothing!" I sobbed.

After a moment, I collected myself, feeling relief but hating that I broke, feeling he broke me, my father, and is still breaking me again and again.

Doctor Harper was still, leaning against the bookcase, arms crossed, watching me as if I were a specimen in a lab experiment.

"I am sure of one thing, though." I smoothed my hair and wiped under my eyes with my fingers.

"What's that?" He stepped toward me. "What are you sure of?"

I looked at the clock, walked past him to the chair, grabbed my purse, headed for the door, and turned back to him. A scorching fire flew up from my belly, breaking free in my throat. I swallowed hard but couldn't extinguish it, and the words flowed like lava oozing off my tongue.

"He's a fucking monster, and so am I."

Chapter 4

A cold wind whipped through the darkness between the buildings as I rushed through Copley Square. It seemed more like mid-February than November, and I pulled my coat up to cover my ears. You never know about the weather in New England. Jerry wasn't pleased in the slightest that I still had nothing to give him. In hindsight, I shouldn't have shown my face in the office with empty hands, but I felt I owed him a face-to-face meeting and knew everyone would be working late, as the deadline for December's issue was tomorrow.

"Goddamn it, Maddie." He snapped his pencil, tapping the shorter half on his desk. "I can't hold out for you anymore," he said, rising from his chair and tossing the pencil in the trash.

"I know, Jerry. Two days, okay?" I pleaded. "I've been working on something," I lied.

He mumbled something under his breath, walked back to his desk, and fell into his chair, nodding as he spoke. "Two days, that's all I can do. I'm not all of Boston Living, Maddie. I have bosses too!" His voice trailed off, and he glanced at the outer office, watching the staff buzz around Maria, the food writer's desk.

"Jerry, I'm sorry. But I'm okay. I'm back." I moved close to him. He looked sad and disappointed, and I hated it.

"Well, you look better anyway." He leaned back, clasping his arms behind his head. The remains of his lunch were scattered on his beard. I looked closer, noticing the coffee stain on his shirt pocket, and smiled, shaking my head.

"What?" He followed my eyes, peering down at his shirt.

"Damn it." He wiped at the stain with his hand, making no difference.

"Some things never change, Jerry." I laughed and made my way out the door.

"Two days!" he yelled, rising from his desk again.

"Two days. I promise," I called behind me, heading toward the elevators.

I hurried through the Common, trying to forget Dr. Harper and Jerry, looking up at the buildings and seeing the city's reflections on the Hancock building's mirrored glass. We spent so many New Year's Eves here, first watching the people's procession, a parade with papier-mâché dragons and butterflies. Those were always my favorite. Summer liked the ice sculptures that sprinkled the park and the Plaza's gingerbread house they created to look like the hotel. Every year, it seemed bigger and better. They kept it in a glass case in the lobby. One year, we were so hungry that we sat up, creating a plan to get into it, but we knew it was useless. "It's probably not real gingerbread anyway," Summer said, and we agreed to go to sleep. In the years we went after, she always felt bad about wanting to eat the house that night, which I'd thought strange because she didn't feel bad about most things. "Live with no regrets," she'd always say, telling me she'd been told that by her father. It was the only thing she remembered about him besides his car, a blue Pontiac Firebird, one of those muscle cars she said he left in and never came back when she was four, just before I'd met her. Once we'd arrived at the hotel, the gingerbread house was the first thing we saw in the lobby. She'd say the same thing every time we huddled over it, looking at the new details they'd always seem to add. "I'd never have eaten you," she'd say, smiling at me. We'd laugh while my parents looked on; it was one of those moments in childhood friendship, the little inside jokes, the glances at one another where we'd both know what the other was thinking. A time when things were simple, and it was us exploring the world, never thinking anything would ever be different.

The lobby appeared exactly the same, except for new furniture, I noticed, trying to remember the events of the last time I'd come. Instead of the red velvet and dark wood, the decor was brighter and more modern. Gold and white fabric with marble accents drenched the lobby. The doorman, of course, was new, and I recognized none of the staff, although they were wonderful and attentive as always. The Park Plaza was one of Boston's most historic hotels. Although I'd been working tirelessly to try and erase my past, standing in the lobby, I only wanted to remember it.

Mom pulling on her white gloves, fiddling with Dad's bow tie. She could never tie it, and he couldn't either. It was the same every year. Then she'd call Bruce, the concierge, and have a clip-on one delivered to the room. Once, they couldn't find one because the stores closed early. So, Bruce tied it for my father, which embarrassed him, and I loved it. The big, powerful man everyone respected and admired had to have help with his tie. I giggled, standing with Summer, watching the scene until Mom swatted us into the other room. After a few cocktails later in the night, I saw my dad and Bruce laughing together while Summer and I counted the crystals of the chandeliers in the lobby. The staff always gave us something to do, a scavenger hunt or a game. One New Year's Eve, we ran the photo booth—well, helped with the props, handing them to the people. We'd run up and down the grand red staircase to the second floor, dancing to the music, waiting for the balloon drop, tired out of our minds. Mom and Dad found us after midnight and ordered pizza from room service while we all recapped the night. I saw them kiss one year at midnight in the ballroom.

Our first New Year's there, Summer and I snuck behind a curtain, watching the adults. The gowns were incredible, royal blues and vibrant reds. Some ladies wore tiaras. "I'll be wearing a crown one day," Summer assured me, whispering from behind her panel while I waved my hand, shushing her. We dressed nicely. My mother made sure of it. I hated my dress: the flared skirt and large velvet bow felt so not me. I wanted to wear my sneakers and jeans in rebellion, but I wouldn't dare. Summer didn't have much for clothes, and I was sure Cat didn't make much money as a hairdresser on the island. When my mom asked Cat to pack something nice for Summer to wear, she was surprised when her tote bag had nothing but a gray wool skirt that was too small and a dinghy T-shirt.

"Did you pack yourself, Summer?" Mom asked, laying out the outfit on the bed.

"Mom told me what to bring. Is it okay?" Summer replied, walking over, seeming not to realize. But turning and noticing my dress hanging on the rack, her face changed, and I could tell she got it. I felt embarrassed for her, praying my mother would stop.

"Why don't we hit Newbury Street, girls? We have time before tonight."

Before I could protest, as I hated shopping, she'd already grabbed her purse and called out to my father, reading the paper in the other room.

The window displays lit up the dimming sky. Chanel, Louis Vuitton, Gucci—my mother loved and wore them all, and I couldn't stand it. Even as a kid, spending so much and getting so little seemed ridiculous, but I was used to it. Summer's eyes widened as she surveyed them.

"Live without regrets, right?" She laughed as we browsed through Mulberry Road, watching my mother pull dresses off the rack while looking for a salesperson to wait on her. Someone always had to help.

"What about this one, Summer?" she asked, holding it in front of her. It was gold and black, with full sleeves trimmed with faux fur. Summer, at first, looked thrilled, nodding her head yes, unable to speak. But then she changed, noticing the price tag.

"It's nice, Mrs. Plympton, but it's too much money. My stuff is fine," she said, shrinking with each word.

"Nonsense, Summer, you deserve the world. I'd love for you to have it."

I was glad my mother spun it that way.

"Okay. Thank you." Summer smiled.

Chapter 5

"Penthouse two," the desk attendant said in a surprised voice, handing me the key.

"Hasn't been used in a while, I guess," I said, smiling awkwardly, feeling like an impostor.

She smirked, seeming unsure about me. I felt her eyes follow me to the elevator, and I began to second-guess why I came here.

The key card was finicky, like always. It took me four attempts before I got the little red light to turn green. Hearing the click, I paused, feeling I may be opening myself to something more than just a room, but I proceeded anyway, thinking Jay may have been right that I should have discussed it with Doctor Harper. I mentioned nothing at our appointment, fearing his disapproval. I left him a message after I left and thought that would suffice. I was only doing it because of Jay. I had enough guilt in our relationship and didn't want to be more deceitful than I already had been. It wasn't intentional, but I always felt I duped him. Selling him damaged goods disguised in togetherness. Like everyone else, I only wanted to be normal and thought I could be. I wanted him, so I worked hard to present myself as something I wasn't. You can't keep that up for long.

The room smelled of linen spray and pine. I'd imagined they do a little cleaning here and there, just in case a ghost wandered in from the past, and here I was. A large vase of white calla lilies was on the table.

They still adhered to my mother's requests, as if I had stepped back in time. The only difference was that the curtains were now white instead of red, matching the ones in the lobby. I missed the red—dark and mysterious. I only remembered them because Summer and I wrapped ourselves in them while spying on the ball. After that, I noticed all the hotel curtains were red velvet with gold lining, and I thought I'd have the same curtains one day if I ever had a fancy house. I sat on the bed, about to lie back and stare at the tray ceiling, when I saw it across the room: the photograph of us, all four of us, from the New Year's with the photo booth. Mom tucked it in the cabinet corner when we returned to the room that night. Shocked it was still there, I went over, pulled it out, and walked back to the bed, staring at it.

I didn't know any of these people.

Dad wore a top hat Mom had put on his head from the prop table. A party favor hung mid-unroll from his mouth as he blew. Summer gave me rabbit ears, wearing a feather boa and giant, gold-glittered glasses. Her hair hung partially over my shoulder as I tucked my head close to Mom, who smiled in perfection, holding on to her champagne glass, lifting it, and toasting. I touched my finger to the picture to see if I felt any connection to the smiling girl raising her eyebrows. I held a single gold balloon, oblivious to life, who my parents were, what Summer kept secret, and what was to come. I studied Summer, seeing if I could spot anything. She looked happy. Why was she happy? Why didn't she tell me? I tossed the photograph on the table and moved around the room, trying to feel past feelings, but I couldn't; I didn't feel anything. Why did I come here?

"Time to get to work then," I said aloud, looking out the window at the ant people below. The clean snow taste of the glass came to mind, and I wondered who cleaned the mess off, feeling a twinge of guilt. Just then, I had an epiphany. I should have come here. I should have done it here. No one would have found me for at least a day. As fast as I thought it, I regretted it. I didn't want to die today and didn't wish for an end. Not now, but I feared I would. I lived more in fear that nothing could help me. I would try it all—the meds, therapy, meditation, and everything else they say—and it would still be there, the feelings of that day, the knowledge that it's the only answer. It tormented and terrorized me that I couldn't move past this. That this was it, and I'd either have to live in the darkness, knowing I'd never see the light, or end it if I couldn't. Since the hospital, I was thrilled to feel at all for a while and didn't care if it was fear or terror, but soon, I was smart enough to know that I couldn't live this way forever either.

I sat down at the mahogany desk and opened the drawer. A Cytrix notepad and pen stared back at me, and I took them both out and started jotting down some notes and ideas for my article after I spent thirty minutes filling in the "fuck you" bubble letters I wrote at the top of the page. After racking my brain, I decided to write a piece about the hotel itself, figuring I could get that done quickly because all the research I'd have to do was right here. Picking up the phone, I dialed nine for the concierge. "Hi, this is Bruce," the familiar voice said on the other end. I nearly hung up.

"Bruce, I can't believe you're still here," I said, realizing it was too late to hang up. Actually, it was nice to hear a familiar voice.

"Oh, this is penthouse two?" He paused. "Mrs. Plympton?" he broke again. "Madeline?" he asked, raising his voice in surprise.

"It's Maddie, Bruce. How are you?"

"Oh, wonderful, Madeline. It's good to hear your voice. We haven't seen you in so long. What can I have the honor of doing for you?"

"I guess I didn't think you'd still be working here. I'm not sure why. It hasn't been incredibly long." I rambled nervously, feeling sure he knew about my family's disgrace. "I'm writing a piece for the magazine I work for, Boston—" I got out the first word when Bruce finished.

"Yes, Boston Living. I read your work all the time. You're a fantastic writer, and we need more attention to the city arts." He cleared his throat.

"Oh, well, thank you, Bruce. Thank you."

"Being a concierge, Boston Living helps me keep abreast of things around the town. I was surprised when I saw your articles. I told everyone I knew that little girl since she was six, sneaking cookies in the kitchen and later champagne at the ball." He laughed in his charming way.

Just as he said that, I remembered Summer and me following a waiter carrying a tray of warm chocolate chip cookies. He passed them around to the guests but never saw us, keeping his head high. We crouched down, sliding between the kitchen doors, watching him put the tray on the metal table and walk away to talk to the chef. My heartbeat was out of my chest, and I thought of turning back when Summer scurried past me like a monkey, reaching up and grabbing a handful. We hurried back through the doors just as Bruce came through. Feeling the resistance, he pushed harder, knocking me backward onto Summer's lap, who nearly choked, shoving the cookies in her mouth to conceal the evidence. Bruce laughed; he didn't care. He never did—the same with the champagne years later. Bruce had an eye for everything going on in the hotel. Summer had already tried alcohol by then. She said she'd sneak a sip of Cat's wine here and there. I couldn't believe she was such a rebel. She'd already tried smoking too. She'd tell me all about it but never pressured me, which I appreciated, although I didn't want to seem like a dork.

Proving I was cool, I took two champagne glasses from a table by the entrance to the ball. Summer looked at me with surprise, putting her hand to her mouth and widening her already large brown eyes. We rushed over to the stairs, hoping no one would see us. As I put the glass to my lips, I noticed Bruce talking to the bartender, watching us. Stunned, I put my glass by my side, shoving Summer, who was in the middle of gulping down hers. She tried hiding her empty glass behind her, but we were already caught. "Shit," I said, eyeballing Bruce, wondering what he'd do. He studied us, seeming unsure of our fate, then put his index finger up, mouthing the words, "Just one." We nodded and smiled, showing thanks.

"You're too kind, Bruce, and you always have been." Sadness swept over me, remembering, and tears began building in my eyes. I grabbed the pen, tracing the "fuck you" bubble letters again until it broke through the paper. Anger was easier than sadness some days.

"So, what can I do for you?"

He hadn't asked about my parents or Summer. He knew.

"I hope it's not much to ask," I began. "I was hoping to write a piece on the hotel from the perspective of art, design, et cetera. So, any history would help." I finished. In that instant, I regretted asking him and coming here. Hearing his voice made me sad, and seeing him, I was sure, would make it worse. This was a mistake.

"That's great, Madeline. Oh, yes, we would love that. When is your deadline?"

I cleared my throat and faked a cough, delaying my response, feeling awkward and unprofessional.

"That's the thing, Bruce. I need it in two days," I said, closing my eyes.

"Well, we can do that. Come down to the lobby in an hour," he said, not seeming to mind. He appeared happy, and I felt relieved.

"You're a lifesaver, Bruce. Thank you. See you then."

It was nice seeing Bruce. He was someone from the past, but not close enough to be of any issue, so I kept my composure. Speaking with him, I felt a connection, and that I existed and meant something somewhere once upon a time. His dark brown hair now had flecks of gray at his temples, and he was still tanned as ever. While I knew he was dark-skinned and Greek, I was sure he went tanning. No Caucasian person, Greek or not, living in Boston during the colder months was that bronzed. He spoke with an accent, almost sounding British, but he wasn't. I had heard him talking once about growing up in Scranton, Pennsylvania. I figured he wanted to sound cultured because his role was dealing with many difficult people with money.

Bruce and I spent hours walking the hotel while he gave me the building's creative history, past and present. He showed me some of the most famous pieces, which I found interesting, explaining why they were chosen. He furrowed his brows and scratched his chin when speaking of the design change and the difficulty of modernizing while maintaining the history and the Boston feel. I enjoyed how much he anguished over this and loved the place. We all did once. Bruce knew details no one would need to know, like how many lightbulbs and steps were in the whole building. Bruce was the Park Plaza, and I considered incorporating him into my article.

"I think I have all that I need, Bruce. You've been so helpful."

"Not a problem, Madeline. It was so lovely seeing you. Are you staying long?"

"A few days, I think. I have some other things I need to do and need the quiet." I felt anxious to get the piece written and sent to Jerry so I could dive into the trial, but I was also relishing the opportunity to enjoy my work again.

While we sat at the bar, Bruce's face changed, and he moved his hand to mine. He put his head down.

"I heard about your father, Madeline," he said, raising his head and meeting my eyes. "I'm sorry. I didn't know if I should say anything but felt I should."

My hand stiffened under his, and my jaw clenched. I started to speak, but the words didn't come.

"Don't say anything. It's okay." He patted my hand and stood, moving his hand to my shoulder. "Call me if you need anything, anything at all."

"Thank you, Bruce," I managed to say.

"You're welcome." He smiled and hurried through the door out to the lobby.

◆ ◆ ◆

I spent all night and into the next afternoon writing my article, only stopping for room service consisting of cold French onion soup and a stale croissant. I wondered when the food became unfabulous, hoping it was just an anomaly. Tired and wired, I pressed send, and off it went to Jerry. It wasn't my best work, but it was pretty good. I just needed Jerry to feel the same. He'd be emailing me times to schedule photographers, and I let Bruce know, who was more than thrilled.

The white curtains didn't darken the room like the red ones, and I desperately needed sleep. I put the Do Not Disturb sign on the door and the room phone so as not to be bothered. I was sure Jay would call the hotel if I didn't answer. After all, it was daytime, so I texted him my day-of-sleeping plan. The voicemail icon glowed green, and I realized I had a missed call, seeing it was from Doctor Harper. I didn't want to explain anything now or hear what he had to say, unsure I cared. The heavy down comforter felt smooth on my skin, and my head sunk into the pillow as its sides surrounded me. The onset of sleep started to come, and just as it did, I gasped, sitting up, unsure where I was. Sweat ran down my back, and I couldn't catch my breath.

"Jesus," I said, huffing, holding my heart, feeling it thud against my skin.

I lay back down, trying to calm myself, staring at the ceiling, thinking how many nights I'd done that here in this room, knowing every crack and corner. After an hour of tossing and turning, my eyes unable to shut, I leaped from the bed, pacing the room.

"Goddamn it." I grabbed my hair from underneath, running my fingers through it. A pale, older face stared at me in the mirror on the dresser: lifeless brown hair and tired eyes.

"I shouldn't look this bad, being so young," I whispered, knowing how desperately I needed to sleep.

I touched it, the mirror. Pushing my face close, I felt my planet, Jupiter, tapping the mirror and my nose.

"Fuck." I walked back to the bed, sitting on the edge, wondering what to do.

The black padding of my headphones stuck out of the side pocket of my bag, and I walked over, pulling them out and grabbing my phone, finding the trial download. Everything in me said not to listen again before getting some sleep or speaking to Doctor Harper.

Stubbornly, I plugged into the aux port and pressed play, picking up where I left off, ignoring it all—Jay, what Doctor Harper would say, and myself. I'd never be ready for this, but it was the only thing that mattered in the world.

Chapter 6

"You're up, Ms. Martin," Judge Stone said, her voice echoing in the courtroom.

I'd imagined it was near empty during the trial. It was the day I testified, so I figured it was the whole time. Cat didn't have much family, and the ones left were back in Indiana, where she was from. I thought I remembered her saying she didn't speak to them. At sentencing, only a few of her friends from the salon and a few other island stragglers, whose faces I knew but not their names, were scattered on the benches behind her. For my father, no one was there except his brother, Uncle Mark, who flew out from LA. I was surprised my father told him because it was all a secret, and my mother followed orders. At sentencing, Uncle Mark spoke, but I wasn't sure how helpful it was. He only talked about how close they were as kids and said nothing that would mean he didn't do it.

"Thank you, Your Honor," Sarah Martin said, shuffling some papers. Someone cleared their throat and coughed.

I'd already listened to the introductions and jury instructions. It was boring and monotonous, but I didn't want to miss anything except when Judge Stone read the charges. It stung hearing them, just as they had when I found out that day when Attorney Heinz read them in his office while preparing me to testify. Right after he began, I stopped hearing. Sounds melted together, and occasionally, one word would be clear, ringing out against all the muffled ones. At the same time, my body sank into his chair as I slid down to the floor, hoping I'd disappear, dissolving into his oriental rug. Dad repeated his mantra, "It's all a big misunderstanding." My mother hummed, drowning out the words, and tidied things whenever the conversation arose. She'd adjust anything in front of her, changing its place, standing back to admire it, seeing if she liked its new home more. She'd move pictures and knickknacks in the house. Things that had held a permanent spot now rotated continuously. I'd always know if something happened—a letter or a new appeal date, a call from an attorney—by where the things were in rotation. I was glad not to know anymore.

"Good afternoon. My name is Sarah Martin, and I am the assistant district attorney representing the state of Massachusetts. In this case, you'll hear a victim who will tell you that she had a best friend, Madeline, the defendant's daughter. Madeline had a big house on our beautiful island that she lived in with her mom and dad—the defendant. The victim and Madeline went there at least weekly, if not more. She went on vacations with this defendant and his family. She got junk food galore at that house, beautiful dresses, and whatever she wanted. The defendant would buy apple fritters at Back Door Donuts for her and his daughter and take them fishing when he was home. You will see that she got anything she asked for from the defendant. It was a little girl's dream to have these friends and this house that she could go to, where she had a best friend and all these things at her disposal. But it came with a price tag, and that's why we're here today. The price tag was staying quiet about the crime William Plympton committed against her. You will hear testimony from Summer Starr, the victim in this case, that her relationship with this defendant began when she was just out of diapers. Her mother is Cat, and you'll hear from her as well. She's a hairdresser on the island, and she'd cut the defendant's and his daughter's hair. You'll hear from Madeline too, about how Summer and she met in the salon and how the defendant offered to help Cat and Summer when they struggled to find housing. They stayed in his house, the defendant's large home, on the water. There, they met Melissa Plympton, the defendant's wife, who agreed to their stay. After some time, Mrs. Plympton found affordable housing for Cat and Summer, pulling some strings, as she is a significant contributor to the island's affordable housing committee. Soon, Cat and Summer had their own little home, and by then, Summer and Madeline were best friends. All through elementary school, they were inseparable. You'll hear from Cat that Summer was a happy kid. She was a good kid, but something changed in her around age nine and ten.

"She started having issues with eating. She didn't want to eat, and when she did, she would sometimes make herself vomit. She was also depressed a lot. Cat talked to her about the vomiting and wasn't sure what was wrong. She was soon entering her teenage years. She got Summer into counseling but didn't think anything else of it, and who could blame her?

"Summer had a major secret and didn't want adults to know what was happening to her. Even at thirteen years old, which is how old you'll hear she was when the police finally got involved. She knew the price tag attached to her telling the truth. Summer knew it would mean she would lose her best friend, and she worried she and her mother would lose their house and be homeless.

"Summer also knew in the back of her mind that what came with the best friend, vacations, and big house on the water were interspersed with all this bad stuff, which would end too. Summer didn't know if it was worth it.

"Summer will tell you details about what happened and that she thinks it all started around age eight to nine. The first time she remembers it was when . . ." Sarah's voice trailed off as I repeatedly tapped on my phone, trying to stop her from talking and me from hearing. I tore off my headphones and tossed them on the bed. I stood, staring at the phone. This small device had all the answers I thought I was ready for but realized I'd never be ready. I pulled at my shirt collar, feeling suffocated, wondering if it was the heat, and walked over to the thermostat to adjust the dial, unsure what I was doing. I paced back and forth in front of the bed. Pulling off my sweater, I tossed it over the phone and headset for a minute of reprieve. The photograph caught my eye, and I picked it up again, studying our faces. Summer went through all this, lived this, and lost me too. It was the first time I considered how much she cared about me. It was too painful to think about. I had been fixated on what happened to her and what I could have done to see or stop it. God, how selfish I'd been.

The wine fridge hummed. I peered through the gray glass at the shape of bottles that desperately wanted to be opened, but I couldn't with these fucking antidepressants. Could I? I glanced at the photo again, feeling everyone staring at me: the ghosts, the before, the ones I longed for sometimes, the pretenders. I returned to the bed, pulled my phone out from under my sweater, and placed the headphones back on. Not being present for Summer is what I'd done for years, and as much as I didn't want to be in my skin and wished I could puncture my eardrums with a sharp instrument, I was going to listen. It didn't matter that no one knew because I did. It had killed me and everything around me since it happened. It exhausted me to understand that this moment was the start of any healing or the beginning of the end. Now, after everything, it was just the start, at least for me. I wasn't only listening for me and closure, to know and hear her say it. I'd listen for Summer, to hear her tell her truth and give her the voice we all denied her. Even me, until now, now that it was too late and didn't matter to anyone anymore except me. But it still mattered; it was all I could do for Summer and all that held hope for me. I pressed play and lay back, my head sinking into the pillows, feeling the world close around me.

◆ ◆ ◆

"She was young, and she remembers it happening; she can't forget it," Sarah continued.

I braced myself, waiting for it, closing my eyes tightly, clenching my jaw, feeling for the phone, but I stopped and grabbed the comforter with both hands, pulling it as hard as I could, inhaling deep, and holding my breath.

"It was in the ocean at State Beach in Edgartown. Summer remembers she was trying to float. She and Madeline were goofing around, and the defendant was in the water. It was a hot day, and he had taken the girls for ice cream and then to the beach to cool off. Both girls had yet to jump off the Jaws bridge, the one famous for being in the movie. As some of you know, it's a rite of passage for all the island kids and vacationers. Both girls were scared to do it but would keep trying, thinking next time they would actually jump. The defendant made a bet with them that he'd give fifty dollars to whoever did it first. The girls went to try and jump as the defendant waited; this time, Summer did it. She said it was a great day, and she was feeling good. They all went into the water after, and Mr. Plympton, the defendant, swam over and gave her a high five. He then offered to help her learn to float as he saw the girls trying to do this. Summer said she remembers him putting his hand on her back, moving it down to her buttocks, and then sliding his hand . . . asking her if it was okay . . ."

Sarah Martin's voice faded as the sounds from that day filled the in-betweens of all she said until her words disappeared into seagull calls against a slight summer wind created by the waves pushing their way to shore. I'd left my body and traveled back to the comfortable predictability of the island with ease. Summer's face smiled hugely, not in her mischievous way, as her brown eyes greened in the bright hot sun. I could tell how proud she felt as she climbed the rocks from the water. I ran from the bridge to meet her, happy and envious, because I was too chicken to do it. I loved that she had and then hated her for it, seeing my dad praise her, clapping as he walked up the sand.

"You did it!" I said in my best artificial, excited voice.

"Great job, Summer, great job!" Dad still clapped, walked over, and handed her a towel.

"Thanks. It was so cool. Maddie, you have to do it so we can together," she babbled excitedly, wrapping her towel around her.

"Do you want to try?" she asked me, her voice softening, knowing I must have felt bad. She knew how I felt before I did most of the time.

"It's okay, Mad. You've just got to do things when you're ready." She smiled in her customary way, nudging my arm.

"Next time," I said, moving the sand around with my toes.

"Next time, we all will," my father chimed in. "Maybe we will even get your mother here."

We all laughed, thinking of Missy Plympton anywhere near the bridge.

"Let's all go for a swim. Then I have to head back to the city tonight."

"You do, Dad?" I said, pouting as we walked to the water. He was always in the city, at least Monday through Friday, but lately, it had even been some weekends. I was sick of it just being my mother and me, but I had Summer. She pretty much lived with us, with Cat at the salon working so much. I knew I'd die of boredom if it weren't for her.

"I'm sorry, Madeline. Let's plan a vacation soon for all of us. You in, Summer?" he called out ahead as she was already halfway in the water.

"In?" she shouted, looking back at us.

"A vacation for all of us! Can you come?" I asked, running to meet her.

"I think she needs to check with Cat, but let me handle that," Dad said as I launched past him.

"I'm gonna float." I laughed, lying back, feeling the water slowly covering my face.

Dad dove in and swam past us while Summer disappeared in the waves, emerging with legs in a handstand.

"Let's try again," she said, remerging, wiping her nose.

"I'm doing it!" I shouted, feeling the water rise past my ears and over my head again.

"Let me help. You need to relax," Dad said, moving over to Summer.

"I'm done with this." I spat, blowing salt water through my nose, and headed to the water line, plopping down in the mud. I tilted my head, banging on my ear, watching Dad help Summer float, thinking I'd ask him to take us to the carousel.

"Summer didn't say it was okay. She didn't say anything," Sarah Martin went on. "And you're going to hear through all the assaults; Summer didn't say anything. She didn't say 'stop.' She would make up excuses and try to get him away from her in those moments, but she was terrified of what would happen if she did say 'stop,' 'go away,' or 'don't do that to me.' She just didn't talk about the incidents at all."

Chapter 7

Except for the glow from my phone, darkness surrounded me. At first, I was unsure where I was. "Ouch." I winced in pain, tugged at my left ear, ripped off the headphones, and realized I must have fallen asleep. I reached for my phone, looked at the time, and sat up, listening to my stomach churn in hunger, unsure where I'd get any food in the middle of the night. Boston certainly wasn't New York. This city went to sleep at a reasonable hour, something I always hated. I flipped the light on and went over to the mini fridge to see if it was stocked. "Ah-ha! Nutter Butters." I grabbed the package and what I was sure was a twenty-dollar bottle of water. Tearing into the pack, I plopped back on the bed, reaching for my phone and thinking about where I'd left off.

Summer at the beach that day burst into my mind, and a stabbing pain erupted in my chest. I hurriedly opened the water and drank, thinking I could flush away the feeling but couldn't. To believe that day was the first time anything happened right in front of me, my belly full of ice cream, thinking about riding at the Flying Horses as I sat pouting on the shore, sickened me. A mixture of feelings flooded me: guilt, foolishness, anger, and sadness. I felt naive and pathetic. I watched the water bottle roll from the bed and plop on the table, slowly leaking all over our picture. Quickly, I reached to grab it but stopped just before seeing the water cover our faces. I headed to the shower, leaving us all to drown.

"And Summer, she will tell you there were other times." Sarah Martin's voice hurt my heart and ears, and I turned down the volume as low as possible to where I almost couldn't hear her at all, hoping I wouldn't. I stared at the ceiling fan spinning slowly, digging my heels into the rug, lying naked and wet on the floor. I wasn't sure I could hear about the other times. I couldn't hear about it any time, even if there were no details, even if it was just Sarah Martin's voice saying my father did this. I couldn't listen to her say it then. I couldn't hear anyone say it without disassociating from my body, leaving on some trip to another planet. Why did I think now I could?

"Most importantly, she'll tell you about when she slept over. The Plympton's house was enormous; it was three floors. She and Madeline would sleep in various places, sometimes in the guest room. Sometimes, they would sleep on the daybed in what they called the art room, where they would paint, draw, dress up, and put on makeup. She will tell you that it didn't matter where they were sleeping. Once Madeline was asleep, and once it seemed she was asleep, the defendant would come in. He would usually wear a white robe with his initials on it. He would come over, kneel next to where she was, and put his hands under the covers, feeling for her. Summer would pretend to be asleep. She was too afraid to say, 'Go away,' or ask, 'What are you doing?' So, she would pretend to be asleep. Sometimes, Summer would start moving like she was waking up, pretend like she was waking up, and he would move away or leave. Sometimes, he wouldn't come back, and sometimes, he would wait a while and come back again and do it all over again on the same night. She'll tell you that she would stay up most of the night after a while when sleeping over at the Plympton's. Summer was afraid of this happening, but you'll hear from her that she still went there. She still wanted to hang out with Madeline. To be honest, Summer will tell you that she liked the defendant. She enjoyed hanging out with him. She liked it when he would, for instance, take her fishing. Summer will tell you that the defendant was nice to her, and she liked being at his home, even though this stuff was happening.

She could overlook it because she got to hang out with her best friend. She got to be around the defendant, whom she didn't dislike as long as he wasn't touching her.

"Summer Starr will tell you what happened in the bedroom while she was sleeping, and it happened almost every time she slept over at Madeline's house. She'll let you know that that was usually once a week. You may or may not have heard of the term 'trauma bond,' ladies and gentlemen of the jury. It is also known as Stockholm syndrome. It happens when there is a deep bond between the victim and the abuser in an ongoing cycle of abuse with intermittent positive reinforcement. It's not uncommon for abuse victims to develop a sense of loyalty to the person hurting them. You'll hear from an expert about this cycle of harm and how common it is.

"And those are just some of the details that Summer will share with you. As I said a few minutes ago, she's not just going to come in here and say, "I was sexually assaulted." She will tell you specific details about this abuse at the defendant's home. And Summer will let you know that when she was around thirteen, the assaults largely stopped. The defendant stopped coming into the room. Summer doesn't know why they stopped and doesn't have an explanation for it. It's not because she said anything or told anybody. It just stopped.

"She still went to the Plympton's house and was still very close with Madeline. But what led to her disclosing was what happened when she saw the defendant at the funeral of Nonie, Missy Plympton's mother—Madeline's grandmother. The defendant came over to her and hugged her, and while hugging her, he whispered, 'I miss you.' As she tried to pull away, he wouldn't let her go. That rattled Summer because even though it wasn't like the other times, it was just enough for her to wonder if it would start again."

I synced my phone to the Bluetooth speaker on the nightstand and had the volume turned up, hearing sweet Sarah's voice echo throughout the room. I wanted to open the windows for everyone to hear, so it wasn't just me. I envisioned them gasping and hanging their heads, clutching their chests, whispering to one another words like *filthy* and *shameful*. I hoped someone was next door and would wake up and come knocking on my door. I'd answer wet and naked and invite them in, and we could listen to it together. Every time she slept over? Many times? I racked my brain, trying to think, remembering the dreams, him kneeling by her and me turning away, feeling I shouldn't see, closing my eyes, and returning to sleep.

Why didn't she tell me, give me a sign? Why didn't I know? But did I know? Did I turn away? Was that real?

"And so, because of this incident, Summer told a friend about what happened. You'll hear she went on an overnight trip with her school just before starting ninth grade and was in a cabin with some other girls. There were about six girls in her room in the cabin, and they were all chatting. She told her friend Kaia, whom you'll hear from—Kaia asked her why she appeared sad, so Summer told Kaia what was going on with the defendant. She said it was a friend's dad—she didn't tell her the name. When Summer did that, she didn't think we would end up here. She didn't mean for the police to get involved and for all of this to happen. She just needed to share with somebody what was going on.

"Summer thought it was between friends and told Kaia to keep it a secret, but Kaia told Summer to tell an adult and convinced her to go into the teacher's room. The teacher's name was Joyce Paul. She was one of the chaperones in the cabin, so she was right next door. You'll hear from Ms. Paul, and she'll tell you that Summer came in with Kaia and several other girls in that room in the cabin—and Summer sat on the bed looking down. She had her knees drawn into herself. When prompted by Kaia, Summer told Ms. Paul what was happening."

Sarah Martin didn't come up for air; sometimes, she seemed emotional, tearful even, in her statement. I tore the robe from the bathroom door and threw it around myself, tying it as tight as possible. Hearing that's when it all came out—the camping trip I didn't go on—filled me with rage and jealousy, which enraged me even more because of how twisted that was. I ripped the earphones from the bed and plugged them into the phone, holding them tightly to my ears, feeling exposed and filthy. I didn't go on the overnight trip with the class because I was sick that day. I'd just gotten my period and cried to my mother about the cramps, hating everything about being a woman. I cried so hard that I gave myself a migraine and slept the whole day. When I woke, Mom had already canceled and thought I wouldn't like the camping experience anyway. I was furious, desperately wanting to camp to prove I wasn't like her and could rough it in life, not some spoiled, privileged jerk.

"Ms. Paul told Summer that she had to tell—that she couldn't keep this to herself. She was a mandatory reporter and was required to tell the police. Once Ms. Paul explained this, Summer was okay with it. And ladies and gentlemen of the jury, the next day at the Oak Bluffs police station, Summer described everything that happened to her for the first time. Summer then had to repeat it all at the Child Advocacy Center, then again to a forensic interviewer, then again to a medical examiner, along with having a medical exam, then again to a psychologist, and then again to us, representatives of the state of Massachusetts. Over and over, Summer had to tell this story . . . which never wavered." She breathed deeply before continuing.

"Four years have passed between her disclosure and when she will walk into this courtroom and tell you about what happened. During that time, ladies and gentlemen, she's been involved in this court process. She's had to be aware that the trial is coming, and she's been preparing for it, having it hanging over her head. But she's still here, and she's still willing to come in here and tell sixteen strangers what the defendant, William Plympton, did to her.

"In this case, you'll also hear from police officers about text messages between the defendant and Summer. You'll see that the police interviewed the defendant. You'll see part of that interview. In that interview with the police, they ask him repeatedly if there is a reason why Summer would make this up. Is there something going on? Was there a rift? Was there a fight? Is there any reason why Summer would come forward and say this about you? The defendant repeatedly said, 'No, there is nothing. She's like a second daughter to me. Our families are very close. I cannot think of why Summer Starr would make up these terrible allegations against me.'

"You, ladies and gentlemen, will be asked to judge all the witnesses and their credibility in this trial. You'll need to ask yourself if you believe each person. Is what they're saying making sense? Do they have a reason to come here and tell me something untrue? Is their body language suggesting that that is the case?

"After you hear from all the witnesses, you will be the people who decide whether or not this defendant, William Plympton, is guilty of the offenses. After you've heard from all the witnesses, it will be apparent that Summer Starr lost a lot in her life. She gained nothing from coming here and telling you this, and there is no reason that anybody could come up with, including the defendant, why she would make this up and come in here and tell you something that wasn't true. And that for a long time, too long, she didn't come forward with these allegations because she knew what they meant. She knew everything that would happen—most notably, losing her best friend. That's why she delayed her disclosure until she couldn't carry the burden of it any longer."

Chapter 8

A chair moved, and the microphone squealed, hurting my ears. Garbled voices mumbled, but I couldn't make out what was said. Then Judge Stone spoke.

"Mr. Heinz, are you ready to give your opening statement?"

More shuffling, and someone sighed.

"I am, Your Honor."

All I thought I wanted to hear was Summer—her words telling what happened. I'd been desperate for so long to listen to her voice. I didn't know what I was looking for. I'm not sure anyone does in any tragic event that changes one's life, but we all do it . . . search for an answer or deeper understanding to find the reason behind it.

I pressed pause and got dressed, moving over to the chair in the corner by the window, seeing the sun begin to rise. I opened the drapes and sat staring out at the waking city. I thought about running, although I hadn't in years. I glanced over at my bag, seeing one old sneaker on top of the small pile of clothes spilling out. I wanted to run long and far along the Charles River, over and over, until I collapsed.

Maybe I'll run?

"Good morning, guys," I said to the doormen, inhaling the crisp fall air.

"Going for a run, miss?" the tall one said, holding the door for the *Boston Globe* delivery man wheeling in a dolly full of newspapers.

"It would appear so." I smiled, unsure what I was doing, attempting a stretch against the building. I tried a braid in my hair to hold its wildness back, but I had no elastic, and it had already come loose under my hat. Zipping my sweatshirt tight to my neck, I popped on the headphones and pressed play, figuring I'd head toward the Common and then over to the river.

"This is William—or Bill is what his friends call him—Bill Plympton." Gabe Heinz coughed, then cleared his throat three times.

"This is a man who is quite accomplished. He served in the US Air Force special forces. He was born in 1970 and was raised by a single mother of two until she lost her life to a drunk driver. After the accident, he had to live with his grandparents. His grandparents ended up raising him. He's from Kansas and went to high school in a small town you've probably never heard of called Cottonwood Falls. After he graduated, he worked in the farming industry for several years, tinkering with the machines and fixing them. He quit his job at some point and joined the Air Force. After an honorable discharge, because he always loved history in school, particularly American history, he came to Boston and attended Boston College to pursue a career in computer science. That turned out to be his forte. During that time, he met his now-wife, Melissa Steele, from a highly regarded local family. After college, he reenlisted in the US Air Force and served as an intelligence specialist. After four more years in the Air Force, he was offered a position in a national security agency. He worked for the United States government in cybersecurity, had top-secret clearances, and was very successful. He and Melissa married during this time, and her family had a cottage here on Martha's Vineyard that they often visited.

"I think everyone here knows what it's like to fall in love with the island, and Bill is no different. He loved it and decided it was here that he wanted to have his family and raise his daughter Madeline, whom you'll meet later. This was also when he started his company, Cytrix, the largest cybersecurity company in New England and one of the top in the world. You may have heard of it or seen the enormous glowing blue sign on the gray, fortress-looking building lit up on I-95 when you're off-island, headed to wherever it is you're going." He coughed and cleared his throat again. The sound of shuffling papers and a female's voice mumbled.

"For the last twenty years, he worked for various companies doing cybersecurity," he went on. "Bill built his business from the ground up. A poor boy from Kansas after serving his country. He's currently in a position where he does cybersecurity for several well-known companies, most of whom you know well and use their products. He has a global team of thirty-five thousand people. He's very successful at this, and that's why he was able to buy his family a big house on East Chop in Oak Bluffs, his wife Melissa's dream house. He started with nothing, went to school, and worked, and that's why he is where he is today."

I hated how he read, detailing who my father was as if he was some character in a movie another actor needed to learn to play. Everything was so linear and blah; a timeline of events that seemed in order and perfect must mean he was perfect. Maybe Heinz wasn't so far off. It all seemed robotic, too perfect, straight, and unswerving without a bump. Everything magically fell into place, dull and drab in the correct order. So, all this must mean what? That he didn't do anything and wasn't capable because he was successful and had a good, clean story? Because he fell in love with the right girl? Because he married her, and they moved to the magical place? Because he was from humble beginnings—some golden boy who served his country and became successful? Everything was too spotless and shiny. I'd always felt it, and it was hard to live up to. Where were the feelings and messiness that people who live real life had? It had never been there—never once. Now it was the most enormous mess possible, and I longed for the perfect.

I'd give anything to be the flawless us again, Mom and her perfect house with nothing out of place. Dinner at five with talks of her next cause. Dad's nightly call at eight if he wasn't home. His assistant Jennie's weekly email provided his schedule so Mom could pencil him in for events on her calendar, which rested perfectly on the antique rolltop desk that was her great-grandmother's. On weekends, when he was home, changing from his suit to his chinos and polo shirt, always red or blue, taking us fishing and stopping at our regular island haunts. Our conversations about nothing real, only surface things like school and island happenings. I'd give anything for it all to have stayed like that. I'd never complain once.

Gabe Heinz coughed again, then continued on his soapbox, "He lives in his home with his wife Melissa, whom everyone calls Missy, and his daughter Madeline. Madeline is just about to turn eighteen years old. You won't see Madeline or Melissa in court today because they're on the witness list, and the rules are that if you're a witness, you're not supposed to be watching what other people say in court. They would be here if they could, and they'll tell you that because they'll be testifying. You'll hear from both Madeline and Missy. And it's critical you do because they were there throughout the period of these allegations, and they know this didn't happen."

I passed the Boston Common and slowed my pace to stop in front of a Starbucks. The street was busy with delivery people and workers opening their businesses and shops for the day. I leaned on a metal fence, watching a man fiddle with the Starbucks door, dropping his keys while balancing his coffee on a box. I wanted to scream at him for help or see if he could sit with me until my heart rate slowed and my head cleared. Hearing Gabe Heinz say my name made me wince. His certainty of my and my mother's belief in his innocence—I couldn't catch my breath. At the time, it was how I felt. I was sure of my father's innocence and didn't think anything else was possible. I let go of the fence and approached the man at the door. He turned, glancing up at me, staring with a look of concern.

"You okay, girl?" he asked, nearly tipping the coffee but catching it quickly and dropping the keys.

I'm not okay, I wanted to scream and burst into tears. Something compelled me to want to tell it all to a stranger, this man, the chosen one, and see what he thought. See if he thought I was a monster and

Summer was okay. Not that he could know, but I wanted an opinion from someone who had nothing to do with me.

"Oh, I'm fine." I reached down, picking up his keys. I came around him, went to the door, put the key in, opened it, and turned back to him, attempting to smile.

"Cool. Thank you. You sure you're good?" He stepped in, glancing back again.

"I'm fine." I shrugged and pressed play, starting again to run.

I made it to the Charles just after passing the Cytrix office they kept in the city, forgetting it was there. Had I remembered, I would have never cut down Beacon Street and stayed on Berkley to get to Storrow Drive. I looked up at the building, unsure what I was trying to see. They kept this office for out-of-town clients who came in for meetings so they didn't have to travel far. It was the whole top floor and had a beautiful view of the river and across it to Cambridge.

I remember being up there once with my father when I was little. Mom and I would visit him in the city on occasion. I could tell she missed it, seeming to come alive when we arrived. She talked faster and pointed at every landmark and shop window. She had a story for each one. On the island, she only spoke of her charities, not seeming to care as much for the beauty and nature as my father did. I had a little of both in me. The island and everything about it was home, and I couldn't imagine not hearing ocean waves, osprey cries, and the ferry whistle. But I liked the city's energy too—so many people from all walks of life doing all different things. Like my father, I also loved American history. I'm sure it's because he'd often reference things our forefathers said, quoting Washington or Andrew Jackson, odd quotes that were usually nonpolitical. "It's better to be alone than in bad company," he'd say to my mother when she'd drag him to another event, reminding her the first president was rarely wrong. She'd laugh, telling him to stop it, and smile. In college, I minored in art history, which didn't interest me initially, but I thought it went well with my creative writing degree. It's not that I didn't like art. I did, but I'd much have rathered American history, and, really, I chose differently to defy him and remind myself I wasn't like him, although I did all the historic tourist things locals didn't in the city. My roommate would laugh and roll her eyes when I occasionally asked her to go. She wouldn't, and I didn't like her much anyway, so it didn't matter. I enjoyed being alone, living in other characters and times long gone. Taking a ride with Paul Revere and visiting the graves of American Revolutionaries took me out of my head, the last place I ever wanted to be.

"See the Charles, Madeline? I knew I'd one day overlook it somehow. Back in college, when I met your mother," my father said as I spun around in his chair, my feet skimming the floor. He turned his back to me, facing the floor-to-ceiling windows and staring at the river. "My grandfather wanted me to stay in Kansas. He never left Cottonwood Falls."

"That's a funny name." I laughed, envisioning cotton balls falling from the sky. "Why don't I know him?" I stopped spinning, looking past my father at the rowers gliding across the river.

"Who, my grandfather?" He half turned to me.

"Yeah, Daddy, my grandparents and great-grandparents. Why don't I know them?"

It only then dawned on me that at seven years old, I'd never met my grandparents, his parents, or the grandparents who'd raised him. The ones from Kansas no one ever spoke about.

He paused, clasped his hands behind his back, and took a slow, deep breath.

"You wouldn't want to know him; I barely knew him, Madeline. He died some time ago."

"What about your mom and dad? What were they like, and your grandmother?" I spun around again, picking up a pen and tapping it on the desk with each turn.

"They are all gone, and I never knew my father."

"Why—" I began when he interrupted, calling for his assistant to bring in his calendar.

The air was warming, and the sun was full over the Longfellow Bridge and just about over the city. I took a right and headed toward it, passing the esplanade and the hatch shell. Gabe Heinz went on about my father and his accomplishments. Then it came: the defense, the bashing against Summer, with which I was on board at the time. Although I wasn't in the room, I could imagine what was being said about her. At home, we didn't speak of the case and only lived as if it was understood that my father was innocent just because he was ours. Attorney Heinz convinced me of what happened the day in his office when he prepared me for trial, and to me, it all made sense. Summer must have been carried away to invent a story to impress Kaia, although I'd never known her to do that except the one time when she had a crush on Cooper Collins. He made fun of Bridget Cox's accent and made up a story that she came from moonshiners in the Tennessee backwoods. She'd just moved up from somewhere down south, and Summer joined in, hoping to get his attention. Summer told me she felt terrible about it, and we all became friends with Bridget later, but I could see how maybe she got carried away, made a mistake, and now had to stick with it.

I fiddled with the volume button, trying to find the perfect setting to accommodate Gabe's voice, but the only one that would work would be mute, so I left it alone. "She didn't tell her counselor, who her mother had her seeing because of her eating issues. She didn't tell any adults. She told friends. And she told friends after they brought it up about someone else they'd heard it happened to, sharing gossip." His voice became higher pitched as he tried to emulate the girls. "'So and so was sexually assaulted.' Then, Miss Starr said she was also and described what happened. Then, one of the little girls, Kaia Kent, said, 'Oh, we've got to tell Ms. Paul.' And Ms. Paul had no choice. She is a mandatory reporter; this is where the story took on a life of its own. A mandatory reporter is somebody who, if they hear any allegation, must report it to the police. If they don't, they're committing an offense.

"This is where Summer could no longer turn back."

Chapter 9

The sun warmed my face, which felt good because the morning air chilled me, and sweat began to form at the base of my back. The crew teams were out from local colleges: Harvard, Northeastern, and BU, my alma mater. I briefly dated someone on the BU team just before I met Jay. Billy Thomas was someone to kill time with, and he didn't have space in his head or love in his heart for anyone but himself. This was perfect because I never wanted to talk about myself and certainly didn't want anyone's heart. I knew I had nothing to give, but I hoped the right person or circumstance could change that. I couldn't see how, but I was sick of being numb and occasionally sleeping with men to feel alive. Someone's body pounding against mine reminded me I was real. Alternating this with drinking to oblivion was how I got by, so I bounced between both.

Jay made me want to be better, at least to a degree. He gave me hope for a future and seemed to love enough for the both of us. But even early on, I knew that would wear on him. I just hoped I'd come around and be able to give him something. I could never get out of my head long enough to think of anything once we got past the lust phase. That worked well for me because hormones and pheromones fuel you, and there is little time for depth. Oh, we pretended; at least I did. Looking back, I realize he was sincere. We'd talk about books and classic movies and visit a museum or an art exhibit, but it was surface, and I could do that in between the sex. But then that slowed some, leaving more time for learning about each other, and then I started to struggle.

Gabe Heinz's voice annoyed me, so I nearly shut off the recording. With his stuttering and constant paper shuffling, I could feel his nervousness or lack of competence even without seeing him. I wasn't sure which. I was sure that defending accusations of harm to children, regardless of the guilt or innocence of his clients, was difficult, but I couldn't empathize—it was his choice. His voice mimicking Kaia and Summer's talk and his tearing down of Summer's character, which I was sure was next, didn't sit well with me even then, and I hated her. He said the same to me in his office about Summer, Kaia, and the girls in the cabin getting carried away. He emphasized "little girls," which infuriated me. I was the same age as them and didn't feel "little" then. We all knew a good amount about how the world worked upon entering high school, and while there was a lot left to learn, the word "little" had left us years earlier. It was derogatory, and I didn't like him after that, even though I had to pretend and have faith, for he was my father's only hope.

I crossed over the Long Fellow Bridge into Cambridge as Gabe went on about mandated reporters and the lack of evidence in the case. He and Sarah Martin both said there's rarely physical evidence in cases like these, and if forensic exams aren't performed quickly, all evidence is gone. They both stated this to me when I met with them, and I researched it repeatedly, googling everything I could about it all, waking up on my keyboard one night to my mother tearing it out from under me.

"You shouldn't be looking up this trash. This filthy trash." She raised her voice slightly, as she could never be accused of yelling or losing her composure. Half asleep, I didn't realize what she was talking about until I noticed the words *vaginal tearing* displayed on the screen as she held it, looking at me in disapproval.

Memorial Drive started filling with cars for the rush-hour commute. I stopped to tuck my hair under my hat, feeling the heat of a warmer-than-usual fall day beginning. Jogging in place, I stared at the rowers, hoping they'd somehow relax me with their uniformed behavior. I fast-forwarded through the rest of Heinz's rants about Summer's difficult childhood and food issues. I knew her. Her childhood was difficult because she didn't have a father, and Cat struggled with money and was always working, but she was happy. To me, she seemed happy, and she told me everything.

I didn't lose sight of the irony in thinking this as I continued toward the Harvard Bridge to return to the city. She told me everything except the biggest thing, so maybe I didn't know her. But I knew I did. I knew my best friend, except for that. I knew she had liked Cooper Collins since fifth grade and wanted him to be her first. I knew she went to search for her father and snuck on the ferry, making it over to Woods Hole and almost on the bus until one of the Steamship Authority guys grabbed her, recognized her, and sent her back on the next boat. I knew that she hated her bare feet on grass, her hair in her face, her toes being long: everything about her, I knew. When she became withdrawn and the eating issues started, I asked her about it all, feeling worried.

I saw she'd lost weight and refused Ben & Bill's ice cream or apple fritters from Back Door whenever I suggested it, changing the subject. She told me she was depressed, and when I asked why, she shrugged. I didn't press her; I just figured it had to be typical preteen stuff or sadness that she hadn't seen Cooper much of the summer.

It was just before everything came out, the reason for all her feelings—the reason I should have known or seen if I had been looking.

Why didn't she tell me? Why didn't I see it?

We walked to the carousel that last summer night. We'd been riding the carousel together every year for nearly all our lives. Unbeknownst to me, it would be the last time we'd be together—the last day of our friendship before that day in court. It was just before the start of school and before the world exploded, but I couldn't remember anything more about that night. I could only remember the summer before, just before the start of eighth grade, and weirdly, in vivid detail. It drove me crazy. I tried repeatedly to remember our last ride, but there was nothing except our walk there. Sometimes, when patterns are repeated, we don't know how we got there or what we did as we went through the motions, but I remembered every other time before, and what it felt like—just not the last time, the time that should be the clearest—the year before, with Coop and Hank, replayed in my head. That day, her face and words were my last memory of the carousel, and although I longed to remember our true last time, I gave up on trying.

"I'm sad sometimes," she said as we passed through the white metal gate.

"Where is this coming from?" I took her arm, stopping her.

"Sometimes I'm sad I don't have a father." She said she had no one to protect her.

"I'll protect you. I'll always protect you," I assured her as we chose our horses, the usual pair, the high and low purple and blue. We'd always grab them if we could. We named them when we were small—Lilac and Blue. Summer had laughed when Blue was all I could come up with, especially when I was the creative one, she said. I ignored her, sticking to my name.

"I'm just being stupid," she said, waving her hand.

The small circular room filled with the sounds of giggling children and excited parents as the carousel waltz played and the horses took flight. We rounded the room, and I watched her face as she sat on Lilac above me. Her hair blew back, and she smoothed away some strands that clung to her lips. I brushed out my faded blue horse's hair, revealing its yellow glass eye, cracked and cold, staring at me and somehow at everyone else.

"Are you okay? Seriously?" I blurted without looking up, running my finger over the eye and feeling its smooth surface, which surprised me. I didn't hear anything except the music and turned, seeing her looking ahead, gripping the brass bar, seemingly lost in thought. She missed grabbing the ring as we rounded; she didn't even try, and I knew something was wrong.

"Summer?" I roared, breaking her from her trance.

"What?" She turned, looking confused, and I wondered if she'd heard me.

"Are you okay?" I asked again, watching her face change.

Just then, she smiled and waved at someone as we passed. I turned back to see, noticing Cooper and Hank Brown.

"Let's see what they're up to," she said, climbing off the horse before we were supposed to and fixing her hair.

"Ugh, but Hank?" I groaned as we circled the platform toward the gate. Hank annoyed me. All he talked about was fishing and all the tournaments he and his dad won. Every tournament on the island, you were sure to see Hank's picture in the *Martha's Vineyard Times* or *The Vineyard Gazette* holding a giant fish.

"Hey, Coop," Summer called, nudging me and walking over to them.

"What was that for?" I asked, watching her walk ahead, ignoring me.

Cooper smiled at Summer, taking her hand. It caught me off guard. I didn't know anything had advanced between them since the one kiss they had had on the pier a few weeks earlier. Suddenly, I felt I was losing my friend.

Hank sidled up to me. "We were gonna head to the Jaws bridge for a jump," he said, eyeballing me.

Summer and Coop were whispering. She smiled large as she tapped his shoulder. I liked seeing her happy, but with boys entering our lives, I couldn't help but think things would be different.

"It will be dark by the time we get there," I said, looking out to the street and seeing the clouds move slowly in the dimming orange sky.

"Oh, come on, Maddie. We can get your mom to grab us there instead. She won't mind. She never gets out on time anyway."

My mother was at her Vineyard Historical Society meeting. It was the first Wednesday of every month. She was always nearly an hour late getting home from the meeting, and Summer and I would wonder why. She sometimes seemed a little off and would tell us some island gossip after: "Do you know that Annie Brokaw had the gall to use the same flower arrangements I did at the Community House event for her daughter's art exhibit I wasn't even invited to? Macey Swanson told me. She even had pictures!"

She had told us this during our last pickup and then went on about how Sissy Martin, her best friend, constantly flirts with the entire staff at the yacht club. My mother never talked like this, and Summer and I would try to keep from giggling and making faces at each other while she went on. I was sure there couldn't be much to talk about for hours on the island's history. I figured it doesn't change, it just is, so there must be some wine and chatter.

"Okay, let's go, but we need to hurry," I said in my most likable voice, trying not to put a damper on things.

Summer smiled and skipped up ahead. We had just passed Ocean Park when Hank stopped and set his backpack down, rifling through it. I was waiting for him to throw some nightcrawlers at us or chase us with fishing hooks, but he pulled out two cans and handed one to Coop.

"What's that?" Summer asked, grabbed one, and read the label. "Summer Shandy?" she read aloud.

"It's beer, but it tastes like lemonade," Cooper said, taking back the can.

"I'll take one," she said, beaming at Hank, who reached back in and handed her a can. She cracked hers open and took a giant swig. "Oh, my God, it does," she exclaimed, wiping her mouth with her arm. "Here, Maddie, try it." She shoved it toward me.

I'd tried beer a few times and some champagne or wine at a few parties at the house this summer season and last. Summer and I would sneak a glass from a waiter's tray after he set it down, just like at the Park Plaza New Year's party. At all my parent's events, there was always one waiter, Rick. He smoked, so he'd disappear, leaving his tray sometimes, and we would wait patiently for our opportunity.

"Wow, it really does," I said, taking another sip, concerned about how easy it went down.

Hank handed me one of my own and, along with it, a small bottle.

"Smirnoff?" I read as we crossed the road onto the bike path.

Hank dumped the bottle into the can and tossed it in the grass. "Dump it in the beer for an extra kick."

"Hey, don't freaking litter, Hank." Summer shoved him and grabbed the bottle, stuffing it into his pocket from behind.

"Oh, that felt nice," Hank teased.

Cooper put his arm up. "All right now, everyone, simmer down."

We all poured one into our beers and continued to walk. It was better without it. Now it tasted like a warm, lemon-scented cleaner, but I continued to choke it down. Summer turned, walking backward, and stuck her thumb out as a Jeep came toward us. It slowed, pulling over to let us in. Although hitchhiking was never encouraged, it was common and not unusual on the island. We'd done it a handful of times but kept it quiet, knowing our parents would kill us. When we got to the bridge, the sun was low in the sky, and the last beachgoers were headed toward their cars, leaving for the day. I looked over at Summer, who appeared sleepy and smiley. I wondered if I looked the same, feeling the effects of my drink as I slurped the last sip.

"I think I'm drunk," I said, moving close to her. Our eyes met, and we broke out into a fit of giggles. The boys looked at us, rolling their eyes.

"Let's go sit," Coop said, pointing to the jetty stretching into the water on State Beach.

The remnants of the burnt-orange sun bled into the gray night sky against the horizon, pouring down into the ocean until nothing was left except the contrasting darkness of sky and sea. Coop moved closer to Summer, who put her head on his shoulder. I thought about what she said at the carousel and how she seemed. Just a short time later, she appeared content and looked happy, and I felt at ease thinking she was only having a moment before. I do; we all do.

"I'm going to jump," Hank said, leaping from his seat.

Everything felt warm and wonderful. I pushed my toes into the warm sand and lay back, closing my eyes, feeling the ocean breeze, and listening to the sounds.

"Anyone coming?" Hank's voice interrupted. We all stared at him. No one seemed eager to move.

"C'mon, Coop. Not many jumps left before school starts."

"All right, I have to show off for the girls." Cooper laughed, taking off his shirt and tossing it at Summer. As they made their way up to the bridge, his thin, tan body became a silhouette in the darkness.

"You really like him?" I asked, moving closer to her. She had her back to me, watching the bridge.

"I can barely see them," she said. "C'mon, let's go up there; let's jump." She stood, taking off her top and shorts, leaving them in the sand, revealing her red and white bikini. On the island, everyone wore a bathing suit under their clothes in the summer for moments like this, which happened frequently.

"It's dark." I looked at her, concerned. She put her hands on her hips and gave me the look she always did when I was being a killjoy.

I'd only ever jumped once, and although everyone thought I did it voluntarily, I didn't. I had stood at the edge of the rail, which I had many times before, only to climb back over in cowardice. Summer had been next to me, giving me her usual pep talk, and my foot slipped after a truck drove by, hitting a bump and making a loud bang, startling me. My dad was with us that day and proudly leaped from his seat, where he was sitting patiently for me, which he'd done so many times. When I emerged from the water, I saw him through blurry eyes, his perfect white teeth beaming and clapping in his usual slow, hard way. Summer's head had popped up next to me in the water.

"You did it! You really did it."

"Yeah, well. It's about time, I guess." I had forced a smile, feeling she could see right through me.

We headed up the sand, meeting the boys who jumped from the top rail right when they saw us, splashing into the darkness below.

"You guys okay?" I shouted down, unable to see them.

"Yup," Coop's voice called back as I made out Hank climbing up the rocks.

"You can't even see down there."

"Maddie, it's fine; we'll jump together." She smiled, then took my hand, squeezing it.

Hank and Coop came up and met us.

"You can't even see if someone ever comes up. I don't know." I leaned over the railing to look.

"I can see. Look, there's a buoy in the waves." Hank pointed to something I couldn't make out, and they couldn't either by the looks on Summer and Coop's faces.

The truth was, I was scared to jump. I'd never done it voluntarily, and now, in the dark, I was sure I wouldn't be able to. It was also stupid and unsafe, I justified repeatedly.

"Live with no regrets," Summer came by my side and whispered.

I raised my eyebrows, turning to her. "I'd just like to live, thank you very much." I laughed nervously.

"Hey, I know!" Summer shouted, standing on the first rail above us. Her hair blew back in the wind, and she raised one arm, circled it around, and pulled her knee up, balancing herself on one leg as if she was about to break out into a cheer. "Let's have a code word." She jumped down and spun toward Coop, nearly falling into his arms.

"A code word?" I asked.

"For what?" Hank asked behind me.

"To let each other know we're okay. Like, say Coop and I jump, and when we surface, we yell the word, so you guys up here know we're good."

I couldn't argue that it wasn't a good idea, but I still didn't think I could do it.

"And what if we're not okay?" Coop climbed the railing and balanced on the top. He pushed his wavy hair from his face and half turned to us, smiling.

"Then I guess we're going in after you." Hank gestured to push him, and I swatted at him to stop it.

"Okay, what's the word?" I asked reluctantly, wishing my mother would respond to my text and come early.

"Hmm," Summer said, climbing up with Coop.

"C'mon now, let's pick a word before you go!" I said, annoyed.

"You pick." Coop pointed at me from above; the beer taste rose in my throat just then.

"Lemonade," I answered.

"Lemonade!" Coop jumped, the word echoing behind him.

Summer sat down on the rail as Hank tossed himself over.

"Guys," she shouted down.

"Lemonade?" I yelled over.

"Lemonade," a voice yelled back, followed by laughter and splashes.

I watched the silhouette of Hank climb up the rocks again. I could tell it was him because he was shorter and stockier than Coop. *He isn't so bad*, I thought, *and sort of cute when he isn't talking about fishing.*

"Come up here with me." Summer waved me over.

I climbed over the railing and sat with her, feeling my heart quicken. The warm and fuzzy sensation from the beer concoction faded, and my head began to throb.

We sat swinging our legs as the warm summer air cooled quickly, as it often did this time of year on the island.

"I'm waiting for you guys," Coop yelled from below as car lights approached us, advancing across the bridge. I could just make him out in the water beneath us.

"Here I come," Summer said, standing. "C'mon, Maddie."

I stood slowly, gripping the railing as hard as I could with my feet.

"Ready, one, two . . ."

"Wait!" I yelled.

"I'm not doing this, Maddie. Jump or don't jump. Your mom will be here any minute, so I'm going. If you don't want to, it's okay." She looked at me, smiling; her eyes crinkled at the corners.

I knew then that she knew I hadn't jumped on my own that

time, and I was determined but remained frozen, unable to envision launching myself into the black void below.

"One, two, two and a half . . ." She looked at me before yelling three, then disappeared. I heard a splash and stared, trying to see her reemerge. Everything went quiet, and the water was still. I waited a moment and still heard nothing.

"Hey, lemonade?" I yelled, pausing. I heard only what sounded like water hitting the rocks. I laser-focused my vision below but could see nothing but blackness.

I looked over, and Hank was walking toward me on the bridge.

"Guys, lemonade, lemonade," I yelled, panicking. I looked at Hank again, and he was too far away for me to yell or explain anything.

"Lemonade!" I screamed again before closing my eyes, hearing nothing, and leaping from the rail, pointing my toes and holding my nose.

"Lemonade, lemon—" I heard Summer's voice ring out, and then there was nothing as I went under.

"Maddie, I'm here, I'm here," Summer shouted as I gasped, coughing. My heart pounded against me. I reached out to her, flailing. Tears poured down my face, and I clung to her arm.

"C'mon, I'm sorry. Just swim. Follow me." She half-pulled me toward the rocks.

Car lights came close, and Coop climbed the rocks just ahead of us. I let go of her, gaining my composure.

"Stop!" I yelled toward her. I felt my feet touch, and my heart slowed. Tears still came, and I wiped my eyes.

"You jumped." Summer swam back to me as Hank splashed down a few yards away.

"Don't give me that crap, Summer. Lemonade? I was calling for you. Lemonade?" I said, lifting my hands above my head.

"Coop and I were kissing," she started and came closer to me. "The first time I heard you, the first time." Her nose touched mine. "When you said it again, I tried to pull away from him, and he pulled me close.

Then I went to say it back, and you had already jumped. I'm sorry."

She smiled and widened her eyes, telling me she meant it. We climbed up the rocks, and she turned back to me. I saw her glowing in the car's headlights, slowing close to the bridge.

"You jumped to save me," she said softly, turning to me, seeming to realize.

"I guess I did." I just realized it too.

Our eyes met, and a horn beeped.

"It's your mom," Coop called, picking up our belongings. The three of us walked up the sand while Hank trailed behind.

Chapter 10

"I call Summer Starr to the witness bench, Your Honor," said Sarah. After a long pause, I could make out the faint sound of a door opening and footsteps. I'd always been jealous of Summer's name. Summer Starr. It sounded like someone famous and much more fabulous than Madeline Plympton.

"It's an old lady's name," I remembered saying in a huff that day in the art room, Summer's favorite room in the house, signing my watercolor and practicing my signature.

"No, it's not," Summer said, shading in a dress she had drawn on her self-portrait, although I'd rarely seen her wear a dress.

"Your name is so much cooler. Starr is a good last name." I put down my brush, waving my hands across the painting for it to dry.

Summer put her pencil down and exited her seat, sitting on the floor and crossing her legs. She always moved around, changing positions, and I never knew why.

"It's English. I guess my dad was." She paused, looking to the ceiling. "Or is, I should say, if he's still alive."

"What's it mean? Like stars in the sky?" I asked, avoiding the comment about her father, unsure what to say.

"I don't know. I never asked." She got up, moved to the daybed, tossed the pillows to the floor, and stretched across it.

"If it was 'star,' like in the sky, then why the extra r?" I reached behind the computer, turning it on. "We should look it up."

Summer sat up, interested. "Okay," she said, coming behind me.

"Hey." I giggled, her hair tickling my neck as she leaned over my shoulder.

"Click this one." She pointed to a web page.

I scrolled down to the Ss. "Here it is. Starr, it's English."

"Duh, I told you that." She slapped my arm.

"Stop." I rubbed the spot, although it wasn't sore.

"Oh, my God." She laughed, pointing.

"What?" I asked as I read.

I turned to her and widened my eyes, and then we both laughed hysterically. I remembered her running to the daybed and curling up in a ball, laughing uncontrollably.

"I guess we're both old ladies," I said, wiping the wetness in my eyes.

"I can't believe it means someone with—"

"Gray hair," I said simultaneously, and we laughed again.

I turned the chair around, pretending it was a walker, making my best old-lady impression. Summer leaped from the bed, grabbed my twirling baton in the corner, using it as a cane, and we fell on the floor, laughing our heads off.

My heart flipped inside my chest, and I suddenly felt I couldn't be still, anticipating hearing my friend's voice. I knew she'd be the first witness, but I wasn't ready. Instantly, I regretted fast-forwarding past Gabe. Listening to papers shuffling and murmurs in the room, I stopped as I hit the bridge and leaned on the railing, catching my breath. Running while listening to this made my heart race faster than I thought possible.

"Can you state your name for the record?" Sarah asked in her sweetest voice.

"Summer, Summer Rose Starr," Summer mumbled.

A rising fire flushed my face. She felt like a memory or a dream, part of a life I wasn't sure existed most days. Tears filled my eyes, and I tapped my foot uncontrollably. She was nervous—I could tell. Her deep, hushed voice, I knew. I pictured her, head down, hands fidgeting, and looking up with only her eyes, embarrassed or uncomfortable. I wasn't sure which, but I imagined it was both.

"Summer, can you say that again?" Sarah asked. "Sorry, the court has to hear it loudly so it can be transcribed into the record by that woman right there. See her typing?"

"Yes," Summer answered, then repeated her name louder but with the same uneasiness.

"That was perfect. Just like that. Okay?"

"Yes," she answered.

"Summer, how old are you?" Sarah asked.

"Seventeen." She breathed, causing a crunching sound in the microphone.

"And where do you live?"

She hesitated. "Well, I live here on the island."

"Which town?" Sarah questioned.

"Vineyard Haven."

The questions went on this way for a while, and I was unsure why they mattered. Who do you live with? Do you have any pets? What do you like to do for fun? I'd guessed this was to establish a relationship and show the jury she was a person. I knew the answers to all the questions, saying them simultaneously as Summer answered them. She knew me the same way, and she knew me better than anyone. I walked along the bridge, not seeing anything—not the cars, the people, or the city. It all blurred, like the backdrop of a movie.

Hearing her voice again solidified her. She had existed in my life, and I cared deeply for her. I hoped somewhere she more than existed. That's all I did until I couldn't anymore. I'd imagined her worse. After what he did, what I did, she was worse. I was sure of it, but I hoped she somehow found a way to live and forget everything about us.

"She still knows me," I whispered loudly, repeating it. There wasn't much more to know of me since—just the facade I portrayed. I walked through life, the shell of a once-someone covering nothing except the particles of a lost island girl.

In the distance, I saw it—the Citgo sign. I blinked away tears, allowing it to come into focus. Suddenly, I wanted to run faster than ever home to Jay to make it all stop. For him to take the recording from me, to punch him for getting it for me, to beg him to check me back into McLeans and call Doctor Harper. I wasn't ready. I'd never been, but I'd never move on if I didn't hear her story. If I didn't honor her in some fucking way. The most pathetic way, listening to her years later on a fucking bridge alone in the middle of a city of thousands.

I stopped and stared at the river, thinking how I felt in the bathroom that day and the weeks before, that it might be the only way out. But then I felt relief that I'd figured out the difference this time; I was scared. Ending my life scared me. I'd instead continue running, whether from it or toward it, I wasn't sure. Everything became quiet, and I saw no one on the bridge, no people, no cars. I closed my eyes, listening to the traffic from Storrow Drive. Just then, a horn beeped behind me, startling me. A man was pulled to the side, waving me over.

"Can I help you?" I asked, wiping my eyes.

"Hey there, can you tell me how to get to Faneuil Hall?" an older man asked with a grin, looking at a GPS on the dash and then back at me. "Thing's not working."

He looked like he'd never left the '90s, wearing a flannel shirt and pushing back his long, wavy hair. A stack of cracked leather bracelets circled his wrist, and he tapped his fingers on the steering wheel.

"Sure," I said, stepping back from the car and explaining the route.

"Thank you," he said, sticking his hand out the window.

Just then, I noticed the symbol—the blackbird on the blue hood.

"Enjoy your run," he shouted, driving off.

Pontiac, it said under another image of the bird etched into the strange taillights that weren't reminiscent of any car I'd ever seen. It was the only car on the bridge. I watched it disappear into the city's congestion, wondering what the odds of seeing a blue Pontiac Firebird were, not just at this moment but at any time. Although I knew it wasn't possible that Summer's father would ever still be driving the same car this many years later, I still wondered and thought of his words—his saying. It was the only thing that I knew about him and the only thing Summer ever said about him—*live with no regrets*.

Chapter 11

I ran past McGinty's and by so many familiar spots as if on autopilot; my feet knew the way as I continued to listen. I craved the numbing effect of alcohol, and had the bar been open, I would've been sitting there, chatting with Pete, trying to lose consciousness, drowning in his stories of Ireland and his former life, trying to escape mine, meds or no meds. Drugs might make it even better. The thought crossed my mind as I raced down Commonwealth Ave, dodging the traffic and pedestrians that now littered the streets. Summer's voice and words strangely made me feel safe and whole until she spoke of things. The things that I didn't believe then, the things I struggled to believe still—the things that no daughter should ever think about her father, the things a father, a man, a human should never be. Monsters walk among us. We're taught this, and we seemingly know, but it's not until it lands on your doorstep like a bomb or you're their victim—violated and destroyed, unable to defend yourself—that you're sure. I guess we are all their victims in some way—his victims. The thought had never occurred to me. I only thought of myself and my mother as coconspirators, but weren't we casualties too? I turned left and headed toward the Park Plaza, suddenly needing to get there as fast as I could and hide in my room where the past remained—perfect, untouched, and unsealed until I opened the door that, right now, I wish I never had. I was now envious of my mother's ability to blind herself.

"Okay, Summer," Sarah continued. "So now that we've talked a little bit about you, I'm going to ask you some more specific questions. Do you know someone named William or 'Bill' Plympton?"

"Yes."

"And how is it that you know him?"

There was a pause, and Summer's voice lowered. "I'm best friends with his daughter." She cleared her throat. "Or I used to be."

I miss you. I missed all these years of you.

"What's his daughter's name?"

"Madeline."

"Do you see the person we are referring to as Bill Plympton in the courtroom today?"

"Yeah," she said nervously. I could tell she was nervous by her hesitations, and her voice sounded embarrassed or put on the spot. I envisioned her struggling and wished I was there to help her. I ran as fast as possible, nearly colliding with a cyclist turning the corner. "Being friends with fucking me and meeting us caused this," I roared, watching a passerby stare. I glared at her, asking her with my eyes what the fuck she was looking at. *Go ahead, say something back, say something. Anyone, I fucking dare you.*

"Can you identify him by where he's sitting and what he's wearing?"

"Yeah. He's right there with the blue tie on."

"Okay, I would ask the record to reflect that the witness has identified the defendant."

"Do you remember how old you were when you met the Plymptons?"

"Like, four."

"You mentioned his daughter; Madeline is her name, correct? How old is she?"

"Right now?"

"Yes."

"Almost eighteen."

"You are seventeen too. Is she a little older?"

"Yeah."

"When you lived with the Plymptons, do you remember how old you were?"

"Four or five, maybe? I know that I started my first day of kindergarten while I was, like, in the middle of living there."

"Okay."

"And my room was, like, the art room, so it was, like, a desk—I don't know—it was, like, my room."

"Okay. So, when you moved out of the Plymptons' house, where did you go?"

"My house, in Vineyard Haven."

"You'd still spend time there?" Sarah Martin asked, her voice louder.

"Yes."

"How often would you spend time at the Plymptons'?"

"Every Monday and Tuesday, and probably every weekend."

She was there every weekend, and even more than Mondays and Tuesdays, but these were set days because Cat worked late, and we'd go to my house straight from school. This continued for years until Summer was old enough to stay alone, but we were still together nearly every day after school and on weekends.

"When would you sleep over?"

"Weekends mostly, but sometimes during the week too."

"Would Madeline ever spend time at your house?"

"Yeah, sometimes."

"Would it be more common to spend time at your or Madeline's house?"

"At Madeline's house." Summer sighed.

"And why was that?"

"Madeline's house was bigger. There was a lot more to do, and I did—I don't know. My house embarrassed me."

"Why were you embarrassed?" Sarah asked, sounding concerned.

"It was really small and not nearly as nice as hers."

"And what made it so—other than being small? Was there anything else specific that made it not great?"

"I, I, I don't know," Summer stammered. "I thought my house was ugly then and didn't want anyone over."

I hadn't realized she felt that way.

Sarah Martin asked to approach the bench and discussed entering exhibits. The judge asked if Gabe Heinz had any objection, which he didn't. It appeared the exhibits were diagrams of our houses—mine and Summer's. She asked Summer if she recognized certain things, like the bedrooms and patio, and asked what rooms we spent time in. I wasn't sure where she was going with it, but I assumed it provided a layout to the jury of where things supposedly took place.

Sarah went on about the windows, doors, and furniture placement. I thought about the house and my mother still living there, by herself in all those rooms with nothing changed and everything untouched; even her rotation of items had stopped. I had noticed some time ago when things had been in the same place the last time I'd visited, which felt like it was ages ago. There was little news nowadays about anything; everyone was gone, so things remained perfect, in their proper homes, untouched. I slowed to a walk when I hit Arlington Street, realizing I'd be back at the hotel soon. A man sitting on the bench at the T stop was reading the paper. I plopped down next to him, wiping the sweat from my eyes and pushing my hair back under my ball cap. I could feel it was wild and large, and I imagined my appearance. He looked at me from behind the paper and quickly nodded. Feeling ill, suddenly, I rested my elbows on my knees and lowered my chin to my hands. I should see my mother—call more.

Sarah finally made her way upstairs, detailing the house layout with Summer, whom I could tell now was exhausted by this.

"Did anyone sleep in the art room, I mean, after you moved out? I know it was your room when you lived there before," Sarah asked.

"Yes."

"Who slept in there?"

"Well, whenever I stayed the night, Maddie, I mean Madeline, and I would usually sleep in there."

I pinched my nose, shut my eyes tightly, and held my breath, hearing her say my name, *Maddie*, with the ease of a friend.

"Why do you call it the art room?"

"Oh, because Maddie and I would do, like, a bunch of art in there. We both loved painting watercolors, and she, Madeleine, I mean, liked to write stories." She coughed. "Sorry, is that too much? Sorry," she stuttered.

"That's okay, Summer," Sarah said sweetly. "You guys slept in there, where?"

"Sometimes we would make little, like, beds out of blankets on the floor and just sleep there, but there was a big comfy couch and a daybed thing that I usually slept on. Maddie, I mean Madeline, liked the couch because it was close to the window, and she didn't—umm, she didn't like the dark sometimes." Summer hesitated, not wanting to break my confidence, I was sure of it; she knew I felt silly for being afraid.

The trolley screeched loudly, muffling Sarah's voice, and pulled up to us on the bench, causing a breeze and cooling me.

"When you were at the house spending time with Madeline, would her dad, Mr. Plympton, ever be around while you played together? Would he be checking in on you at all?"

"I mean, yes, mostly on the weekends. He would ask what we wanted for, like, food or whatever, and he took us places like fishing and the beach a lot."

"If you wanted anything like food or to go somewhere, who would typically go get it, and who would you ask, Bill or Missy Plympton?"

"Bill. We'd always ask Bill."

"Did he tell you to call him Bill?"

"Yes."

"Why would you always ask Bill?"

"Missy was busy with her charity and island things. Bill seemed to like us more."

"So, you said Mr. Plympton, or Bill, took you to the beach a lot."

"Yes."

"Did just you and Madeline go in the water, or did Bill sometimes go in with you?"

"He went in sometimes."

"Do you remember a time when you were trying to float on your back?"

"Objection, leading," Heinz exclaimed.

"Ask it differently," said the judge.

"Summer, has Mr. Plympton—Bill—ever taught you anything in the water?" Sarah Martin rephrased.

"Yes."

"And what was that?"

"To float."

"And do you remember how old you were when that happened?"

"Like eight or nine."

"What helped you remember that you were eight or nine?"

"I don't know. Because I was in, like, third or fourth grade."

"On this occasion, was Madeline in the water with you?"

"She was and then got out."

"Was anyone else in the water with you?"

"Yes."

"Who else was in the water with you?"

"Bill."

"Do you know where Madeline was?"

"I think on the beach."

"Okay. When Bill was in the water with you, and you were trying to float, what was he doing?"

"Like holding my back."

"What was he holding your back with?"

"His hand."

"Did he touch any other part of your body besides your back?"

"Yes."

"What part of your body did he touch?"

"My butt."

"Was that over or under your bathing suit?"

"Over, at first."

"Okay. Did you say anything to him about touching your butt?"

"No."

"Did he say anything to you at that point?"

"At that point, no."

"You said he not only touched you over your bathing suit but also under. Where did he touch you under?"

"Like, my vagina."

"What part of his body was he using?"

"His hand and fingers."

"And were they outside or inside of your vagina?"

"Inside."

"Okay. Did he say anything to you while that was happening?"

"Yes."

"What did he say?"

"He whispered in my ear, 'Is this okay?'"

"Did you say anything back to him?"

"No."

"Summer, was this the only time this happened?" Sarah asked, raising her tone slightly.

"No."

"How often did things similar to this occur, where Bill Plympton touched you?"

There was a long pause and a screeching sound like someone moving a chair. Another trolley came, and I got up and walked, zombie-like, into the cluster of people exiting the car and dispersing into the street.

"Hey, watch it," a man yelled, shoving his middle finger out his car window as I stepped into traffic, leaving the crowd at the curb.

I suddenly fell backward, feeling pulled. "Lady, get off the phone!" A man lifted me to my feet, and my right headphone slid from my ear just as Summer answered the question.

"Too many times to count."

Chapter 12

I shuffled through the hotel entrance, trying to muster a smile to the doorman, praying I didn't see Bruce in the lobby. The judge called for a break so the jury could use the bathroom and stretch their legs. My eyes stung from the tears that flowed as I walked from my near-death experience down the long sidewalk while people quickly maneuvered around me, hurrying about their day. The man's face who lifted me—saving me—appeared angry and confused. He stared at me, perplexed, and scrutinized, probably thinking I was high or insane.

I envisioned myself now looking back at him, scrunching my brows, and roaring something, angry that he had intervened. I hadn't done it on purpose this time. I had stepped mindlessly off the curb, sinking into the street, listening to what I had already known, but Summer and Sarah's words made it more real—more real than my father in jail and the collapse of my life, the loss of my best friend, my sister, and my island. The life I'd known, the mother I knew, the Summer I knew before, and the me I knew, if I'd ever known myself, was gone. And none of that seemed to make it more real than hearing Summer say it. I'd always known it would. I had no choice but to not be in the courtroom, but I was glad that I hadn't been there. I would have testified for my father over and over again if it allowed me to avoid seeing Summer and hearing her because then I would know deeply what I already did intuitively—that my father, the strength of us, the proud, strong, successful man who was my everything, our everything, and so much to so many, was a monster of the worst kind. When you know someone as well as we knew each other, you know when they are truthful and when they lie. You know every detail about them, even the ones they didn't know about themselves. Summer would never have lied about this or been swooped up in gossip. This, I was sure, was the hardest thing she'd ever done: testify against him—and lose us. I never thought it was possible for us not to be *us*. But it was, and I had believed Gabe Heinz and my father and had followed my mother's blind faith, asking no questions. I had walked with them in solidarity off the cliff of everything we knew, never to be seen again.

My legs barely held me, and my insides felt black, filthy, and numb to existing and to what I was hearing, but I couldn't help but think it was meant to be. Getting pulverized by a bus or trolley at that moment would almost be beautiful, poetic even. Then that fucking moron jumped in, ruining God's plan. Most would think the opposite: the man saving me was a divine intervention. You hear all the stories of those who've experienced things like it, talk about it being a wake-up call, and go on to live their lives somehow better. I wondered if they did or if it was just for a few days, months, or years; then, they'd fall right back to floating in the dead sea of humanity, unable to swim, spinning round and round on this thing, this giant ball, lost, doomed, and untethered.

If divine intervention worked that way, then it most certainly worked the opposite, but no one wants to talk about that. Maybe I was meant to die that day in the bathroom or just now in the street, and then Mrs. Janson and the guy on the sidewalk messed up the plan, setting things in motion that shouldn't be. Why isn't that a thought in people's heads? No one likes to speak of things that aren't pretty, and I knew that better than anyone.

I kept my head down and rushed through the lobby to avoid eye contact if Bruce or anyone familiar was around. Appear rushed and busy, then people tend to avoid trying to talk. I learned that from my father, the master, especially at my mother's charity events. "If you look tense, move quickly, and look down at your phone, people tend to think something more important is going on than whatever they've dragged you there for," he'd say, laughing, the two-huff way he always did as my mother nudged his arm. He didn't do this at events, at least that I saw, but he pretended he did. He was only always at his best, especially if they were on the island. There, he smiled and took his time talking to everyone in the room, no matter who they were. He spoke to everyone on the island equally. He chatted with Lou, the gas station attendant in Oak Bluffs, in the same way as the attorney general, the senator of Massachusetts, and Hollywood A-listers who summered here and showed up to all the island events that nine times out of ten my mother was running, where the who's who come to throw their money around.

"This place is the land of equals," he said one night, smoking his cigar out behind the tent with the waitstaff and making a bet about who out of the elite big shots got drunk first after having just talked with the president and first lady at the Possible Dreams Auction for over an hour. "Maybe not equal money or status as far as the mainland is concerned, but we aren't on the mainland, and that's fine with me." He took me with him, saving me from Sissy Martin's son, who spit when he talked. I couldn't hear who they were talking about, but I hung on his every word, studying his face as he puffed on the cigar, watching the smoke come from him slowly and controlled, dissipating into the night air. The one thing I was always sure of was how much he loved the island. Although it was all I'd ever known except our vacations and Boston, his love for it made me love it that much more.

The mini fridge looked like a life raft from a sinking ship, and I knelt, throwing it open, then glanced at my phone for the time: 9 a.m.—too early for a drink? I kept coming close to drinking since the hospital, thinking thoughts like this, staring at bottles in liquor store windows and the open signs of bars whenever I'd walk past. Maybe tomorrow. Just one. I'm sure the medication will mix fine with just a few. I felt better saying these things to myself, knowing I wouldn't act on it, at least not yet. It's as if almost committing and stopping myself meant I had control, but I was secretly preparing myself for the day I would give in because I hadn't all the other times before. That would make it okay and mean that I didn't have a problem. I wasn't even sure I had a problem, at least with the alcohol or sex or whatever else I'd use to numb myself. The problem was *the problem*, and the alcohol, men, and other things I did that I might not even be aware of were the Band-Aids—the temporary solution.

I plopped backward, sitting by the fridge, surveying the contents, and reached for the nip of vodka on the top shelf, putting it close to my face. I felt this need to talk to it, to let it know why I planned to drink, wondering what it would say if it could talk back. The orange letters, trimmed with gold, were mesmerizing. Closing my eyes, I tried to remember what it tasted and smelled like, feeling I couldn't quite grasp it unless I did.

"Hey," a voice sounded, loud and firm.

"Jesus!" I shuddered, dropping the bottle and watching it roll under the desk.

It was Jay. He stood holding the door. His mouth was slightly open, and his wide eyes quickly narrowed, catching me in my near-criminal act. I sighed loudly and fell back to the floor, stretching out my body, surrendering. *Fuck.*

"Really, Maddie, is this why you came here? To hide and drink?" He walked in, sitting on the bed.

I need to remember to lock the doors, I screamed in my head.

I didn't respond and shut my eyes.

"Don't be a child." He huffed. I couldn't see him, but I knew he was smoothing his hair or scratching his chin, the shit he always did when he was concerned or out of hope.

"Nothing, Maddie? Just ignore me?"

I jolted upward, twisting toward him. "Then stop treating me like a child, Jay." I threw up my hands. "Stop!"

"Is that why you're here? To drink?" He ran his fingers through his hair and paced.

"No! I came here for the reasons I said." I stood up in front of him, coming close to his face. "I just went for a fucking run, Jay, a run—see my outfit, see the sneakers? Feel the sweat on me." I grabbed his hand, pulling it to my shirt. He pulled it back and moved to the window, opening the drapes. "I just heard Summer say my father assaulted her not once, Jay, not twice, but repeatedly! Do you hear that, Jay?" My voice became louder and louder, and tears burned my eyes. My head throbbed, and I wanted to punch or collapse into him. Either one would be fine. "Fuck, Jay! Fuck!" I grabbed my head and squeezed. The now blurred photograph of us all stared at me from the table. I reached down and grabbed it, tearing it into pieces wildly.

"Okay, okay, Mad, come here." He pulled me backward into him and wrapped his arms around me. My hands fell to my sides, and what was left of us floated to the floor.

I relaxed my head to his chest, then turned into it, shaking, crying, convulsing until I couldn't breathe and pulled away, sobbing and gulping for air.

He looked down at my face, studying it. I wondered what he thought. What a disaster I was. Why was he with me? I'd imagined this running through his head, and pressure filled my chest—the words simmered in my mouth like molten lava before the explosion.

"Why are you with me, Jay? Why? I want to know." I feverishly pulled away from him and stumbled to the bed.

"Don't, Maddie," he began.

"Don't what?" I asked, glaring. "Don't fucking what, Jay?" I reached for my phone, wanting to throw it. The sound of something hitting a wall, breaking—smashing was the only relief I'd get right now, but I stopped myself; it held all the answers and what was left of Summer and me. It was all I had.

Jay walked over and sat beside me, smart enough to keep space between us. "I'm not explaining this anymore, Mad. I love you. You have something going on, some struggles—fine. Can't I get that *and* just be there for you?" He paused, taking a deep breath, struggling. "You're not as damaged as you think, Maddie," he whispered, turning to me. "This doesn't define you."

I wanted to scream, run, anything to escape his calm, know-it-all demeanor. What the fuck did he know? What defined me then?

He smoothed back his hair again and inched closer, moving his hand to my leg. I tensed at his touch and turned my body, stiffening my shoulders.

"Let's move forward, listen together to the rest of this, and stop wherever you want to stop." His arm was around me now, and I softened into him. "Let's define the rest: us, life, all of it. Let's write our own script. Let's play this one out and then put it to rest, Mad, okay? Start looking ahead and not backward. There's nothing you can do here—nothing except listen and—"

"Listen and move on, Jay? Listen and what? Put it under the mattress, lock it up, and throw away the key. This is me, this shit, all of it. Summer is me. She was the only thing real about me, and I never knew it until she was gone. My parents, the island, the perfect life, the persona of it all, the things we didn't say, and the feelings we didn't feel were like a dream, someone else's life in which I was some avatar. That's what it feels like, Jay. Who am I? I don't know."

He reached for my hand and squeezed it as our eyes locked. "You're my love." He smiled, his dimple showing. I smiled back and rested my head on his shoulder.

"Let's do this together, the rest. Okay?" he whispered.

"Okay."

Chapter 13

I showered while Jay got us coffee and bagels, and then I relaxed in his arms, tucking my body into him on the bed. I picked up the phone, seeing the date. "Jay." I flipped to face him. "Don't you have to work?" I asked.

"Don't worry about me." He stroked my arm.

"But your deadline, isn't it tomorrow?"

"I got an extension," he said, kissing my forehead.

Why does this man love me so much?

The doubt and guilt returned to the forefront of my mind. I was sick of him doing things for me and me giving nothing in return.

Did he have a need to take care of me? What if I got my shit together and was okay? Would he like me then? To wrap my head around that he loved me for me was something I struggled with because I was nothing more than made up—a lie, someone born with installations of false input. Nothing about me was real, but he saw something was, and many days, that was the only thing I clung to.

He and I at McGinty's came into my head. All the time we spent there talking about writing and where we'd be, wanting to travel, see the world, and experience more. "So we'd have more to write about—expanding our minds," he had said. It was then I began thinking more about getting farther away, escaping somewhere and then somewhere else, anything to run from my life, thinking all I needed was a change, but with him. I wanted to run with him. My New York City guy: intelligent, caring, and handsome. His parents were still together, and he called his mother every other day like clockwork to check in. Women wanted him; I could see it wherever we went: the captain of the baseball team in high school who almost made it to the minors and still coaches Little League every season. What wasn't to want? He wanted love, real love, and a real life with someone. I never knew why he chose me, and I wondered if there was more to his childhood bubbling below the surface. Maybe he was too perfect, and I feared behind his perfection lay something dark and sinister like my father. But I knew it wasn't true a few months into our relationship when he lost his mind in city traffic after someone cut him off. That he had road rage comforted me as I realized he might be real. I always told him I'd fallen in love with him the night we danced drunk in Boston Common, then smoked a joint laying on the damp grass looking up at the reflection of stars in the cities mirrored buildings, but in truth, it was that day, when he screamed and cursed uncontrolled when the driver swerved in front of him on State Street. In that, I felt safe.

Times were okay then when I was distracted by us. I stared at him, wishing for another distraction, wishing something had happened to avoid all this. It was so good while it lasted when we were consumed by each other. Were we more than that? Were we real? Are we real?

"Maddie," he said, raising an eyebrow.

"What?" I leaped from my thoughts, my eyes meeting his. He said nothing, studying my face. "What?" I asked again.

"I lost you for a minute." He smiled, nodding his head back and forth.

"Oh, shut up." I flipped around again, taking his arm and throwing it over me. I leaned over and pressed play, closing my eyes tight.

"We are going to go over some of those times, Summer. The times Bill Plympton touched you. Is that okay?" Sarah Martin said.

I tensed my body and moved slightly from Jay, instantly regretting agreeing to listen with him. Shame washed over me, and I felt desperate for another shower. This was my filth, not his, and sharing it with him made me feel worse. I didn't think of that. I didn't want him to hear—to know more than he did and think anything more. A tear ran down my face and hit his arm. He held me tighter, and I chewed on my lip, hoping the feeling would end.

"Was there another time at the beach, Summer?"

"Yes," Summer said, sighing.

"Do you remember how old you were?"

"I was eleven. It was just before it stopped."

"Is that how you know how old you were?" Sarah asked.

"Yes."

"Who was there? Was Madeline there?"

"She was in the car. She didn't feel good."

I held my breath. The room was hot, but I shivered under Jay's arms, remembering the day. It was the hottest day of that summer, and we'd been fishing on Chappaquiddick for most of it. Dad hadn't been home for a few weekends, and I was happy he was back. My mind raced, thinking of how and when this could be. How could this have happened in plain sight, right under my nose, and I didn't notice? No one did? How could I not see the monster take over my father, the monster that is him, or my best friend's reaction to it? Where was I? I racked my brain, remembering a stomachache from too many molasses cookies. I touched my cheek, remembering the hot leather seat of the Wagoneer against it, recalling laying down in the back, hot and nauseous, while they went for a swim to cool off.

"Are you sure you don't want to come?" my father asked, holding open the door, staring at me from above. "Cooling off might help." He leaned down, touching my head, feeling if I was warm.

"No, go ahead." I sat up slightly, holding my stomach, wincing. "Just hurry up."

"I told you not to eat that last cookie, and they were bigger than usual today," Summer called from the back, shutting the hatch and giggling.

"Be back in two shakes," Dad said, closing the door softly.

"So, Madeline was in the car, and you and Bill Plympton went swimming?" Sarah Martin continued.

"Yes," Summer said.

"What beach were you at?"

"State Beach, at the bend in the road."

"And you both went in the water?"

"Yes."

"What was Bill Plympton wearing?"

"Like swimming shorts."

"What were you wearing?"

"My bathing suit," Summer said, clearing her throat.

"Was it a one-piece or two?"

"A one-piece. It was orange and white."

"How do you remember the colors?"

"It was the only one I had then."

"And did something happen that made you uncomfortable?"

"Yes."

"What happened?"

"He pulled me close to him."

"While you were swimming?"

"Yes."

"How did he do that?"

"He grabbed my hands while, like, I was swimming."

Papers shuffled, and footsteps clicked.

"Then what happened? Did you touch any part of his body?"

"Yes."

"What part of his body did you touch?"

"I could feel, like, his penis."

"What part of your body was his penis touching?

"My upper thigh area."

"Okay. What did that feel like?"

"Like something hard."

"Okay. And how did you know it was his penis?"

"Because it didn't feel like hands."

"Okay. Did he say anything to you while that was happening?"

"Yes."

"What did he say?"

"He whispered in my ear, 'Is this okay?'"

"Did you say anything back to him?"

"No."

"When you talked about feeling his penis on your . . . the back of your thigh, was that happening at the same time as something else?"

"He touched me," Summer said. "My vagina, with his finger—like before," she continued, her voice shaking.

"I'm sorry, Summer," Sarah said sympathetically. "I know this is a lot."

"Yeah." Summer sighed.

I remembered them getting back into the car. I wasn't sure how long they had been gone, thinking I must have dozed off. It was a quiet drive home, and I was happy I felt better. That's all. I felt better, and it was quiet.

I squeezed my eyes as tight as I could, trying to see her face, a change in it—his face, the evil, the killer of us all. I tried so hard to see the sickening garbage that could do this, but all I saw was my father driving the same way he always did, and Summer, just herself, the same Summer I'd known.

"Summer, you said these events with Bill Plympton happened numerous times. Is this correct?

"Yes."

"Were they mostly in water, at the beach?"

"No."

"Okay," Sarah went on, "where did these events mostly happen?"

"Mostly in the art room or Maddie's room, like wherever we slept."

"Was Maddie in the room when these things happened?"

"Yes."

"What was she doing?"

"Sleeping."

"Did you ever want to ask for help or tell her? Wake her?"

"I don't know."

"What do you mean you don't know?"

"I-I'm not sure I wanted her to know."

"Why?"

"Because if she knew, then how could we be friends?"

"Do you think she ever woke up? Saw anything?"

Summer didn't answer.

"Summer, did you hear the question?"

"Yes."

"Do you think Maddie ever woke up when this was happening?"

"Well, Maddie was a deep sleeper. We joked about that sometimes." Summer laughed nervously. "She, like, didn't wake up."

"Objection, Your Honor," Gabe Heinz chimed in. "The witness can't speak to Madeline Plympton's sleeping depth," he stuttered.

"Your Honor, the witness—" Sarah spoke, but the judge interrupted.

"I'll allow it—overruled."

"Go on, Summer," Sarah said.

"Once, he came in the room and—"

"Wait, who's he, Summer?" Sarah interrupted.

"Bill. Bill came into the room in his robe and went over to my bed like he sometimes did. I pretended I was asleep, but he put his hand under the covers. I turned to the other side, still pretending, and opened my eyes. Maddie—she was awake."

"How do you know she was awake?"

"I saw her eyes open."

"Did she see yours open? Did she see you and her father near you?"

"Objection—leading," Gabe Heinz roared.

"I'll rephrase. Summer, what did you see?"

"I saw Maddie. She looked at me. We saw each other."

"Then what happened, Summer?"

"The same thing that always happened."

Chapter 14

I grabbed my phone and stopped the recording, flinging Jay's arm off me.

"What day is it?" I yelled, spinning toward him, tears spilling down my cheeks.

"What?" He looked at me, confused, unsure of what was happening. "It's Thursday. Why did you stop—"

"Thursday," I said to myself, trying to think. I hadn't been there in so long that I forgot which days I could visit. I walked to the window, scrolling through my contacts, hoping it was there. "Yes," I whispered, dialing.

"Who are you calling?" Jay sat up, swinging his legs to the side of the bed.

"Concord Correctional, this line's being recorded," a robotic voice said on the other end of the phone.

"Hello, yes. My name's Madeline Plympton. My father is William Plympton, an inmate. Am I still on the visiting list?" I asked, watching Jay about to speak. I wiped my face with my sleeve, then put my finger up, shushing him.

"Yes, ma'am. Yes, you are."

"What's his visiting day? When can he have visitors?" I asked hurriedly, feeling out of breath. My heart beat hard in my chest, then sank in my stomach when the voice answered.

"Today, ma'am. His visiting hours are today from four to six."

"Thank you," I said, hanging up while the man's voice kept speaking.

I ran my fingers through my hair wildly, then hit the side of my leg repeatedly, pacing in disbelief.

"Maddie, what—what are you doing? Visiting him, your dad? You haven't in years—what, why?"

It all came rushing back—the dreams. I'd had them for years, but I convinced myself I made it up after everything happened. I tried hard to remember seeing something, wondering how I couldn't have known. I thought I made it up, him—the robe, near her in my room. I thought I dreamed it then or made it up later, but I dreamed about it constantly. I could never *not* remember dreaming about it; it felt like I always had, but I could never remember when they started. I thought college, but I wasn't sure if that was because I remembered them or started waking up to the possibility. This, and that last ride on the carousel, on our flying horses, with Summer, made me crazy.

"The dreams, Jay. That dream." I chewed my lip, plopping in the chair at the desk, feeling my legs nearly buckle.

"What dreams?" he asked, reaching out for my hand and putting mine in his; he squeezed.

"I told you. I know I told you once. At McGinty's, the time after, I told you about all this. We were drinking but—"

"I remember," he whispered. His eyes darkened like a storm was coming. It was.

"It was real. I saw him near her. I saw her face, Jay; her eyes met mine. It was real," I said, trembling. "I could have stopped it. I must have known!" My voice escalated. "I saw her. She looked different. I saw, Jay!" I screamed, shaking violently in his arms now around me.

He smoothed my hair as I continued screaming into his chest.

"Shhh, Maddie, you were a kid. You didn't know. You didn't see him do anything. Maddie, please," Jay whispered in my ear, rocking me like a baby.

"You were a child, Maddie. A child," he went on.

"I saw her eyes, Jay." I lifted my head, looking at him, crazed. "I saw her, and things seemed different. It wasn't a dream, Jay," I said, shaking my head back and forth. "It wasn't. It was her and me, her needing me, and you know what I did? I went back to sleep. I went to sleep," I repeated over and over.

I cried until I had no tears left, and my head felt on the verge of explosion. The anger came rushing in next, and I collected my thoughts. I thought it was a dream that next morning and all the mornings after that when I'd dreamed about it again for years. Then, when the accusation and the trial happened, I convinced myself I had dreamed it, forgetting when they started, as it was all a blur. It was never a dream, and after hearing Summer say it, there was nothing left for me to do but confront the devil himself, my devil, because he was the only thing worse than me now, and he was all mine, or I was his. It didn't matter because he created me. He created everything, and I needed to look at him, in his eyes, and see him, the real him, and what he truly is. I just hoped I'd be able to.

"Maddie, you shouldn't see him, not by yourself. You're not ready for this," Jay pleaded as I threw my stuff in the bag.

"How did you get here?" I asked, ignoring him.

"Kevin's truck. Maddie, listen—"

"Jay, I love you. You're all I have in this world, but please—please stop. I have to do this," I said, turning to him and giving him a moment of undivided attention that he more than deserved. I touched his face, attempting a smile. My eyes felt the size of golf balls.

"Let me go with you," he said.

I hated seeing him look so helpless.

"It's something I have to do alone. All of this, Jay. You've held my hand long enough." I reached into his pocket for the keys. "Tell Kevin I borrowed the truck for a day or two." I stuck them in my pocket.

"Wait, I was going to move some stuff, but I guess I can after. I don't think he'll care." He scratched his chin, thinking out loud. "Wait—a day or two?"

"Just in case. I'll see you later, but in case I can't drive, I might get a hotel. I don't know," I said, grabbing my bag and kissing him. He held my arms, pulling me toward him.

"Are you sure about this?"

"No, but it's all that's left, Jay. I think it's all that's left." I put my head down, not knowing what I was doing or the answer. Listening to it all didn't fix it, so I was unsure this would, but something compelled me.

"Please call me after. Got it?" His eyes softened, and he leaned in, kissing me long and hard.

"I will," I said and headed out the door toward the elevators. I wanted to turn back, as I knew he was at the door, watching me go, but I didn't, and I didn't need his concern to stop me.

I'm not second-guessing a thing.

◆ ◆ ◆

There was hardly any traffic on I-95, which was shocking. Boston and the surrounding cities had exploded since the Big Dig finished in 2006. The project rerouted major routes under the city and created tunnels to accommodate the increased population. With it came more jobs and even more people, so traffic seemed worse to everyone who had lived there before and still does.

Gabe Heinz kept to his defense that Summer had gotten carried away in gossip. Listening to him grill her destroyed me, but she was unwavering. Her story never changed, not when he tried to trip her up, but once, he came close. I could tell it wasn't that he was catching her lying, but he wanted to confuse her whenever he could, and I heard her becoming tired.

"Summer, I want to go back and talk more about the beach and the incidents in the water," Heinz mumbled. "You told the children's services interviewer what happened in the ocean on State Beach, correct?"

"Yes," said Summer.

"Okay. And you agreed that Madeline Plympton was in the water too, right?"

"Yeah."

"The first time?"

"The first time that anything happened?" she asked.

"That's correct."

"Maybe. I don't remember."

"You're talking about the time floating at State Beach. I'm on page thirty of the interview if you want to follow along. You describe laughing with Madeline."

"Yeah."

"Okay. So, that means Madeline was there in the water?"

"Yes."

"I'm asking you, was Madeline in the water with you the first time it happened?"

"Yeah, but that doesn't mean it was the first time; I don't really remember."

"Well, in fact, didn't it only happen once at the beach?"

"No."

"Didn't you tell the interviewer that the beach incident so traumatized you that you never went in the water again and were afraid?"

"I mean, yeah."

"Do you remember saying that?"

"Yeah."

"Well, that sort of wasn't true, right?"

There was silence and a sigh.

"Summer?" Gabe Heinz said.

"Sort of. It's not like I stopped going in the water immediately after, but there was a point where I stopped going in, yes."

"But what you said to the interviewer, and I want to be very clear on this—"

"Okay."

"I'm reading what you said."

"Okay."

"'I never went into the water with them again. I was afraid.'"

"Yeah, I'm sure—" Summer began, and then she was cut off.

"So, is that true you didn't go in the water? It was too scary. Is that true?" Gabe asked aggressively.

"Objection," Sarah Martin shouted. "Let the witness finish her answers."

"Sustained," said Judge Stone quickly.

"I'm sorry, Your Honor." Heinz huffed.

"Carry on," Judge Stone said.

"So, when you told the jury yesterday that it repeatedly happened in the water, that wasn't true, was it?"

"No, that is true," Summer said firmly.

"Well, they can't both be true. You either didn't go in the water, or you did."

"I did go in the ocean with them, but after a while, I stopped going in."

"But that's not what you told the interviewer, right?"

"I don't know."

"Do you remember you told the jury yesterday that Madeline was in the water the first time? Do you remember telling them that?"

"The first time with me floating, yes."

"So, she was in the water?"

"The first time . . . yes."

I could tell Summer was becoming confused, which was the point, and I wondered why Sarah Martin wasn't objecting more to something. I didn't know what, but I wanted someone to stop him.

"But you said I never went in the water again after this happened."

"Yeah, but that doesn't mean after the first time."

"So, the first time was okay, but the second time was so terrifying that you never went in again? I'm trying to understand this. Can you explain?"

"What?"

"I'll read you the quote again. You say, 'So I didn't go in the water anymore.' I'm on page thirty-six, line ten." He coughed. "'I didn't go in the water anymore because I was afraid.' You said that to the interviewer, right?"

"I did."

"And you said that because you were trying to tell the interviewer that you stopped going in the water because of what the defendant allegedly did to you in the water, right?"

"Yeah."

"So, that would have been the first time, right?"

"No."

"Why did you keep going in the water then at all? I'm trying to understand."

"Fuck you, Gabe Heinz," I whispered. "She did stop going in the fucking water!" I yelled, turning onto the exit and down the road onto Elm Street. I always found it odd that one of the wealthiest communities in the state was home to a prison.

The concrete fortress emerged in the distance, and I felt my heart speed in my chest. Summer's testimony against the backdrop of the building that housed him and so many like him. I thought I'd throw up.

Summer did stop going in the water with us after Dad took us fishing or for lunch. We always stopped for a swim or another attempt for me to jump off the bridge, especially on super hot days. Summer stopped going in, and I don't remember when. She'd have different excuses that I never paid any mind to, and she did go swimming when it was just us, now that I thought about it. Putting the pieces together, it was when he was there, my father when he went in or had the idea. It killed me over and over how I hadn't seen it when now it was so clear. I glanced up into the rearview mirror, sickened by what I saw—myself.

I pulled into visitor parking, thinking of the last time I had been here and could barely remember how many years it had been. I never thought I'd be back and swore I wouldn't be once I settled into his guilt, a term I struggled to wrap my head around. Doctor Harper told me, "Settling into your father's guilt will never be easy, Madeline." I recalled his words in the hospital. "There would never be anything settling about it," I exclaimed.

I had time before visiting hours and continued listening while rummaging for an Ativan in my purse. There was no way I could do this, see him, without being semi-sedated. I envisioned my heart exploding in my chest or being carried out in a straitjacket. I'd had enough of that for a while, so I figured I'd be proactive. Continuing to listen, I envisioned the long walk down the corridor to see him, unsure how I'd ever do it, hoping the Ativan would carry me. Just to be sure, I popped another. I was so bat-shit crazy in all this; one milligram wouldn't touch me.

"Okay. The first time in the water, at the beach, was traumatic to you, right?"

"Yeah."

"Are you sure?"

"I mean, yes."

"Okay. And you were so traumatized that you never went in the water again. Is that true? Am I right?"

"I mean, yes and no. I didn't stop going in the ocean after the first time."

"Asked and answered," Sarah Martin said.

"Move on soon, Attorney Heinz," Judge Stone's voice followed.

"Well, why is that yes and no? The answer then is no, right?"

"Okay. Then no."

"Let's try it again. After the first time in the water, you never returned to the ocean again; is that true or false?"

"That's false."

"That's false. The fact is, after the first time, after that happened to you in the ocean, you never went in the ocean again; that's what you said."

"Objection!" Sarah Martin said, sounding frustrated. "Form of a question."

"Do you wish to approach?" Judge Stone asked.

"Yes, Your Honor," both attorneys responded simultaneously.

There were some mumblings and whispers I couldn't make out except Heinz's words.

"I'm sorry, Summer. So, we're going to go through this one more time quickly."

"Okay."

"I'm going to read it from the transcript, okay?"

"Okay."

"Good, because I'm apparently not being clear, and I want to ensure I am. But this is the interview you gave?"

"Yes."

"All right. I believe this will be the last time I go over this point, so stand by. I'm going to ask you because it appears from the transcript that this only happened in the water once since you never went back in again."

"Okay."

"You said, 'I didn't go into the ocean anymore because I was afraid.' Did you say that to the interviewer?"

"I mean, I guess that's what I said."

"Okay. And during this time, the defendant is trying to help you float; these things happened, right?

"Yeah."

"So far, I'm accurate, correct?"

"In reading in the transcript?"

"No, no, no, no. In what happened."

"I don't remember. What?"

"You told the interviewer what happened to you in the ocean, right?"

"Yes."

"After you described that to the interviewer, the interviewer asked, 'Did anything else happen?' Do you remember her saying that?"

"Yeah."

"The interviewer asked if there were other times that stood out to you, and you said this, correct? 'I didn't go in the ocean with them anymore because I was afraid.'"

"I mean, yeah."

"Okay. You will agree, then, that seems to suggest that you never went in the ocean again, doesn't it?"

"No."

"Well, you said it, didn't you?"

"I did say I never went in the ocean when he was there again, but that doesn't mean I didn't go after the first time."

"Well, then what you said in the interview wasn't true?"

"The—what?"

"You told the interviewer you never went into the ocean with Mr. Plympton again, but you described later another incident, and now you're telling us that, yes, you went in again?"

"Yeah, and then I stopped going in."

"Okay."

"It just didn't happen when you say it happened."

"Well, I'm not saying anything. This is what the transcript says."

"No, I know."

"So, are you telling me that the first time this happened wasn't scary? Another time was scarier, and that's why you didn't go back in the water?"

There was silence for what seemed like an eternity. Then Summer spoke.

"No." She took a long breath. "I mean, over time, I realized that any time I got in the water with Bill, I got molested, so I didn't want to go in anymore."

My head disconnected from my body. That weird, disassociated feeling you get right before a panic attack. I had felt this another time that day on the bathroom floor, watching the blood leave my body and pool on the floor around me. That time was different, however. My heart didn't start hammering in my chest, and I didn't feel the need to escape my situation. I had lain there, disconnected from the experience, as if it weren't me this had been happening to. It had been a movie or a dream, someone else's life was how it had felt, but I had known enough that I hadn't wanted to wake up or realize it was me, and I hadn't wanted to be there. I had just watched calmly and patiently, listening to the room's sounds, the hum of Mr. Runnal's bathroom fan through the wall, the footsteps in the hallway, and the sound of my breath, hearing them all intensely, each movement an exaggeration. I remembered that moment, blinking with pause and feeling my eyelids become heavy. My mouth slowly began to open, and I rested my head on my arm, feeling saliva pool at the corners. The red river crept toward my face, dampening my shirt sleeve, and I closed my eyes, becoming lost and peacefully disconnected. This was different.

The guards buzzed us in, and the large metal gate opened. When I first visited with my mother after the trial, I had never wanted to return. There's a sense that once you get behind these walls—hearing the hard clanging of cell doors slamming open and shut, buzzers going off, allowing you to pass, and your name being shouted by serious and angry-looking men and women, armed and uniformed, in sync in their actions—that you are indeed never going to leave. I'd come a few times after on my own and then one last time a bit later. That last time, I thought it would be the last. It was when things began to unravel, and I started opening my eyes, like a baby fawn just after birth, seeing the world for the first time. Things were hazy then, but I was on the cusp of it becoming clear.

I waited for the others to find their bad man and disperse into their pods. My eyes scanned the plexiglass, wondering if I'd recognize him. It had been, what was it—three years now? I'd surely see him differently, I thought. I knew who he was now and accepted it as best as I thought I could. I floated down the row, studying each prisoner's face for the one I'd recognized. I was sure I'd see the evil now, which might make him appear different and not like the man I had known, my father, my once everything. I'd notice the difference, even if it were subtle; I'd see it, the evil—the darkness. I was no longer blind, and that's what I came for, to see.

A second door opened behind the glass, and I spotted him next to a guard. He stopped and turned to say something to the man, who patted him on the shoulder and pointed to an open phone. My heart screamed, and I felt as though I was caught in a sudden storm, hiding from the thunder and lightning but shuddering at the sound of my name called as a guard pointed me to sit. I moved, but my legs felt hollow and unable to carry me. I shuffled in his direction, looking down, afraid to see his face, afraid to feel anything good for him, but more afraid to see the devil. When there was no more floor to walk, I put my hands on the chair, still hesitating to look at him. Reaching deep inside of me, I attempted to muster any bravery there. I had to get it right this time. I had to see what was really there, say what I should have said, and ask what I should have asked. Thoughts smashed together in my head, and a pulsing pain pounded my temples.

My head felt in a vise, squeezing until my eyes burst. Breathing in deeply, I exhaled slowly, thinking of Doctor Harper's methodical movements and words, calculating and skilled, then Summer's smile, the brass ring from the flying horses—a complete circle. Here was the circle, part of it, me being here. A sound startled me, and I looked to see him tap on the glass. His eyes met mine, locking. My stomach sunk to the floor as he pointed to the phone, and I reached for it but couldn't grab it, realizing I was still standing. I hurriedly sat down and picked it up, closing my eyes to him, and put it to my ear.

I will not be afraid. I am not a child.

Then, his voice. "Madeline, are you okay? Look at me, Madeline," he said. My organs rattled at every syllable.

"Madeline?" he said again sternly, as he did when he was mad or irritated. I transported back in time, and suddenly, I was a child sinking in my seat, nervously burying my chin to my chest, feeling I'd done something wrong.

I glanced up again, seeing him—his perfection. Not a hair out of place, he was almost entirely salt-and-peppery now at the temples and silver on top. His face was neatly shaved, and he had a bit more weight on him than I was used to. I studied his face, his wide, deep-green eyes slanted at the corners, leading to the canals of crow's feet spreading down to his tanned and leathery cheeks from years in the sun. There was no blackness—no horns. He was just him—my father—and I felt relieved. I inhaled deeply before I spoke and exhaled methodically, hating that there was nothing profound, no demon, no pitchfork, nor darkness. I knew it wouldn't be obvious, but I felt I'd see something, notice something different about him, anything—now that I believed in what he was. Nothing existed except the room's sounds, the murmurs of people talking, chairs dragging across the concrete, a woman faintly crying in the distance, and then the sound of my breath, my heartbeat, hearing them all intensely. I blinked, adjusting my eyes, lasering in on him across from me. My mouth slowly began to open, and I spoke, hearing a voice that sounded like mine leaving my body; then, I went with it, hovering over myself, out of the seat, watching and listening, wanting to disappear and die.

Chapter 15

"Dad," I stammered, adjusting in my seat. He came close to the glass and put his finger to it as a smile grew across his face. My blood was simmering to a boil, and I tightly clenched my jaw, thinking of what I would say.

"Madeline, I am so glad you've found time to come. I know you're so busy with the magazine."

I tilted my head to the left, squinting at him, confused, but quickly remembered there would be nothing more than surface—pretend and phony bullshit. How could I fool myself that there would be anything more? Well, I wouldn't give him his act: his perfect scene. I was done. If I weren't going to die, I'd live, and it would be in a world full of truths he'd never want to be in.

"Stop, Dad. Stop." I sat straight, gathering my strength. I furrowed my brow, letting him know I was serious. Hearing myself felt foreign. I'd never so much as raised my voice to him, and I hated that I was still intimidated. The anger fueled me as Summer's voice swirled in my head. "Too many times to count, too many times to count." It replayed over and over, along with the dreams, him by her bed, his white robe with his initials embroidered in blue, the feeling, the truth.

"Well, how are you? How's the city?"

That's right, dodge and deflect.

He didn't lose his composure. No matter what I said, he never would, but I'd never said anything, so how could I know?

I moved my face close to the glass and pressed my hand to it, feeling safe that it was between us.

"Enough, Dad. Enough, okay? I'm going to talk, and you're going to listen," I said, gripping the phone so hard my hand hurt.

His face hardened, and he leaned back in his seat. Hearing the words come out of my mouth scared me. His face sickened me now, and I heightened, feeling giant.

"Go on," he said casually as if he were indulging me.

Tears filled my eyes, and I angrily wiped them, unprepared for this. I didn't want him to see me weak, but they were tears of rage, and I spoke anyway, feeling empowered and uncontrolled.

"I haven't not visited because I'm busy. You're my father, and had I still believed in you and your lies, I'd have come every week like Mom, who is still blind."

"Madeline," he said firmly, leaning in closer.

"No!" I shouted, watching his eyes dart side to side and then past me.

I turned to look at the guard behind me, who glared, and I spoke softer now.

"I'm talking, and please let me finish. Please let me finish," I repeated through gritted teeth.

He said nothing, and I continued.

"I listened to the trial, I listened to her, to Summer, my best friend, my, my fucking," I stuttered the word, as I'd never said it in front of him. It enraged me more than I cared, so I repeated it clearly and loudly. "My fucking sister. She was like my sister." I squeezed the phone, feeling I'd break it.

His nostrils flared, and he looked about to get up.

"Don't move, Dad. Please don't move." I hardened my tone. I had to get this out, or I'd burst.

"I saw you, Dad. I saw you by her bed. I'm unsure if I did more than once because it's all blurred together, and now it feels like a dream. It's in my dreams too, but I convinced myself it wasn't real, but it was.

I felt it—I felt something wrong, and she looked at me, and I did nothing. I was a"—I refrained from swearing again as I didn't want him to leave—"a kid. We were kids!" I raised my voice, controlled and not too loud.

"Madeline," he said in his sternest voice.

"Please. Please let me finish, Dad." I spiraled, bouncing in my seat. "Please do one thing for me and let me finish this."

"You will not change my mind, although I wish you could." I pulled at my hair with my free hand. "Mom is a shell, a shell of a person," I whispered, hanging my head. "And me, well." I cleared my throat, refusing to look up. "I tried to kill myself." I kept my head down for a minute. The silence on the other end was deafening and spoke volumes. A fury ignited inside of me and increased with every word unspoken. I heard his breath and glanced up, his face still unfazed. "Do you know that—or did Mom try and protect you from it all?" I asked, bracing myself in the chair. His face didn't change. Nothing moved.

"And Summer, who knows what happened to her? Wherever she is, I'm sure it's hell." I sniffed, feeling tears come. I stared directly at him, now watching him blink.

"I'm not going to ask why. I don't even want to know why, and I'd never understand the depths of your sickness, your darkness. But I want you to know that I don't believe you, and I should have believed her then." There was a subtle hint of anger as his eyes crinkled. He looked away. He searched for something, anything except my face. "She never lied. She was nothing but good, and after hearing her, I knew more than ever that I didn't even have to listen to another testimony, not the experts, not the police, not your interview with the police, but I am, Dad."

He rose from his seat and moved the phone from his ear.

"You did this! And Summer's story never wavered. Her story's never changed, not in years. It all made sense, everything she said. You destroyed us—all of us. The cops didn't believe you. And you never said you didn't do it, Dad! Not the words!" My voice cracked, and my rage broke free; I wouldn't let him escape me or this. He'd escaped it for too long. Even being in here, it was still a big mistake, and he lived in denial, enabled by my mother and his lawyers. I stood and dropped the phone as he placed his gently on the receiver and motioned to the guard.

"You never said it! You never once did!" I felt a hand on my shoulder and pulled forward, tearing myself from it.

"Let's go, ma'am," the guard said from behind. I turned to him and then back quickly, watching my father walk away.

"I only exist, Dad; I'm fucking dust; we are all dust because of you," I erupted as tears burst from my eyes. "Do you hear me, Dad? Do you fucking hear me? Dad?" I screamed and pleaded, terrified and crazed. The guard forcefully turned and pushed me to the female guard, who dragged me through the doorway. Buzzers sounded, and the metal gate slammed shut.

◆ ◆ ◆

I opened the door to the truck and plopped my body, falling over on my side. The sun hit the side of my cheek, warming me, and I closed my eyes, feeling exhaustion set in. The desk guard had told me the prison warden stripped me of my visitation rights as I walked through the lobby and out the door, still escorted by the female guard. I had laughed, turned toward him, and raised my shoulders. "Wasn't planning on coming back." I smiled, feeling free, but it had faded as quickly as it had come.

My stomach churned, and acid rose in my throat. I jumped up, throwing my head out the door and throwing up my coffee all over the parking lot. I sat for an hour, feeling stagnant. I didn't see him as evil. The evidence and Summer undeniably challenged my thoughts, and everything in me knew Summer was truthful. Still, without a constant reminder of that or repeatedly hearing her say it, me thinking about it, or talking it through to Doctor Harper, Jay, or whomever, I was left with an emptiness, a hole. The hole grew so dark and big that it ate me from the inside out, and that was when I was my worst: not talking about it, just existing in a life without my father and a barely living mother. That's why I was their half-dead daughter walking on the edge of a cliff, waiting to trip or jump if my thoughts settled on any of it for a length of time. I knew I couldn't live in that again, but I couldn't spend my life reliving it and replaying it in my head over and over to keep the anger I felt for him and the loss of all of us alive so that I wouldn't jump. I had to grieve. It dawned on me just then, lying in the truck. I still saw him as my father, whom I defied and abandoned forever.

I thought that's what I wanted and what I had to do. Put closure to this, give Summer her truth, and slap him with it. I'd read an article about OJ Simpson once. I forgot where, but it was after he wrote his book *If I Did It, Confessions of a Killer*. He explains that if he did murder his wife and her friend Ron Goldman, this is how he'd do it. It was sick and twisted in every way imaginable, but the article spoke to how this man, OJ, and many people who commit heinous crimes, after spending years defending themselves, gradually start to believe it. They think they didn't do it. That saying rings true—others will listen if you repeat something enough. With my father, it seemed it was no different. He believed he was good, incapable of evil. But there had to be somewhere where he knew. Do those like him justify it? Do they think it's normal and others won't understand? Or do they bury it so deep it doesn't exist, and it's dust, easily swept away or taken with the wind like it never happened? Whatever he felt or thought, it didn't matter. I had to find a way to grieve somehow. We died, all of us, the way we were then. Could there be a new way? I grabbed the bottle of water in the console and swished it around in my mouth, spitting it out the door, wondering if Doctor Harper would be concerned or proud at my revelation. I wasn't sure which.

Chapter 16

"My name is Melissa Plympton, P-L-Y-M-P-T-O-N," my mother said coldly. I shuddered, hearing her voice. Her testimony was next, right before mine. I listened to most of the state's case as I headed back to the city: the police, psychologists, nurses, Kaia, and Mrs. Paul. A forensic expert went through text messages between Summer and my father. I knew they texted here and there about food and rides, but there was more. He asked how she was feeling once when she went home sick. He texted asking if she had a good time once and another where he said he liked hair the way she wore it that day and asked if she wanted to go on our next vacation. He said odd things, some inappropriate things, which I see now as an adult. He complimented her appearance and clothing and asked if she needed anything. I had no idea about these exchanges then but wouldn't have thought anything of them as a kid. I was sure Summer didn't either then, or maybe she did, but they seemed innocent enough unless you knew what was happening.

My hands trembled on the steering wheel, and I gripped it tighter, trying to steady them, hearing Mrs. Paul's voice cracking between sniffling. "She is such a sweet girl, Summer. She didn't deserve this," she repeated over and over through Gabe Heinz's objections. Judge Stone called for order and for Mrs. Paul to compose herself and told her to drink some water. It was clear the police didn't believe him. The state played my father's initial interview with the police for the court, which revealed nothing more than his bewilderment at why he was there.

"Is there any reason this young girl would accuse you of this?" asked Officer Brendan.

"No. There is not," my father answered.

"Did anything happen between your families? Any rift? A reason why Miss Starr might make this up?" he went on.

"No, this is all a mistake," he said.

It was said so often that I felt it became our family's motto: the Plymptons—it's all a big mistake.

Cat testified too, which I was unaware of at the time. She didn't say much except how she came to know us and Summer acting depressed for a time, which I'd noticed too. She didn't sound like the Cat I knew, who seemed always to sing when she spoke; everything sounded lyrical, and she made words silly for effect. "How goesy's, girlies?" she'd ask us, sporting the purple smock she always wore with scissors embroidered on the pockets. I'd giggle while Summer rolled her eyes. Cat's hair was always a different style or color, which I guessed was typical of many hair stylists. Purple streaks or bleach blond, she was always changing it. I liked her and sometimes wished we were around her more. She was always fun and light, no matter how hard she worked. Cat seemed to enjoy life and her customers. But there was no joy in her voice as I listened, no song or silliness. I didn't recognize her speaking, and I wondered how she looked when she did, although I was glad I hadn't seen her. It was enough to have seen her at the sentencing. She was different—everything was.

There was no concrete evidence, but as the nurse, police, judge, and Sarah Martin repeatedly reminded the court, there rarely is in sexual assault cases, especially those involving children. It is well documented that most children do not disclose what had been happening until long after it's stopped, and those who do tell are often not believed. I'd listened to Sarah Martin frequently say the exact words over and over throughout the trial to the jury: "After you consider all the evidence in the case, after you think back to Summer's testimony, ask yourself, what did I think when that kid was testifying? Did I believe her?"

"Hello, Mrs. Plympton. Can you tell the jury where you live?" Gabe Heinz asked my mother, sounding confident for the first time.

"We live in Oak Bluffs, East Chop Drive—Oak Bluffs."

"May I ask whom you live there with?"

"I live there with my husband and my daughter."

"Okay. Do you know who William Plympton is?"

"Of course," she answered, sounding annoyed.

"Is he in the courtroom?"

"Yes."

"Can you point him out?"

"Yes, right there."

"And who is he to you?"

"He's my husband."

I drove the long stretch of Route 2 back to the city, thinking I'd avoid some traffic this way, but I was wrong. My head throbbed, and the truck smelled like stale cigarettes, which I found odd because I'd never seen Kevin smoke. My plan was not to listen anymore. I didn't think I could take any more. I still didn't feel relief from any of it, hearing Summer's words, telling my father my belief in his guilt. Actually, I'd never felt worse. I wondered what he thought as I inched along the road. Nothing felt better, and I feared that nothing ever would. My mother's voice calmed me—her tone, not her words. I caught a glimpse of myself in the mirror and laughed at the mess I'd become, startled by my sunken eyes and unruly hair. I didn't even recognize myself.

Gabe Heinz went on with the same crap. A load of questions they always ask that I was becoming used to. How long have you been married? How did you meet Cat and Summer? How long did they live there? When did they leave?

"Blah, blah, blah," I said loudly, rolling my eyes.

"So, when they left, there wasn't any kind of falling out or anything?"

"No, quite the opposite. We helped get them housing," she huffed.

"So, Summer was still welcome, and Cat, as far as you were concerned?"

"Of course."

"Did you maintain a relationship with Summer?"

"Yes, we would take her most days and on Saturdays when her mom worked at the salon and whenever else she worked. Summer was always welcome to stay for however long she liked." She sounded as if reading from a script.

"It appears she became an intimate part of the family. Is that right?" Heinz started before she cut him off.

"I'd say so. Not blood, of course, but yes, she was my daughter's best friend."

"Okay, well, that's important," he finished and then went on. "Well, how did that dynamic work? Were you a mother figure? Was Madeline, your daughter, like Miss Starr's sister? What was the dynamic in the family, Mrs. Plympton?"

"It certainly was important between the girls. I was obviously the adult and a female presence, and Summer's father was not in her life." Her voice lowered. "Bill, he was like a father figure to her. That is a certainty," she said, articulating her words perfectly.

There was a cough, and something slammed, maybe a door or window, then a long pause before Gabe Heinz continued, sounding flustered. "Can you describe the relationship Summer had with Bill, your husband?"

"Well, just normal, I'd say. I mean, he's a very good father."

"Did you ever step in as a parent or mother figure or have to help her mother? Summer's mother, Cat? Melissa—may I call you that?" Heinz chirped.

There was a pause, and I knew my mother was mulling this over. She liked things formal and proper. Melissa was too informal, and she wasn't comfortable with it in even some of her social situations, never mind this.

She ignored his request, going on, "Well, when she was living with us, I had to remind Cat to register her for school. I also took the girls to school and helped them get ready—things like that."

The traffic crept, and I saw flashing lights ahead, figuring there must be an accident that every idiot on the road had to slow down and stare at, making things worse. My father's face, as he stood from his seat, stared back at me with every blink, and I blinked harder, hoping he'd go away. Guilt panged at my insides, and it enraged me.

Why do I feel guilty? He did it. Him! I screamed in my head.

I couldn't help how I felt, though. It sickened me that I still felt like his daughter, his little girl who'd never spoken to her father like that.

I am his daughter.

This, on top of my mother's voice, singing her bullshit diatribe about the perfect husband and father, and her getting the kids off to school when most days it was Marta, the housekeeper. I was on the cusp of some extreme action, although I didn't know what. There had been enough extremes the past few days and months, and it needed to stop. I was trying to stop it by opening my eyes now, putting things to rest, and saying what needed to be said, but none of it brought relief. My mind scrambled for something else, a new action, besides jumping from the Tobin Bridge to make this end.

"So, sometimes you would step in with Summer; is that what you're saying?"

"Yes, yes."

Footsteps paced the floor, and Heinz's voice cleared. "Would you say you and Bill helped raise Summer?"

"Why yes, of course," she said. I could tell she was flustered. "I would say so. She was at our house a lot."

"Okay. Did the girls come to you for things such as rides, snacks, and things of that nature?"

"I-I did give them rides or had Marta, our housekeeper, get them to where they were going," she said, lowering her voice and clearing her throat, knowing how this sounded.

"Was Cat, Summer's mother, helpful at all?"

"Cat was busy working, and, well, after they left our home, we mostly only saw Summer."

"Did the girls come to you—Summer, I mean—to talk about things or 'hang out,' as they say?" He chuckled awkwardly.

There was a pause and a deep breath. I could tell she was getting frustrated or upset. It was hard to know because I only heard her voice, but a deep breath after a long pause from my mother meant irritation, or sensitivity leading to indifference, and I was confident she was feeling it all. I stared at the road ahead, squinting in the late afternoon sun. I felt for her and didn't like her put on the spot to feel inadequate as a mother. She was a good mother, a decent one anyway. She wasn't the warmest and wasn't always present, but she cared, and I knew it. She just struggled to show it. There was a wall there that I'd never seen down. Only in that picture in the drawer I'd found at Nonie's cottage with her in the scarf and dark lipstick did I see she had been someone else once. Sadly, before that, I'd never thought of her as anything other than just my mother. But seeing her dressed like that, carefree and confident, I knew something had happened or that she was someone more. I envisioned her made of glass, and she was cracking. It wouldn't take much for this to shatter her. Maybe it already did, or something did before, and I didn't see her as broken. I saw her as weak. Perhaps it wasn't that at all.

"They often went to Bill when he was home, if I'm honest. Bill was more fun and relaxed at home, but he worked a lot. When he was home, he made our daughter Madeline and also Summer a priority. I, well, kept the house running and on a schedule. I was their structure, I guess," she added hurriedly.

"Let me ask you directly, if I may, Melissa—I can call you Melissa, right?" he asked again.

"Yes," she said reluctantly.

"Sorry, okay, did you ever see Bill with the girls?"

"Of course."

"Were you ever concerned?"

"No. About what?"

"Did he ever seem inappropriate with Summer?"

"Heavens no, and this whole thing is ludicrous."

"Objection," Sarah Martin said.

"Way ahead of you, Ms. Martin," Judge Stone quipped.

"Mrs. Plympton, please just answer the question," Judge Stone said nicely.

"Yes, Your Honor."

"Did you ever see Bill with the girls at the beach?" Heinz went on.

"Well, no. I didn't go to the beach. I've never been much of a beach person."

"Mrs. Plympton, just the question, please," Judge Stone said firmly.

"No, not since they were very little," she whispered.

"Did you and Bill share the same bed?"

"What? Why, of course. We are married." Her pitch heightened.

"Did Bill ever get up in the middle of the night?"

"I'm sure that he did at times."

"Do you know if he ever went into where the girls slept?"

"I'm-I'm sure he checked on them."

"Did you ever see anything inappropriate?"

"No!" she said louder. "I have not."

My phone rang, cutting through Sarah Martin just as she started her line of questioning, and I was happy because I couldn't bear listening to my mother struggle any longer. It became more evident that her cracks were gorges and gullies. Suddenly, I felt for her, guilty I hadn't been to see her and barely called. When we did speak, I turned into the same defiant child I became at Doctor Harper's and now with Jay. I was part of the problem too. If I couldn't fix anything else, maybe I could fix us?

"Hey," I said, clicking the speaker icon and turning off the exit.

"How's it going? I'm worried," Jay said, concerned. His voice was calm and comforting.

"It was—I'm not even sure, Jay; I don't even think I've processed it," I said, feeling my eyes burn from freshly forming tears.

"I hate you driving by yourself. You shouldn't be. Not like this." He breathed.

"You've carried me so long, Jay," I blubbered as I turned up the ramp onto 95 South, seeing the open stretch of road free of gridlock ahead. I fiercely wiped my eyes, clearing my vision.

"I'll carry you forever, sweets," he said, and I could tell he was smiling.

"'Sweets?' You haven't called me that since the early days." I smiled, crossing to the fast lane and feeling the truck shudder beneath me.

"Well, those days were good. Maybe we can get back to them soon."

They were good, except for me denying what was, or maybe that was what made it good. I thought about first meeting him and his ugly shirt, blue with faded black lettering I couldn't make out as the wrinkles ran through it.

"Jay, I hope so. I hope we can. Actually, I hope we are better, and I can be better."

"Maddie, you were never not enough. Why can't you see that you're enough, broken and all? A lot of us are broken in different ways, and it doesn't mean we are disposable. Jesus, Madeline Plympton." He sighed.

Just then, it hit me. He was right. I didn't know if it was how he said it or if I was ready to hear it. He'd said it before in different ways so many times, but this time something clicked.

I had to learn to live with this. I couldn't erase it, pretend it didn't exist, or my father, me, and my mother. I realized we exist in this and after this, never in the way we'd imagined, but we do.

Just as I thought this, my next thought pummeled me. I'd thought about it before, but this time was different.

Does Summer? Does she exist in this, with it, or past it? Or has it buried her?

I'd been afraid to know, I'd never let myself go there, but it was all I wanted to know right then. No matter what the answer.

"Jay. I'm headed to the island. I'm going there to . . . Jesus, I don't know. To see my mother, I guess, see the island, feel it—"

"Maddie." He cut me off. "This is a lot for a few days. I mean, have you talked to Doctor Harper? You're on a mission, and I'm unsure how it will end."

"Jay, the point is it needs to end. I mean, it will never end, but I have control over some things. I've pushed the trial, Summer and my father, my feelings—all of this aside for so long and haven't asked questions. I stuck my head in the sand, and look where it got me. Look where it got us. Let me do this. I can't fight you and do this too. Please, Jay." I cried. "Please. Just be by my side, if not physically, just-just be here with me on this." I cried again, switching lanes and easing back on the gas.

"Okay, be careful driving. Don't get yourself all upset on the road. Okay? Promise me." He sighed again loudly.

"I promise. I love you." It felt vulnerable saying it. I hadn't in a while.

"Call me when you get to the boat." He paused. "Safely."

"Thank you." I smiled. "Sweets." I laughed through the last of the tears, sniffling.

Jay's words rang in my head. They felt like a sign that I was doing the right thing in going here.

A lot of us are broken in different ways, and it doesn't mean we are disposable.

My mother's not disposable; our relationship isn't. Is mine and my father's? I could never envision having anything with him after what he'd done—what he'd put us through—but I couldn't help the feeling. It was there, and it never wasn't. I loved him, and thinking it sickened me because my next thought was always what he had done to her.

Chapter 17

There wasn't a lick of traffic the rest of the way to the Cape, which assured me I was doing the right thing again. I figured I'd make the 7:30 p.m. ferry and wondered if I should call my mother, although I didn't know what to say. What brings you here on a whim? I imagined her asking, but I wasn't sure I had the answer. I'd just get there and see what transpired, but I was nervous, and I wasn't wasting this trip or my momentum to get things out there, no matter what was said or how bad it went. I didn't want to hurt her, and I didn't want to hurt anymore, although sometimes I wasn't sure that was possible.

My heart fluttered as I circled the rotary into Falmouth, seeing the sign to the ferry and wondering if my father had called her. I didn't think of this before, but it's a likely scenario. I might be headed for trouble, but I was bringing it with me, locked and loaded wherever I went lately, so this was no different. Either we'd clear the air and maybe talk—God, could we talk?—or we wouldn't, and we'd end up more distant than we already were. Whatever the outcome, it was a gamble I was willing to take.

I pulled into the Palmer Avenue parking lot just in time to catch the bus to the boat. A man across from me smiled as I sat, making eye contact. He stared strangely at me, along with his chocolate-brown lab by his feet. I smoothed back my hair, figuring it was a wreck, and leaned back into the seat when something red caught my eye. My dingy red bra hung haphazardly from my duffel bag on the seat beside me. I slid my hand over, trying to be stealth-like, and pushed it inside, avoiding the man's glare, sighing loudly enough for all to hear.

The bus bumped along, doing its usual drag race to the terminal. No matter how late the buses departed, they always made it to the dock in time for the departure. The ferry loomed over me as I followed the line inside. We boarded through the car entrance into the boat's belly. It was off-season, and they didn't always use the ramps if there weren't many passengers. I followed the man with the lab up to the top deck and pushed the heavy door, stepping outside, feeling the cold wind from the stern whip my hair in my face. I turned hurriedly toward the bow and inhaled the crisp, salty air. It was too cold to be out there, but I didn't care, seeing the sun setting over the island in the distance.

What the fuck am I doing? I thought, tossing the duffel bag on the floor, resting my arms on the railing, and tilting my head to the sky. My hair whirled wild and free, and I closed my eyes, seeing my father's face again—his disappointment and disapproval.

"Madeline?" a voice said, startling me because I thought I was alone. "Maddie Plympton?"

I opened my eyes, searching. A familiar face stared back at me unchanged, except it was older, like all of us.

"Coop?" I said, feeling I'd gone back in time. A stew of emotions churned in my stomach, and I struggled to catch my breath as I studied his face. He was still good-looking and tan, although it was fall. He was permanently tanned, though, growing up. He had some scruff on his face, which looked odd because the rest of him still looked like a teenager. How he did the last time I saw him.

"It's been so long," he said, smiling and pulling me in for a hug.

"It certainly has," I said into his shoulder and pulled back, feeling uncomfortable and exposed.

Did he know? He must. Everyone did.

"So, what's going on with you? I know you're a big-time writer at that Boston magazine," he said, pushing his hands through his hair and turning his back to the wind, moving his body in front of me.

"I don't know about big-time, but yup. I write for a magazine, *Boston Living*, the arts in the city section." I found it odd that he'd read anything from *Boston Living*. He didn't look like a cultured type, I thought, surveying him and reminding myself not to judge a book by its cover because that hadn't gotten me far. He wore jeans with splashed paint, and his hands were weathered with white flecks. He's a painter, it was clear, and not the Van Gogh kind.

"If I'm honest, I don't read it." He laughed, raising his shoulders. "My mom does and is a fan, and she always talks about it. You know her; she was always your mother's sidekick in any art event on the island growing up. Remember?"

"That's right," I said, smiling, envisioning Brenda Collin's face, forgetting she was an artist and heavily involved in the Vineyard Arts Society. "How is she?"

"Oh, she's good. Still there, same house, same thing. Not many changes on the island. You know that." Just as he said it, his face changed, and he looked down at his feet, then craned his neck, looking past me nervously—he knew. He knew it had all changed on the island for Summer and me, and our lives changed because of my family's sickness and the atrocity that was my father's, his perversion and shame. It was mine, all of it. That's how they looked at me or didn't look at me, or at least they did here. That's why I left and went to boarding school freshman year so that I wouldn't be a plague, a virus that no one wanted. I was unclean and dirty, and being around me dirtied them. I wanted to jump overboard but gritted my teeth and plastered the phony smile I'd mastered on my face. "How's your mom?" he asked reluctantly, breaking the silence between us as the voices screamed in my head. Nothing was silent for me.

"She's-she's okay. Same, you know." I felt moisture forming in my eyes and wasn't sure if it was from the wind or this.

"Well, can I get you a beer? I might have one." He turned, looking at the door inside.

A beer? I'd love a beer, and I can have a fucking beer, and I need a fucking beer. Fuck it.

"Sure."

Just as I said it, a pang of guilt stabbed my heart. It's incredible how quickly it takes to make a bad decision. Good ones take such a long time. We contemplate them and assess what we'll do or when we'll start, but a bad one takes the right person, time, or place, colliding with inner desperation, and it's easy and a straightforward yes. Jay, looking at me with disapproval, popped into my head: *tsk tsk tsk*, he said, shaking his head. I tossed him over the side along with my father and let them drown together in the choppy waters of Vineyard Sound.

"Did you want to go inside? It's freezing out here," he said, already opening the door. I followed him in, grabbing a table near the window. When he returned with our beers, I felt free to give in to the cool amber liquid, feeling it slide down my throat. An instant warmth filled me, and I felt rebellious and satisfied with my decision.

"So, are you living on the island again?" Coop asked after downing half his beer.

"No. I'm, well, I'm just going back for a visit. I haven't been in a while," I said, shifting my eyes from his. "I'm in the city now."

"Cool, cool," he said, finishing the rest of his beer. "Do you want another?" he asked, getting up.

"No. I think I'm good, but go ahead."

He returned, already finishing most of it by the time he sat. He seemed more relaxed, which pleased me. *I get it if you have to be drunk to deal with me.*

We made small talk for a while and settled into each other after the initial awkwardness. I finished the last of my beer, mustering the courage to ask him, although I wasn't sure I would. His being on the boat struck me as a sign of sorts—an opportunity to find out more, to end the wonder, the pretend, and the unknown.

"So, have you ever heard from Summer?" I gulped, squinting instantly, feeling my head hurt.

"Umm . . ." he paused, thinking. "Last I heard, she left the island. I'm not sure if it was her junior year or senior year. It's all sort of a blur now. I remember you left. Where did you go?" he stammered. I could tell he regretted the last part.

"I went to boarding school on the north shore with all the prims and propers. I mean, my parents—my mom—made me," I lied, immediately turning into a teenager, blaming my parents when I was the one who begged my mother at the time. I couldn't take the thought of whispers, feeling like a social pariah if anyone found out. Maybe I could have taken it but having to see Summer every day in class or the hall, looking at me, was more than I could stand. I never could read her thoughts, but imagined she hated me as much as I thought I hated her, but I didn't. I didn't every time I thought of her. I didn't, although I tried. I tried so hard and spewed it to anyone who'd listen in the beginning when it all came out, but truth be told, even by the time we got to trial, it had softened—the hate. I only turned my back on her because I was supposed to. She was the enemy because if she wasn't, my father was something far worse.

"Oh, wait! That's right," Coop said, raising his hand. "I heard Summer took off to New York. Kaia, I thought, told me when I saw her at Back Door Donuts one day. I mean, it was so many years ago, but I remember it. I think she said she wasn't doing so well. Like drugs and stuff." He hung his head. "Stinks, ya know. Summer and I had a thing. I mean, for a while, you know." He half smiled, glancing up bashfully, meeting my eyes.

My heart sputtered, then sank to the floor. I eyeballed the bottles of wine on the metal shelf in front of me. I wanted another drink. I wanted ten, but just then, the announcement came over the loudspeaker.

"We're arriving in Vineyard Haven. Please make your way to the car deck for departure, and thank you for riding the Steam Ship Authority," the captain said.

The beer took away my nerves, and I ached for more to take away all the feelings, but it never did for long. Nothing did for long, so if all

I could get was a temporary reprieve, I would take it. That's what led me to the bathroom floor, years of that, and now I'm here, back in the same shit storm. I needed to face it, but couldn't I tomorrow? I thought of Scarlet O'Hara in *Gone with the Wind*, my favorite book when I was sixteen, saying her famous line: "After all, tomorrow is another day." Scarlet was right. I could figure it out then—tomorrow.

We walked together off the boat into the evening sky. Streaks of orange and red painted the horizon behind the sailboats that dotted the harbor. The air was still, and the wind was nonexistent now.

"So," Coop said, turning to me in the stillness. I stopped as he did, averting my eyes toward the cabstand to see if any were there. "Where are you headed? Your mom's still in OB, right? East Chop? You always had the best house."

"Yeah, I mean, I am eventually. I'm just not sure I'm ready now."

Being on the island both comforted and haunted me. It felt like home—it was and always will be—but nothing was the same. It was always the same when I visited on school vacations or in college. I'd step off the boat and breathe deeply, taking it all in, feeling calm. Then, by the time I hit the bridge into Oak Bluffs, *wham!* A sickness washed over me that I was unable to recover from. Then it started before I hit the bridge, and sometimes I just reached the street past the ferry terminal before it hit me. It was then that my visits became fewer and fewer. I couldn't take the high of being here, home, where I had loved so much, to the low of it all ruined. I longed for the island to wrap me in its arms and make it all better. I tried to separate over and over the island from the events that happened on it, but I couldn't, no matter how hard I tried, and it crushed me like everything else about this did.

"Mom troubles?" Coop smiled, taking my bag from my hand and pointing to a cab that pulled in.

"There's just a lot to unpack." I shrugged. "Are you headed to OB? Is that where you're living?"

"I am. I have a little place on Nashawen Avenue. Nothing special. Winter rental I just moved into. You know the game. I'll be out by

May searching for a summer place like the lot of us."

"No chance staying with the folks?" They had a big house.

"No." He laughed. "There's a lot to unpack." We both laughed together. "Share a cab? I'm gonna head to the Ritz and have another if you want to join me before you head home."

"Sure."

"Great. It will be fun to catch up," Coop said, opening the cab door and tossing in my bag.

After all, tomorrow is another day.

Chapter 18

We drove over the bridge into Oak Bluffs, and the sinking feeling I'd usually get wasn't as bad. I figured it was because of the beer I had on the boat, dulling my senses just enough. This, combined with my anticipation of another, made everything tolerable. We jumped out just across from the carousel, and *wham*. There it was. One beer wasn't enough to kill it all.

I thought, as we headed into the Ritz, *How can something—pain, feelings, and hurt—be so alive in someone who's been so dead?* I still felt guilty—having the beer and about to have another. It felt like I was cheating on Jay in many ways, but I was sick and tired of answering to people, and I didn't care, pushing him and all of them out of my mind. It felt freeing to decide on my own instead of checking in with Doctor Harper or running it by Jay or even my mother. Granted, it wasn't a good decision, drinking while on medication or drinking at all in a fragile state, I guess. But it was my decision, which empowered and polluted me.

The Ritz held the usual sorts and suspects. It was still early, but the after-work types were there, and they had been for a while by the looks of them. I didn't live on the island when I was twenty-one, so I didn't frequent bars. I had my haunt, McGinty's, which was similar in many ways. The usual bartenders and crowd, although college kids mainly at night, and the regular older ladies and gents hovering over their drinks during the day, escaping the realities of life for a while. Both bars were dimly lit with dark wood but different smells. The Ritz smelled like a mixture of patchouli oil and tobacco. The island had some artsy, hippy types that frequented, and McGinty's routinely had the odor of stale whiskey with the occasional musky scent of Old Spice or some other lousy cologne one of the older regulars at the bar wore that lingered for days.

"Hey, Coop," a few guys shouted, and he walked over and shook hands. I put my bag on the ground and sat on a stool by the door in case I wanted to make a quick exit, still questioning my decision.

"Another beer, Maddie?" Coop called to me, and I nodded and smiled.

I'd never drunk here, but I often frequented it with my father as a kid. He'd say they had the best burgers on the island, and we'd come every so often to reevaluate it, laughing; then, he would shake his head after the first bite. "Yup. Still number one in my book." My mother would never be caught dead in the Ritz, and he'd joke with me about taking her there on her birthday or Valentine's. We'd laugh at the thought of it, and I loved that we shared special things like this just between us. The Ritz was where the hard drinkers frequented, at least the Oak Bluffs' ones. It was a honky-tonk bar with music most nights in the summer and weekends in the winter. I'd also come in a few times as a kid with Summer and the other island kids for Cokes. Henry, the bartender, never charged us and let us sit on the stools at the bar if the place was slow in the afternoon. I looked at the young bartender, wondering if Henry was around or even alive. He was pretty old then and was always so lovely to us. I wished I knew.

Coop came back to the table, delivering our beers. I sipped while he guzzled. The awkwardness was back again; the first beer's effects had worn off slightly, but Coop seemed to be getting primed for a big evening.

"So, Maddie," Coop said, clearing his throat. "What's going on in the big city? You got a guy there?" He smiled and continued before I could answer, which I was glad about. "I mean, I'm sure you do." He nodded his head nervously, then smoothed his hair back. His right dimple appeared as he smiled sideways. I was sure his boyish good looks got him many girls, but he was still Summer's—off-limits to me. As soon as I thought about it, I realized how ridiculous that was, and it confirmed how stuck I was in the past and life.

"I have a guy," I said as Jay's face returned, leering at me with disapproving eyes while a pang of guilt pulsed in my chest. I sipped beer and rubbed at my shirt, trying to massage it away, watching Coop's face change and his eyes dart around the room.

Great. Did he think tonight might lead somewhere?

"So, what's the gent's name?" He sat straight, seeming to recover. He sucked down the last of his beer and raised two fingers to the bartender. "Two more, Mikey!" he shouted.

"Hey, I'm not even done here." I laughed, shaking out my hair, wondering what I looked like, and realizing I could be a wreck. I didn't care much anyway, but my mother would certainly be concerned if I were drinking and appearing a mess.

"I'm gonna run to the bathroom," I said, rising from the stool and adjusting my sweater. I looked down, forgetting what I had on, not surprised it was the standard black sweater and leggings. Same thing I wore most days. It was easy, and as of late, I didn't care much about appearances, and everything I did was what took the least amount of effort. Black suited my moods, anyway, living in the city for years in the throes of a suicidal spiral I wasn't fully aware of.

"His name is Jay. He's a journalist at the *Boston Herald*," I blurted.

Coop looked at me, confused.

"My guy?" I shrugged my shoulders.

"Oh, nice," he said, realizing I was answering his question.

"Be right back." I leaned in, brushed my hand across his shoulder, and headed toward the back corner where the lady's room was.

Maybe I should add some color soon, I thought as I looked down at my outfit again.

"Jay what?" Coop called from behind me.

"Huh?" I said, turning back to him, shouting over the men talking.

"What's your guy's last name? Maybe I've read something." He threw up his arms, oddly animated.

"You a big *Boston Herald* reader?" I winked, nearly laughing, saying the words.

"Depends on how the Pats and Sox are doing." He stood, walking to the bar.

"I figured."

"What?" he shouted.

"Why are we doing this?" I laughed out loud, and he did too.

"Jay Moore."

"What?" he said again, coming closer.

"Jay Moore," I said again. Saying Jay's name, I suddenly missed him and felt naked without him.

I should go.

"Hey, I read his stuff," the large, scraggly man in the group huddled at the bar said, raising his beer. "He's a good writer."

Coop was closer now, and I pointed to the bathroom. He nodded and turned to walk back to the table.

"Wait!" Coop yelled, and I turned again.

"Can I go to the bathroom?" I shouted, smiling.

The scraggly guy laughed, scratching his chin.

"Let the lady go to the bathroom," one of the other men called out to Coop.

"Didn't he cover some of the Hernandez trial? And wait!" Coop stepped toward me excitedly, jostling his glass, and I watched beer spill down his hands and onto the floor. "Deflate-gate too. He wrote about it. Brady and the balls." He laughed. I could tell he was feeling the alcohol now and wondered if he'd started even earlier.

"He writes mostly investigative stuff and not sports, but these two happened to be both, so I think he did," I said, seeming to remember Jay talking about Aaron Hernandez and the murder. I think once going to Connecticut, where the footballer and, by then, ex-New England Patriot grew up.

I waved and headed to the back. "I'm going now."

"See you soon," Coop said.

I turned back, shaking my head and laughing.

I fixed my hair in the bathroom, trying to tame the wild and large waves by running my fingers through it without much of a difference. After splashing some cool water on my face, I stared in the mirror, questioning what I was doing, but I had no answers. I was living on impulse, attempting to gain some closure, I'd convinced myself, and initially, it was true. Now, I wasn't sure. Now, I was just drinking, but I wouldn't be that honest with myself or even question it for long. I swiped on some lipstick I had in my pocket and rubbed my lips together, telling myself I'd leave soon, knowing that nothing now was carved in stone, and I was easily swayed into having another, avoiding what I came here for.

By the time I finished my second beer, the bar had filled with all sorts of island characters. So many faces I recognized. Some names I remembered, and some I forgot. A few people I'd grown up with came over, and we made small talk. Coop seemed oddly protective of me, watching me talk, staying quiet, listening to conversations, and then giving me the real scoop of what was happening with the person when they left the table. Marnie Eustes, whom I'd gone to the Sailing Camp with a few summers, was having an affair with the married bartender at the Vineyard Haven Yacht Club. Jeremy Flint, my first crush, came in, said hi to Coop, and leered at me in silence until I finally said hello, reminding him who I was. He looked like he'd seen a ghost. Coop informed me he was a pill fiend and a thief and to keep an eye on my bag. He came back and brought us shots, which I knew was the worst idea. But I drank one, enjoying being out among the living, catching up with familiar faces in the most familiar place, the island, my home, or it used to be. The alcohol fueled it all and simultaneously allowed me to hide and play; let's pretend my father isn't a pedophile, that he didn't sexually assault my best friend, our friend, and let's pretend you all don't know about it. I took the shot, then another, and stared out the door onto Circuit Avenue as the people came in, seeing the white lights winking at me in the trees. I felt my mother close and suddenly wanted to crawl into her arms.

"Madeline Plympton. Is that you?" a voice said, breaking my trance. I spun my head around, seeing a face I didn't recognize.

"Hi," I said, staring at the man, wondering where I knew him from. My phone vibrated, and I saw it was Jay—shit.

"It's Rick," he said gruffly, scratching his chin.

"What's up, Rick?" Coop said, slapping his back and twisting his face, giving me the hairy eyeball.

I nodded my head, trying to keep from laughing. Coop was suspicious of everyone.

"Rick, hi. How are you?" I wondered how this man, the waiter from my parent's parties, even recognized me. I hadn't seen him in years.

"You look the same as you did as a kid." He smiled, scratching his chin again, appearing to study my face.

"Thanks, I guess," I said awkwardly.

He felt his pocket and pulled out a pack of cigarettes.

"I'm going to smoke. Anyone want to join?" he asked, turning to Coop and Jeremy and returning his eyes to me.

"I'm good, bro," Coop said as Jeremy waved his hand.

"I think I'll have one," I said, getting up and surprising myself.

Everyone smoked in the nut house. I never had, but I had a few to connect with someone one-on-one instead of just talking in our groups. My roommate only rocked and talked to her stuffed animal about her mother. Plus, it was a chance to get outside and breathe natural air, not the stagnant dirty duct shit from the hospital.

Coop looked surprised and mouthed the words "Be careful" as I followed Rick to the street. I was sure he'd give me an earful about him, too, when he could. The music started, and the sound traveled out to the street. Johnny Hoy and the Bluefish were playing, an always popular band on the island known for their bluesy soul and off-beat stage antics.

"So, you back living here?" Rick asked, handing me a cigarette. I put it to my lips, covered it as he lit it, and inhaled deeply, blowing out into the cold night air.

I wondered how he knew so much about me, staring up at the sky and swaying to the music.

"How did you know I wasn't?" I said, scrutinizing him.

"I've heard rumblings. I know what happened," he answered boldly, inhaling and waiting to see my reaction.

I took offense at first that he didn't pussyfoot around it all or say nothing and pretend like most. I went to say something snarky or thought about walking inside but didn't. My eyes caught his under the streetlight, blue and beady. He was handsome in a grifter sort of way. I remembered him some more, always attentive to the guests at my mother's events, but in a phony way. You could tell he resented them. I was feeling that from him now but second-guessed myself. I could be wrong, but I wouldn't run from what he said; if anything, I appreciated his candor, but only because I was drunk and my guard was down.

"Oh yeah?" I smiled, feeling my phone vibrate in my pocket again, ignoring it. "What do you know?"

"You've turned out to be a looker." He flicked his cigarette into the street and pulled his flannel shirt close around his neck.

"Don't change the subject." I stubbed mine out and stuck it in the coffee can on the ground by the door.

"How about another drink? I'll tell you what I know. I'll tell you what they all know."

I was drunk. I knew as I followed behind him that I cared what this man—who meant nothing—knew or thought, which sickened and intrigued me simultaneously. I raised one finger to Coop, telling him to give me a minute, and scooted beside Rick at the bar.

"Beer?" he shouted over the music, turning to me and leaning against the brass rail, his shoulders hunched up to his ears.

"Sure. Whatever you got." I grabbed the stool and tilted my head back, stretching my neck. I turned my head from side to side and stopped, seeing my hair brush against his arm.

"Sorry." I laughed, biting my lip and almost breaking into a fit.

"What's so funny?" he asked, waving a twenty to the bartender, who wasn't Henry.

"That's not Henry," I said, pointing.

I should get out of here.

"No. It's not," he said, pushing my beer in front of me.

"Well, I like Henry." I took a sip, turning to him.

"Henry's dead."

"Fuck," I said, becoming teary.

"You're not gonna cry now, are you?"

"Maybe. So what?" I said, dabbing my eyes with my sweater.

"I didn't know you and Henry were close."

"He gave us Cokes."

"Yeah?" He lowered his shoulders, scratching his chin again. A piece of his dark hair fell in his face, reminding me of Jay.

"Yeah."

We stared at each other without a word for a beat, and then a smile cracked on my face, then his. I burst out laughing and flipped my head over, shaking my hair. When I returned upright, his laughing turned to a smile plastered on his face. I grabbed my beer and gulped half of it down.

"Whoa there," he said, motioning his hand. I peered over his shoulder but couldn't see Coop anymore as the bar crowd filled in around us.

"So, what do you know, Mr. Rick?" I shouted over the drum solo I recognized from the bars on warm weather nights when Summer and I could occasionally stay out late and walk around the harbor.

"I'm a caretaker now, I guess," he said, leaning into me.

"No," I shouted. "What do you *know*?"

He stared at me, seeming unsure of what to say. "Forget it." I waved my hand. "A caretaker where?" I shouted, figuring I'd stick with small talk. The room was hot now, and my face felt flushed. I fanned my hand in front of me and sipped the last of my beer. I turned to find Coop again but recognized no one in the sea of faces. A blond girl sitting at a stool turned to talk to an older man with a scraggly beard, and a clean-cut-looking kid moved his hands around quickly, talking to a group of guys. I watched their eyes of all shapes widen, and their teeth appeared and disappeared. The blond girl's hair spilled into the old man's beard, and the room closed in as more people filled it. The music hurt my ears, and I closed my eyes, trying to find quiet in the noise.

"The movie theater and the carousel."

I felt Rick's breath hot on my cheek and could tell he was right in front of me. I opened my eyes, seeing him smashed into a kaleidoscope of colors. I blinked methodically, trying to make him whole again.

"Are you okay?" he asked.

Pieces of him moved to form a mouth, and his nose shaped above it; then, his censorious eyes glared at me.

"Carousel?" I asked, feeling the word ping-pong around my brain.

"Yeah." He shrugged. "Wanna go for a ride?" He laughed, turning to the bar and searching for the bartender.

The room fell silent, and my mind emptied. Coop came into view, but he didn't see me, and I moved, silhouetting Rick so he wouldn't.

"Yeah," I said, putting my hand on his arm as the bartender set down two overly full, red-colored shots before us, and some spilled onto the white napkin on the bar.

"Really?" he asked, picking up his and drinking it. He nodded thanks to the clean-cut kid and picked up mine, handing it to me. My head throbbed, and I watched the red bleed across the napkin toward me. I touched it, expecting it to be warm like blood—my blood—but it was cold, which made more sense. Everything was cold except my face. I shivered, grabbed the shot, and tossed it down my throat.

"Let's go."

Chapter 19

We slipped out of the Ritz, into the night, and walked across the street around the corner to the front entrance. The words "Flying Horses" in white against the burgundy clapboard were haunting. The carousel was one of the oldest in the country, I remembered someone telling me once. I think it was Cat, who dated a guy who operated it for a while—Ben was his name, or was it Bob? I touched the building, ensuring it was real, unsure I was even there. Rick fiddled with the lock, pushed open the door, pulled me in quickly, then turned to shut it, giving the outside a once-over before he did. It was pitch-dark with the door closed, and I felt for something in front of me, wondering if I'd gone blind or died. Then lights came alive, and a twang of music, loud, then soft, then silent.

"Hey, over here." Rick motioned for me across the room.

I ignored him, mesmerized by the horses' sleek lines and glaring eyes that found you no matter where you were in the room. My hand reached for the rail, and I followed it, walking the path I had so many times through the turnstile and onto the platform, absorbing all the different hues of aged reds and golds. The room looked different, smaller, with boarded-up windows and the big, wide entry closed. Everything glowed, and I was back in time—a time machine. Footsteps chased me, hands on my hips, and laughter close to me, sounding muffled and underwater.

"Have to be quiet," it said, the voice echoing through my insides.

"Shhh." I put my finger to my lips, bouncing on my tiptoes in front of him.

Who is he?

I pushed away from him, connecting him to the voice, searching, slowly making my way around.

"Do you want the brass ring?" He laughed farther away, but I felt him watching.

My hand wrapped around the pole, forcing my fingers into the grooves. The darkness, the trenches deep within the gold filled with children's laughter and parents' joy capturing it there—stuck. *Is my stuff in there?* I wondered. My secrets with Summer, our sisterhood.

"Oh," I gasped, stumbling ahead and seeing Lilac. I ran my fingers down her side and spun quickly to Blue. "Oh, Blue, my boy, Blue." I leaned down, pressing my face against his, closing my eyes as the tears fell, and I rubbed them into my horse's side with my cheek.

"Are you okay?" a voice said from above me.

"What are you doing here?" I asked, knowing it didn't sound right, hearing the words.

"What?" Rick swayed, looking like he'd fall, and I shuddered, waiting, not moving.

"I'm not leaving Blue," I whispered, holding the horse's bent leg and clenching his hoof.

"We should go," he said, and I jumped up, looking at the man in the face, not recognizing him.

"No. No. Please. Please." I patted his chest. "Can I take a ride? Just one?"

I closed my eyes, begging God to make him say yes.

"I think you're fucked up. How much have you had to—"

"No. It's okay," I said, panicking. "Just one. Please." I moved close to him. "Just one," I whispered, touching his hand.

"All right, one, then we're out of here." He disappeared into the darkness, and I felt a jolt under my feet, then the music.

I moved to climb Blue, lifting my leg. Then Lilac's engineered eye moistened, and a tear hung onto the corner. She needs me, and I need her too. "I'm coming," I said, reaching for her. "Next time, Blue."

The platform swirled, and I climbed onto Lilac, winking at Blue, then buried my head into her mane, smelling the years. Summer was taller and always rode Lilac, who was higher. *Where is she?* We passed by the ring dispenser, and I reached, nearly missing it, touching the ring at the end with my fingertip, pulling it, but unable to grab hold, hearing it clatter on the floor. As Summer and I aged, we'd laugh at how silly it seemed, reaching for metal rings, hoping to get the brass one, which would mean a free ride. Yet, we still did it, and I, no matter what age, still enjoyed it. I knew she did too, but we were becoming cool then, or at least we thought we were, and had to say the right things that made us that way.

Rick waved as I whirled past, forgetting who he was, then remembering his words: *I know what happened.* We passed him again, his arms crossed, as he leaned against the railing. I stood, my feet in the stirrups on Lilac, and pushed out my chest, opening my arms in the air. "You know what happened?" I screamed. "What fucking happened? What happened?" I yelled again, missing the rings altogether. Just then, it came to me like a wave on South Beach, toppling you upside down, then right side up, but you have no idea which until it's done with you. Summer, our last time. Her on Lilac. She stood in the same way, arms opened and palms down. She leaned forward. I leaned forward. I sat on Blue, watching her, unsure what she was doing. It was the last ride, our last ride of the summer. The one I could never remember—the summer just before.

Someone yelled something I couldn't make out. I didn't care. I closed my eyes and was her—Summer—whirling, flying. "Maddie, I wish our horses could fly," I remembered her saying as we reached and pulled, looking at our rings, seeing they were iron and not brass. "I think we're beyond fairy tales," I said, watching her face as she pulled her hair out of the ponytail. It unfolded, the straw-colored waves onto her shirt, and she flew. "I want to fly out of here with you and Blue, Maddie. Why can't we fly?" I stared at her: her eyes closed, and her arms still out, balancing in the stirrups. I never knew it would be our last time as us.

I collapsed into the saddle, feeling it stop. Everything went silent, and I climbed off Lilac, falling over onto Blue.

"What the fuck is wrong with you?" Rick's voice said. He stood me up. My face met his, and I stood at attention, animated and foolish. "I-I'm fucking flying. Why didn't I fly?" I asked, my lower lip trembling. He glared at me, and I broke into laughter and simultaneous tears. "She knew. She knew it was all over and wanted to fly with me. Let's fly." I grabbed his hands, pulling him toward the horses.

"Let's fly." He breathed, touching my back and pulling me toward him.

"Can I have a golden ring?" I asked, sulking and plopping down onto the platform.

He sat beside me, reaching behind him and pulling out one iron ring after another until the golden ring appeared. "One per ride," he said, pulling me near him again, his breath on my face, then lips—wetness.

"Wait." I touched the ring's smooth surface and glimpsed down, staring at it in my palm. The night of our first ride together on the carousel, we each got the brass ring, her on Lilac and me on Blue. She got it first on her side, then two more turns around, or was it three, I got mine. I held the ring up just as she did. "Sisters!" I yelled, the same as we had done that day, and stood, shoving my arm into the air and holding the ring high. It happened too fast for my impaired brain to register—he was on me, pushing me against the chariot behind Lilac and Blue and pulling at my leggings.

"We were sisters then because of the ring," I said, holding the ring in my outstretched hand and ignoring his movements as he lay me back on the hard, cold seat. His lips hit my neck and moved down my throat. I stared at the ring, entranced. "Sisters," I whispered as the tears returned. I let the ring go, hearing it rattle on the floor. All at once, the past disintegrated, and the present materialized—the sights and smells, him and who I was now, and not then, where I was and why. His weight on top of me—his breath and smell—everything moved fast, and I squirmed out from under him, falling to my knees. He got up and spun me around. His kaleidoscope eyes were back, but the rest of his face was his, Rick the waiter, the smoking waiter. I got up and moved to the end of the platform, feeling him grab my arm and pull me back.

"Hey, rich girl. You got the brass ring. I gave it to you. Let me give you something more." He pulled me into him and put his hands in my hair, pulling.

"Get the fuck out of here." I put my hands on his chest and pushed, meeting his resistance.

"Are you serious?" He let go, glaring at me. His eyes were wide and angry.

"Let's just go back to the bar, okay?" I changed my tone, trying to sound friendly and sweet, hoping to calm him. My head swirled, and I suddenly felt sick.

"I know what your Daddy did to that friend of yours." He held me against the wall and raised his arm. I thought he would hit me, but he stroked my cheek with the back of his hand, moving my hair behind my ear. "Did he do it to you?" he whispered and moved in to kiss me.

I closed my eyes and let him. My head spun, trying to find a way out of this, but I was too drunk to think clearly.

"Did he do it to you?" he asked again.

My insides twisted, and an explosion erupted in my chest. I put my hands on his shoulders and quickly pressed down on them with everything I had, then raised my knee into his groin as hard as I possibly could. "Fuck you!" I yelled, clawing at him as he keeled over, taking me with him and pulling us both to the floor. I kicked and screamed on top of him, closing my eyes and wailing.

"Maddie!" Maddie!" a voice yelled, and I felt someone pull me back. I slid across the ground, moving against the wall, terrified, blinking quickly, and hurrying to my feet, seeing Coop's face come into focus. A police officer stood behind him, and I recognized him.

"Maddie? Are you okay? Jesus."

"Hank? Is that you?" I asked. Coop moved me toward the door as Rick moaned on the floor, mumbling.

"It's me, Maddie. Good to see you. It's been a while," he said, removing his hat and pushing back his blond hair, then returning the hat to his head.

"Stand up, Rick," Hank said, standing over him and touching his side with his boot.

"I fucking can't." He rolled side to side on the floor.

"He tried to attack you, Maddie?" Coop asked, putting his arm around me.

Hank turned to see my answer.

"How did you find me?" I asked, grabbed the turnstile, and adjusted my clothes.

"I know Rick works here and in the movie theater. He's a shitbag, and I was worried when I didn't see you at the bar," he said, dropping my bag beside me. "I saw some lights on through the boards and figured he took you over here. Saw Hank on the way patrolling Circuit Avenue and thought it might be smart to have an extra hand." He smiled and put his hand on my shoulder.

"Thanks, guys. I appreciate it. God, I feel stupid."

My stomach rumbled and quickly soured. My head throbbed behind my eyes.

"I think I'm gonna be sick."

"Coop, take her outside while I deal with this asshole." Hank leaned over, pulling Rick up by his shirt.

"Get up!" I heard Hank yell as we went out the door.

I rushed along the outside walls, holding onto the sides, seeing a few other officers head in. A set of trash cans was in the small alley behind it, and I fell behind one and threw up.

"Jesus, Maddie. How much did you drink? Think he slipped you something?" Coop asked, leaning against the wall until I finished.

"I don't know." I breathed, wiping my mouth, mortified.

The air was still, and the lights from the Oak Bluffs ferry terminal shimmered in the distance. The gentle lull of waves came between his words, and the moon glowed over us. I felt protected in my childhood and these men from it in a way I never had. I knew he probably didn't slip me anything, or he could have, but my medication, with copious amounts of alcohol and, I was sure now, a low tolerance, didn't help.

Blue lights flashed, and doors opened and shut. Hank appeared from around the corner. The uniform and his confidence and presence of authority didn't match the fishing-obsessed goofball kid I remembered, but it suited him now.

"Can I ask you a few questions, Maddie?" Hank asked, nodding to Coop, who nodded back.

"I'll be back at the Ritz if you need anything, Maddie. Just call or get me. I can get you home," Coop said, smiling and reaching his hand to mine.

"Thank you, Coop," I said, hugging him. I held onto him tightly for longer than I ever would normally.

"You're all right, kid." He winked and tapped Hank's arm.

"She'll be fine, Coop. I'll get her home."

"Jesus." I sighed as my feelings sloshed around in my gut, and I wanted to crawl into bed and pretend I never came, that I never lived here. That none of this happened, none of it right down to my birth.

"Let's go sit in the car," Hank said, walking. I followed behind him and got in after he opened my door.

"Did you arrest him?" I asked, leaning my head back and closing my eyes.

"We're talking to him; arresting him is sort of, well, up to you."

I opened my eyes again and looked at Hank. His jaw was square and chiseled, and his chest protruded in his shirt. He was safe, and I was safe.

"Listen, Hank, I'm not even sure I know what happened. I don't even know if I know what's happening now." I turned to stare out the window. The white lights of Circuit Avenue lit the path to so many memories. I envisioned myself following them alone, past the square into the darkness, then right up a sandy way to Inkwell Beach, jumping in the water and following the moon.

"Did he assault you? Are you okay?"

"I'm okay, Hank. I mean, I think I am. Nothing got anywhere."

"You got him good, Maddie. I didn't know you had that in you." He laughed. "Are you the same girl afraid to jump from Jaws bridge?" he asked, laughing again.

I laughed with him, enjoying him.

"Odd, we're seeing each other again under these circumstances," I said, embarrassed but needing to say it.

"Where are you staying? Your mom's?" he asked, starting the car.

"I am," I started. "Shit, what time is it?" I reached into my pocket for my phone.

"It's ten-thirty." Hank pulled out, made a U-turn, and drove toward the harbor.

"I have to go. She's in bed for sure now. Shit."

Hank cleared his throat and fiddled with something on the dash. "Well, I'll take you home, but I want to talk to you about what happened with Rick. You really should come to the station."

"Hank, I appreciate it, and I don't want him doing this to anyone else, but I'm not the witness you need. Trust me."

Recent suicide attempt, McLean's. No.

"What the heck were you doing over there with that dirtbag anyway? Sorry, Maddie, but I have to ask."

I explained without getting into detail, blaming it mostly on being drunk and mixing it with medication. I wouldn't tell him anything more. I was sure Hank knew about Summer and my father, but he may not have put it together. I was just a ghost from his childhood, and him mine. I'd leave here and become a ghost again, and things would go back to before, at least to yesterday, before I arrived.

Chapter 20

"Busted," Hank said, seeing the porch lights come on as we pulled up on the gravel. Many homes on East Chop are summer ones and stay empty this time of year. The waves hitting the cliff below in rough seas, the occasional cry of an osprey, or the haunting sound of the ferry whistle blowing were the only things you'd hear during the cooler months. A car coming at night on the cusp of winter was noticeable. She always sat in her Morris chair by the windows in the front room. There was no TV. She'd sit or occasionally read by the dim light of my grandmother's Tiffany lamp next to her, which stayed on no matter what time of day. It was odd because she never sat when I was growing up and was always on the go, moving swiftly, planning and coordinating with whomever she was working with for her next event. Even between events, she'd be preparing the house for the holidays or redecorating. She was never still, until now—after—and the front room was her haven. I never asked why. I only wondered—wondered what she was thinking. *Maybe nighttime bothered her*, I thought. It can be soul-stirring, and losing yourself in the dark is easier—this I knew.

"No sneaking in quietly, I guess." I shook my head, feeling slightly dizzy. "Let's do this," I said to myself, opening the car door.

My mother's form appeared on the steps, silhouetted against the lonely New Englander with its mixed roof pitches and walls of windows. I tilted my chin, gazing at the turret, where the art room was in the tower. It was still there, unchanged. At least it was my last time here, although it had been a while. I tried to remember when it was and couldn't because the few times I'd visited as of late blurred together, and everything was blurred now.

"Madeline, is that you?" she asked, craning her neck into the night.

"Yes, Mom. It's me. Hi," I answered, picking my bag off the car's floor.

"Are you under arrest? Should I call the lawyers? I'll call Bernard," she shouted, not moving from the step.

I laughed quietly and turned to Hank. He smiled, shrugging his shoulders as he got out of the car.

"She's not, Mrs. Plympton," Hank said. "Not at all," he finished, walking around the cruiser.

"Oh, Hank, is that you?" She waved and then hugged her sweater close with one hand while fixing her hair with the other.

"It is. Good evening," Hank answered, attempting to be charming.

"What's going on then?" Her voice turned suspicious.

"I'll let Maddie here fill you in. Have a good night, ladies," he said, tipping his hat and turning to me.

"Give me a call if you want to say anything more. We have Rick at the station now, questioning him. If you can think of anything helpful," he added, leaning into me and handing me his card.

"Thanks, Hank," I said, meeting his eyes.

"Madeline," my mother's voice chimed.

Hank and I smiled, knowing I was a full-blown adult in trouble.

"Hey, Mom," I said, passing her on the steps as Hank pulled away. I felt her eyes burning a hole through me. I opened the French doors, tossed my bag on the oversized chair in the corner, then hurried to the bathroom. She followed close behind me, but I pretended not to notice, nearly shutting the door in her face.

"Madeline," she said. I could tell she was right there, at the door, listening.

I ignored her, splashed my face with cold water, and opened the closet, searching for mouthwash and gargling silently. Examining myself in the mirror, it was apparent I'd been drinking or crying, but crying didn't smell. Maybe I could get away with it, as ruddy noses and cheeks with slightly bloodshot eyes could be either, but drinkers or those familiar with them could always spot the difference. My mother was both a drinker—casual, but not always—and familiar with them. She and Nonie would say Big George, her father, loved his whiskey. It surprised me that she married my father, who barely touched a drop. He could never be out of control or anything but clean as freshly fallen snow; who knew his facade cloaked something more sinister? I was screwed, and I knew it—plus, she's my mother. "Let's do this," I whispered again, finger brushing my hair.

"Maddie," she repeated, tapping on the door as I pulled it open. She had put the lights on, and it felt like I was on stage—breaking a leg.

"Mom, I'm tired." I stopped, trying to keep my distance. She moved closer to me. Of course, she was already suspicious because I'd shown up unannounced at night and in a police car. *I'm not even trying hard with her*, I thought. *I don't have the energy.* I breezed by her to the front room, which was still dimly lit, and plopped down on the chair next to my bag, kicking my legs out and stretching. I was here for a reason: I wanted to talk. But I was still drunk with the beginnings of a hangover from the alcohol, my father, and all that transpired. I didn't have much left in me and nearly forgot the point of my visit entirely, wishing I could teleport to my apartment with Jay and curl up next to him in the quiet—no questions or talking—just sleep.

"Madeline, for God's sake." She followed behind me and turned the lamp twice, brightening the room. She switched on the chandelier above us.

"It's light enough, Mom. Can you shut that off?" I asked, squinting and covering my eyes, feeling my skull vibrate when I spoke. "It's been a long day, and I just want to go to bed," I said, grabbing my bag, getting up, and heading back to the living room.

"Well, what are you doing here?" She followed me again, shutting the lights off. "Why are the cops dropping you off?"

I turned to her, feeling hidden in the shade of the room. "Not cops, Mom, Hank." I could barely get his name out when I saw it. Her face changed, and she was scrutinizing me now.

"Have you been drinking?" She put her hand to her heart, and her sweater fell open, exposing the white nightgown she always wore. She had at least fifty copies of this one from Garnet Hill. "I smell it, Madeline."

Just then, my phone vibrated, and I answered, feeling saved.

"Hi, Jay," I said, turning my back to her and walking to the front room.

Her voice called out behind me. "Does Jay know you're drinking?"

"You're drinking, Maddie?" Jay's voice was alarmed.

I clenched my jaw, feeling my face contort with rage. "You know I'm an adult, and I've been for a while." I spun to face her and spoke purposefully into the phone, emphasizing my words. "I'll be glad to tell you all about my day and the hell I've been through, but I will not be treated like a child. Got it?" I hissed. My heart began beating out of sync, flipping in my chest like a wild bird tossed in a cage. I held my breath, trying to slow it before I ran out the door, screaming into the night.

My mother stepped back, resting her hand on the sofa table, seeming to try and steady herself. I'd never talked to her like this, and I could see it caught her off guard. I felt both powerful and ashamed.

"Jay, I'm safe. I love you. I'm at my mother's, and clearly, she and I need to talk. I'll call you in the morning, okay?" I said quietly into the phone, becoming softer, trying to smooth things.

He paused and let out a long, dramatic sigh. "Make sure to call me, okay? I'm getting a little tired of chasing you when all you do is run, Mad," he said, breathing heavily.

"I know," I whispered, feeling the sting of his words. I hung up and looked at my mother, who remained in the same position except her head turned to her hand as she fiddled with the gold and blue Fabergé egg on the table, moving it to the right and back again. Her thick red curls fell in her face, and she tucked one side behind her ear. I stood firm in my tracks, waiting for more questions, but they didn't come. My vision narrowed, fixating on the Fabergé egg, thinking it wasn't right; it wasn't supposed to be there. It was always on the credenza by the opening into the butler's pantry. I squinted, my temples beating like a drum as I tried to focus on the other objects in the spinning wheel of whatever new angst regarding my father arrived on my mother's doorstep. Nothing was new for some time, except me and my visit—he must have called and told her. The Paul Brant portrait of my mother as a girl sitting on the steps of the State House in the city was now on the mantel. It was supposed to be on the shelf in the corner. The bronze stallion sculpture was now there in place of it. I stopped there, knowing the rest.

"Did Dad call?" I asked, unsure if I needed to suit up my armor or wait, knowing the latter could finish me.

"Madeline, I'm worried." She closed her sweater and walked over to the couch. She pulled something out of the sweater pocket, rolling it in her hand—her rosary beads. He had called.

I pulled on my armor halfway, leaving my heart narrowly exposed. I came here for a reason, and as much as I wanted to wait, sleep, and talk in the morning, it seemed it was happening now, and I had to be open.

"So, you know I went to see him," I said, sitting beside her on the couch, carefully keeping my distance, hoping she'd forget the drinking. Watching her sickened me. She fidgeted and rolled the red and gold beads compulsively as though prayers and beads would save us. They were her grandmother's—blessed by the Pope, one of them, I forgot which, but Nonie always told the story. I didn't understand her faith; I never did, especially in all this. I was also raised Catholic and spent every Sunday at Our Lady of the Sea Parish. We all did, but I never had an unwavering conviction. I liked Jesus and Saint Michael, but most of it made no sense to me. Any faith I'd acquired burned up and disintegrated, rising as ashes to the heavens after what happened. I hated her unfaltering belief and synchronously envied her for it, but I wasn't entirely sure it was even real.

"He called today after you left. He calls every Thursday if I don't visit."

I took a deep breath, wanting to be careful with my words.

"I'm sorry if that upset you," I responded coldly, tracing the woman's outline in the painting above the fireplace with my eyes, attempting to keep my composure.

"Do you want some tea?" she asked.

"Sure," I answered, hoping to buy time to figure out what to say. I didn't want to distance myself further from her. I wanted us to find a way to coexist in our differing opinions or for her to see the light, although I could never see how. I couldn't fathom her belief in him, with all the evidence, the police, his nonadmission, Summer—she knew Summer. Did she ever question it? But she didn't listen to the trial. She didn't want to know, and I wasn't sure I could ever accept that, but I wanted to. I needed her. I didn't think I did and spent so long trying to erase my past that I nearly erased myself. I needed a connection to her and the island. It may not be the same, but I hoped there were some scraps to cling to. Seeing Hank and Coop reminded me that I was alive before, and here—I existed. But I wanted more than proof of my existence in my relationship with my mother. I wanted my mother, Missy Plympton, in any way I could have her. I knew I needed to compromise and be vulnerable, which I wasn't sure was possible. But I was here to try. I was also here to say my piece, which I knew could break us for good, but there wasn't a way forward if I kept living in the lies of the past. That's why I came. Clear and unmistakable: the truth, feelings, and urgency to see her as I headed here took form in my haze.

The kettle whistled, and I curled up on the sofa, closing my eyes and feeling myself drift; then, I heard her return with two steaming cups. I opened my eyes, one by one, as she handed me one. I smiled, taking the small cup with the pink and white flowers and gold edging.

They were from her wedding china set, and I could drink its contents in one sip. I preferred a large coffee mug, and she knew that, but tea was supposed to be served in teacups, so that's what she did.

"So." She breathed, sitting next to me softly on the sofa, blowing onto her cup, then taking a sip. I did the same, unsure what to say. I thought I'd think of something, but all I could think of was sleep.

"It seems like you're struggling," she said, reaching for a coaster and putting the cup on the coffee table.

"How so, Mother?" I replied, feeling like a defiant adolescent.

"Madeline, you show up here in the middle of the night—"

"Mom. It's eleven," I cut her off, rolling my eyes.

"Eleven. Fine." She picked up her cup, taking another sip. "You show up here unannounced at eleven, in a police car, no less."

"I have to announce myself now?" I quipped, putting my cup down without a coaster and watching her struggle.

"Madeline, you know what I mean." She pulled my cup onto a coaster.

"And you've been drinking. I thought you couldn't with your medication. Are you still on your medication?" Her eyes widened as she shifted in her seat to face me.

I began to retreat within myself and sat there stiffly. The air was stagnant, and everything was silent except a ringing in my ear that grew louder and more intense with the grandfather clock's heavy ticks in the study, counting the seconds. I was about to get up and head to my room, running from her voice and avoiding the questions. Then, the picture of her as a girl in the city came into view. I got up and drifted to it as if there was a magnetic pull, and I thought of the other picture of her in the scarf and the dark lipstick from Nonie's.

"Madeline, why can't you answer me? I'm worried." Her voice lofted from behind me.

The reflection in her eyes, I'd always loved the picture. You could see the city buildings in them. She looked hopeful and full of promise, as we all did once.

"Mom," I said, picking the picture up off the mantle. I walked across the room, returning it to its proper place on the shelf.

"Do you think I am troubled or damaged?" I asked, clutching the bronze stallion.

"What are you doing, Madeline?" She leaned back in her seat. She knew exactly what I was doing.

"Is it me? Am I the problem? My problems?" I questioned, moving through the room and returning each item to its rightful place.

"You've been having problems, Madeline. Yes!" she said, exasperated.

"Why do you think I have been having problems?" I stuttered.

"Madeline, I guess depression. That's what your doctor said." She lowered her voice.

"Okay, and why? Was I a depressed kid, Mom? Did you know me to be sad before?"

"You were a fine child," she interrupted, becoming defensive.

"So what's wrong, Mom? What is wrong?" I shouted, and my head felt on the verge of exploding.

"Don't shout at me—your mother." She lowered her eyes, looking away.

I came back over, sitting next to her. "Mom, I don't want to shout. I'm sorry," I said, pulling her arm to take her hand. It was in her pocket, and she took it out, switching the beads to her other hand. "I've been struggling because of Dad, Mom. You must know this," I pleaded.

"Well, as you know, this is not his fault," she began, avoiding my eyes as her face hardened.

"No, Mom. Stop!" I cut her off.

She pulled her hand from mine.

"Mom, he did it." I softened my voice. She leaped from the sofa, startling me, and marched toward the staircase.

"Mom, don't run." I got up, moving toward her.

She spun around at the banister, jutting her arm out toward me.

"How dare you. How dare you come here and say all of this. You know that girl, your friend," she emphasized. "She lied, and you know she did. She lied, Madeline, and look what it did to us. You know!" she scolded, pointing her finger at me.

Her words were a cannon fired into my chest, taking the wind from me. I was sober now, completely, and I wanted to be anything but.

"My friend?" I seethed as if, somehow, Summer, being my friend, made it my fault.

"We were kids—little girls, Mom. Why would she lie? Why?" I screamed.

She huffed loudly and started up the stairs.

"Don't you run away from this, Mother. Don't! He did this, and I told him I didn't believe him. I told him I believed Summer. Today, Mother. Today, I told him all of it." I ran to the stairs, watching her disappear around the corner.

"Mom," I yelled firmly, heading up quickly and following her into her room.

"Madeline, please leave. Please go to your room," she said, her lips quivering in the moonlight that shone through her window. She looked translucent, and I reached to touch her.

"I'm sorry, Mom. I know this is upsetting, but haven't you ever wondered? Haven't you ever thought this could be true? Why would she—"

"Because she did! How would I know why she lied? She's troubled and got caught up in the gossip, as Gabe Heinz said. He's your father, Madeline. Your father!" She wailed, moving past me, back out the door, and down the stairs. I trailed behind her, unrelenting. It was out now, my feelings and questions, at least some of them, and I wouldn't stop, although I thought I should.

"Madeline." She turned to me at the bottom of the stairs. She closed her sweater and smoothed back her hair, composed now, although her shaking hand gave her away. "Madeline, I am done with this conversation. It is inappropriate and not right. I think you should call your doctor."

"My doctor? Am I crazy? No. No, no, no," I said as I bounded down each step.

"I'm not crazy, Mother. I've lived a life that is crazy," I said close to her face, clenching my jaw and trying to keep from yelling. "Everything was perfect; everything had to be perfect, crisp, and clean without a wrinkle," I said through gritted teeth. She moved over to the corner shelf, clutching it. Her hand trembled, and I rested mine on top of it.

"Summer was good; she was always good. We were good. She wouldn't lie. I wanted to believe she did, and I did think it, Mom." I moved to her and caressed her hand. "Because I couldn't not believe him."

She stayed silent and still but with wild eyes. I wondered if I'd shattered her, and she'd break onto the floor in a million pieces.

"Mom, I listened to the trial. I heard the evidence; I heard Summer, the police, the psychologists. We never talked about this. We just went along and accepted that Summer lied and Dad was gone. We never even discussed it. Is that normal? Is it okay?"

She turned to face me, and I wasn't sure if she'd collapse or murder me, but I persisted.

"I saw him, Mother—by her bed where we slept. I fooled myself into thinking it was a dream for so many years, but it wasn't," I went on, my eyes pleading. "She looked at me. Summer did. She looked at me for help. I knew something wasn't right—I felt it," I said, my voice trailing.

She stared at me blankly, and I watched for a sign, anything to know I hadn't pulverized the already broken pieces of her. I watched as she looked back at her hand and grabbed the picture of her, young, with the city in her eyes.

"No!" she screamed wildly, taking hold of it and pausing—staring at the image before hurling it across the room. I stood in horror, seeing it break against the bookcase and the image sail to the floor through the storm of wood and glass.

"Mom." I grabbed her and tried to pull her to me, knowing I'd gone too far.

"No!" she yelled into my chest. "Madeline, no." She pulled away from me and dropped down onto the steps.

Crouching in front of her, I took her hands in mine, feeling her grip on the rosary beads tighten. Her eyes were closed, and she mumbled something I couldn't understand.

"Mom," I started again, pausing, wondering if I should go on. I'd never seen her like this. I'd never envisioned it was in the realm of possibility, and I didn't know if she was irreparable now—if *we* were. I was the one who did it, but to me, she needed this because it was evident that she had been hanging on by a thread. But it concerned me that there was no light on the other side and that the threads were all that she had, stringing together the pieces of her, and without them, there was no other side; there was only the memory of who she used to be without hope of any way back. Who was I to determine what she needed? What did I do? I thought all this and knew it wasn't my decision to make, but I'd already driven into her a truth that she had never considered. If there was hope for us, I couldn't stop and wouldn't, no matter if it was selfish, and maybe it was, but I needed her, and I felt sure she needed me.

"He never said he didn't do it. Has he? Has he once to you ever?"

She mumbled again, and I tried moving closer to hear what she said, feeling her breath warm my cheek. "Our Father who art in heaven," she repeated, not finishing the prayer.

"Mom." I cried. "Open your eyes. Can we talk about it? Just talk?" I said, watching her lips mouth the words. Her eyes were squeezed shut, and she tapped her slippered feet on the ground. "Mom," I repeated, shaking her. She opened her eyes, glaring at me with fear and fury. She closed them again and started the prayer again, this time finishing it.

"Mom!" I yelled and reached for her hands, grabbing onto the rosary.

"Stop praying. Stop!" I yanked, feeling a release. The string let go, and my arm slung backward as I stumbled from my stance onto the floor. Beads shot into the living room and rolled along the floor. She crawled over me, hitting my leg, and scurried on all fours to the living room, wailing at the top of her lungs.

"I'm sorry!" I called after her, watching her chase the beads in a frenzy, stuffing them in her pocket.

I came up behind her and reached my arms around her, pulling her in between my legs on the floor. She leaned back, not fighting, and let her head fall onto my shoulder while crying. I'd never seen her cry. Not even at Nonie's funeral.

"I shouldn't have come. I guess I just shouldn't have come," I said, holding her tightly and feeling the tears spill down my cheeks.

"He couldn't have done this, Madeline," she whispered, pulling her head away from me and moving my arm. She slid across the floor and leaned against the coffee table to face me. Her head fell forward, and she brushed the hairs from her cheek.

"How, Mom? How could he not have? Why?" I breathed, exhausted, feeling that we'd only divided ourselves more and ripped anything we still had to shreds.

She noticed the photograph of herself and pulled it out from under the shattered frame. She stared at it, then shook her head, touching her finger to her cheek.

"Because he saved me, Madeline." She smiled. "He, your father, saved me from—" She stopped and pointed at nothing, screwing up her face.

"What, Mom? I'm not following." I pulled myself closer to her, my leg touching hers.

"From that—that filth, you know?"

I was confused. She struggled with saying it, but I didn't get it. "Filth, Mom? What? What happened? What filth?" My head spun, thinking, not wanting her to retreat.

"Big George? Your father?" I said in alarm, wondering. I couldn't think of anything else, and I didn't know him. He died when I was small, but I couldn't imagine what she was talking about.

She stared at me icily, her eyes as big as moons.

"No. No. God help us, no." She swallowed hard, curled her legs under her, looked at the picture again, and breathed an exasperated laugh.

"I was . . . I was assaulted, Madeline. There, I said it. I was." She put her thumb up to her mouth and rested it on her lip.

I said nothing, trying to figure out what she meant. Minutes went by, and I finally spoke. "What? When?" I exclaimed. "Assaulted? Mom?" I reached for her. She didn't move. I'd never seen her look more tired. She looked old, something I'd never seen her as.

"That's it," she said. "I was assaulted and never thought I had to discuss it again. But clearly, I must." Her eyes filled, and she waved the picture, fanning her face.

"Where? When? I'm just trying to—"

"Trying to what—understand? You can't understand these things, Madeline. These aren't things meant for understanding," she said firmly. "These are things you don't talk about, the horrible devil things that happen that are unspeakable." She leaned in close to me, then pulled back her head, shifting her legs and pulling her nightgown over them.

"Where? When?" I asked again, knowing I was pushing.

Thoughts banged against each other as I tried piecing this puzzle together in seconds, feeling I'd run out of time and would never know if I didn't right now.

"In the city—Boston." She shrugged, shifting her eyes to the floor. She turned childlike, and innocence took over her voice. "In college."

"Who?" Fire rose in my throat, thinking this had happened to her.

Assault, violated: these words so many use to downplay what happened. I knew by her demeanor that she was raped—raped, not assaulted or violated. She was raped, and I could tell. One expects the act to be downplayed by defense lawyers who rarely say what the crime is, but what saddens me the most is us—women who say it— assault—as if to lighten the perpetration somehow. Rape, penetrated— these words bring damage: unforgettable and life-altering destruction. And no one wants that. No one wants to feel forever broken—robbed of something for eternity. So assault me, violate me—this sounds temporary, and that there's a chance of recovery.

I thought of tonight and where I'd be if Coop hadn't come in. Would I have been raped or penetrated? How would those words now define me? I looked at my mother—a paper doll, crumpled on the floor, telling me this when everything in her thought she'd left it somewhere behind. Maybe back in the city. Things started making sense.

"Dad saved you?" I looked at her intensely. I didn't want the conversation to end, but she was exhausted.

"He was in the service when he reenlisted. I let someone walk me to my dorm while he was away. I shouldn't have. I shouldn't have." She hit her hand on the floor.

"Mom, you did nothing wrong!" I pleaded, trying to convince her.

"I did—I did something wrong. I was engaged and let another man walk me home. I thought it was safe. I thought it was fine." She raised her eyebrows, picked up the pieces of broken glass, and put them on the table above her. "I had grown up with him. He was someone I knew." She shrugged, smiling again.

"Oh, my God, Mother. I'm so sorry." I pulled off my sweater, holding my tank top so as not to come with it, immediately feeling the coolness on my arms. I lay it on the floor and began piling the glass and beads.

"Your father was the only one I could tell, except I never said who. I told him I didn't know." She brushed her hand across the floor, watching it. "I tried everything I could not to tell him, but he'd always known me so well, and he knew. And I was, well, you know, you don't do certain things before you get married. I mean. I had to tell him." She stood, adjusting herself, seeming to return to her previous character.

"How did he save you?" I stood, picking up the sweater and folding it so nothing spilled.

"He brought me here to the island."

She headed toward the kitchen. I heard the fridge open, and then she appeared again at the archway holding a bottle of wine and two glasses.

"He loved the city, Madeline. You had to know that. He came to Boston from Kansas, worked, and built his business there. This—" she looked around—"was for me."

She put the wine on the mantel and poured two glasses as I emptied the shirt into the garbage in the kitchen. This had some meaning—the wine—the calm after the storm. I followed her to the porch, and she sat in her favorite chair. I sat near her and took the glass. Nothing and everything made sense. The city she'd always loved. Her eyes lit up every time we were there. She loved shopping and the busyness of it all. We'd never stay long, though, only for New Year's or quick weekend trips, sometimes for a museum trip or a hair appointment. She'd shop Newbury Street with a smile and urgency I'd only ever seen there. She could never be away from the Vineyard for very long. I'd always wondered why she was here. I knew she loved the island and summers here. Still, nothing made sense that this philanthropist and socialite, who could conquer a much larger area and had every connection to do so in Boston, was on Martha's Vineyard in the dead of winter, spending most nights alone in a giant house with just me then . . . and now alone.

"Dad loves the island," I said, confused. I'd never wondered if my father wanted to be here. He fell in love with it after coming to Nonie and Big George's cottage; that was the story. It was him; he never wanted to leave. Just as I thought this, I realized how blind I'd been. For someone who never wanted to leave, he was rarely here.

"He does love it here. I think he convinced himself of it more and more to convince me. He brought us here and saved us from my secret. We built a life in this beautiful place. I've become okay with the loneliness, the long winters, and the quiet. I'm okay. Thanks to him." We said nothing; what more was there to say? It was the most we'd ever said. The most real we'd ever been. I stood and leaned against the chair rail, looking out beyond the cliffs to the darkness. She sipped her wine as our breath alternated, and we dissolved into the night.

"Do you miss the island?" my mother asked, taking another sip. "It is your home." She turned now, looking over at me, waiting for an answer.

"Yes."

"You should come more," she said, to my surprise after the night's events.

My heart sped up in my chest, and my breathing shallowed.

"I wish I could," I said, holding back the tears.

"Yes." She paused. "I understand." She paused again. "I sometimes wish I could leave."

We finished our wine, silent. There was nothing more to say.

Chapter 21

The sun streaked through the shutters. I reached to close them, but they were already. You could never effectively darken a room with shutters, especially my room on the east side of the house. I wanted it dead dark so I could sleep, but even if it was, there was no use with all the noise downstairs. I lifted my head from the pillow, feeling like it weighed one thousand pounds. I'd been hungover before, and there was not much a concoction of prescription-strength ibuprofen, greasy breakfast, and a can of Coke Classic wouldn't fix, but I'd never felt anything like this. My body felt mangled, and I imagined this was what one suffered being crushed by something heavy, like a train or a tractor, in slow motion and lopped back down. I didn't move until I couldn't take the stillness anymore.

"Good morning, Madeline," Marta greeted me, carrying a bag of groceries and putting them on the counter when I finally wandered into the kitchen. I smiled, wincing as pans clanked and clashed behind me.

"Sorry, ladies," my mother chimed, whisking something into a bowl.

"Marta, it's so good to see you," I said, coming into her open arms.

"Look at you, Madeline. You big writer girl." She held me and then pushed me away, taking my hands in hers and stretching out my arms, studying me. "You look tired. Are you sleeping?" she asked as her glasses slid down her nose.

Marta had always called me "the big writer girl" since I got the column at the magazine. She had worked for us forever, and unbeknownst to my mother, she was her best and most authentic friend. She was family to me, and I never realized how much I missed her until I saw her again.

"Not lately, Marta." I forced another smile and walked over to the pot of coffee.

"I love seeing you, though," I said, grabbing the Black Dog Bakery mug I always used.

"No cream?" My mother swung her head toward me while pouring eggs into a pan.

"Black today," I said, raising my cup and awaiting her comment.

She didn't. She continued cooking the eggs as if nothing had happened, and Marta put away the groceries. I walked to the living room, enjoying the warmth from the sun through the windows.

"Ouch!" I cried, lifting my leg and inspecting my foot. I leaned against the mantel, watching some coffee spill on the floor. "Great," I said, wiping the blood with my fingers, catching a piece of glass glistening on my toe, then moved to the couch with my coffee, removed the shard, and applied pressure with my thumb. Aside from the tiny bit of glass, the room appeared as if nothing had transpired there; everything was the same and how it was supposed to be. The Fabergé egg was on the credenza, and the stallion was on the shelf. If it weren't for the blood running down my foot and the missing photograph on the mantel, I would have thought last night had all been a dream. Everything looked perfect, and she had made sure of it. I guess it's just her way, and for the first time, I appreciated it.

"Oh, you're bleeding, Madeline. What happened?" my mother asked, alarmed, rushing over to me, her nightgown billowing in her wake.

"It's nothing," I said, avoiding saying glass. I hated her avoidance of all things, but I did it too. I wanted to pretend last night hadn't happened. I was glad it had, I thought, or maybe I wasn't, but I didn't want to discuss it. Enough had been said, and she wouldn't want to anyway, so not saying it was glass left us much more comfortable.

She returned from the kitchen with a wet tissue and Band-Aid, and I reached to take it from her. She ignored the gesture, sitting next to me, gently wiping my foot, and applying the Band-Aid.

"Did you get it out, the glass?" she asked matter-of-factly. It surprised me, but she seemed fine, so I followed suit. We were fine. Although I knew she wasn't fine. What happened to her changed her life. I looked at her lips, thinking of them painted crimson, smiling like in the picture—her before. I wished I'd known her then, and I never would.

"There," she said, smoothing out the Band-Aid.

"Thank you." I smiled, tapping her knee.

It could have been her control—applying the Band-Aid and cleaning my cut—to do it right and not stain anything. The house was predominantly white, with white rugs, couches, and throws. Color, she brought in through art and refined touches here and there, but I felt it was more her mothering me, and if it wasn't, I didn't care because I liked it. So, I made the decision that was it.

"Your eggs are burning up here, Missy. You want me to finish?" Marta called from the kitchen.

"I'm coming," she hollered, then ran back toward the archway to the kitchen. You're staying for breakfast, right, Madeline?" she asked before disappearing, not looking back.

"Of course she is," Marta said. "You're making her favorite eggs."

I enjoyed listening to the banter between them. They'd grown so comfortable together in their age and aloneness. Marta lost her husband many years ago, and her kids were older and lived on the mainland. One was in California, if I remembered, and the other was in New York. Marta, I was sure, knew everything and more. Not only did she know everything that went on in our house, but there was also nothing she didn't know on the island. Still, she never abandoned us or seemed to think differently or judge; at least, she never made anyone feel that way. She was a vintage islander, born and raised here. She knew judgment only came back to haunt you, especially living here. Everyone knew each other's business, so if you lived here year-round, you better have nothing to hide if you were going to squawk. She told me this one day in junior high when she caught me gossiping about how Meredith Gaffney did more than kiss a boy, and everyone knew it. I had been filling Summer in on the news I'd heard on the porch. Marta, unbeknownst to us, had been beneath us cutting hydrangeas for the table. We hadn't seen her until she popped up, scaring us and giving us a schooling on island ways.

I headed upstairs and changed into my running clothes. They smelled awful, having not been washed from my run in the city, but I didn't care. I'd only sweat them up again and, in a few minutes, wouldn't notice the difference. I laced up my sneakers, hoping my wound wouldn't bother me. I'd cut it short if it did. I grabbed my phone and texted Jay that I'd be on an early afternoon boat and planned to return to the city just before evening. He didn't respond right away, as usual, and I hoped it was just that he was busy. I had to start prioritizing him, and I knew it, promising myself I would.

"Come eat," my mother called as I jogged the stairs.

I grabbed a piece of toast off the plate and took a forkful of eggs, standing over the table.

"Sit, Madeline." She motioned with her hand.

"She's a woman on the move, Missy." Marta laughed, washing something in the sink.

"Are you running? It may be chilly out," my mother said, sipping her tea.

"It's a beautiful day, cool and crisp but sunny. Good day for a jog," Marta said.

"God, what is that smell, Madeline? Is that you?" My mother sniffed.

"Sorry. I ran in the city just before I came and wore the same clothes. I know, pretty gross," I said, lifting the fork to my mouth.

"Go up and put something of mine on."

"It's fine," I said, standing. I leaned against the wall, pulling one leg behind me, stretching.

"Do you have the Martha's Vineyard Film Society benefit details yet?" Marta asked.

"Oh yes, I do. Adam emailed me yesterday. Do you have time to go over it?" my mother asked, opening her computer.

"Yes. I'm a little excited about this one. I saw their documentary on the housing crisis here and thought it was excellent." Marta poured a cup of coffee and sat beside her.

"You're into documentaries, Marta?" I asked, surprised.

"Oh, hush. They had free tickets at Cronigs, and I went on a whim."

Marta was a simple woman who didn't like much fuss. This made her and my mother an odd pair. She enjoyed knitting and baking and used to paint seascapes of various island scenes. A few hung in our house, but she stopped when her arthritis got bad. I wasn't even sure of Marta's role here anymore. She helped with shopping and cleaning, but it seemed like she did some of everything. Somewhere along the way, she turned into my mother's assistant in her philanthropic endeavors. I'd never thought Marta was interested, but she seemed to enjoy it, my mother said, and hearing her today confirmed it. If I hadn't seen it for myself, I wouldn't have believed it and figured my mother was pushing it on her.

"I'll be back," I said, zipping up my sweatshirt and putting on my headphones.

"Be careful," my mother said. She looked rested and youthful, so different from last night. She seemed lighter, and I imagined she was. Secrets are burdensome and can make you mad. Of course, I knew this well, and now, I knew, so did she. She never wanted to speak of what happened to her again, and I was sure she thought this was the best approach. Maybe it would make it go away, or so it never happened, but I'd come to realize it gave it more power. *The dark things fester and feed on you, killing who you were and what you could become.* She freed herself some, and I could tell. I hoped she felt it and continued to.

I fiddled with my phone, trying to find MVY radio. More was left of the trial, but that was nothing I could handle right now. I didn't want to think about any of it, especially the remaining part. Summer's testimony was the reason I listened. That's what I wanted to hear, and it terrified and consumed me. Knowing my testimony was next was something I couldn't think about. I didn't consider how that would be, listening to me and my truth then or what I had thought it to be. It was nothing that interested me, no matter how much I wanted to get this done to move on and have a chance at healing—to see if it was possible, although it nearly paralyzed me in thinking it wasn't. I wouldn't go there—not now. That required no thinking. I'd know it soon enough after all this—everything exposed to ourselves and each other, and now the truth about my mother. There were only two options now: forward or belly up in a dark hole with someone throwing dirt on my face.

I jogged down East Chop, feeling the wind chill my face and my hair fly free behind me. The new hospital had been built a few years earlier, and I wondered what it was like inside as I passed by. I'd only been to the previous one that resembled a large summer cottage, and I thought of the last time I was there when I twisted my ankle jumping on the trampoline my father had surprised Summer and me with on Easter Sunday. My mother hid eggs for years in the yard for both me and Summer. She filled them with chocolates and jellybeans, but my father always hid one large one with money for each of us. This was how I discovered there was no Easter Bunny. That one year, I saw him, Easter morning out the window, walking with two large eggs, one silver and one gold, sticking one under a bush and the other on a branch above the hammock. Summer and I bet our egg money on who could jump the highest on the trampoline. Like her, I soared into the air on my turn, but upon landing, I crashed down, watching my leg twist underneath me. I screamed in pain as Summer ran to get my father, who picked me up and loaded me in the car. We went to the ER, and Doctor Mac wrapped it up in ace bandages.

"It's not broken," he said, examining the X-ray before us.

"That's good," my father said, tousling my hair.

"Ice and rest for six weeks," Doctor Mac finished, handing me a pair of crutches.

"Crap," Summer said, to which I agreed.

The sun sat high in the sky over the Alabama and Shenandoah, the tall ships in Vineyard Haven harbor. It was colder than I thought, feeling the wind pick up as I reached the top of the bridge. I ran fast down the flat road, knowing it would pass and I'd be warm in a moment as long as I kept my pace. I figured I'd head out to West Chop and circle to Franklin Street, then make my way back in time to get the 2:30 p.m. ferry. *I should stay another night with my mother—maybe she needs me.* Still, I also thought we needed some distance to let this settle in and not be on top of each other, feeling the need to rehash what was said or weirdly ignore it the way we do, but I couldn't let us retreat to our previous practices. I thought about saying something to her about that—something where we agree to try and be different—accepting and making more of an effort. It'd be hard as the island, no matter how much I loved it and wanted to return, had memories that kept me away.

I wished there was a way to twist it so the good ones brought me back. But the evil and sickness in it all, along with the what-ifs, never allowed that to happen, and it seemed my mother had the same issue with the city. My face burned from the wind, and anger came, heating my veins. The thought of the man, whoever he was, hurting her and changing the trajectory of her life suddenly consumed me. Every footstep on the pavement vibrated my bones, and my heart collapsed into my stomach. I stopped, grabbed the bench by the library, walked around it three times to slow my breathing, and then sat, putting my head in my hands.

"I'm not thinking about this," I said, watching a bus pass. I started shivering as MVY radio announced its classical hour, and Richard Wagner's "Ride of the Valkyries" began to play. The song moved me because I chose it to be one of the cultural artifacts in nineteenth-century art and culture class junior year as a follow-up to a previous paper on Norse myths and history, researching a painting by artist Peter Nicolai Arbo titled *Valkyrie*. It depicted warrior-like women with armor, shields, helmets, and spears on their wingless flying horses, and for whatever reason, I loved it. For an art project, a classical piece of music was unusual, but my professor allowed it. It was played in the *Opera Die Walküre*. The Valkyries are female messengers of the god Odin, who soar down from the heavens into battle to take the souls of dead soldiers to Valhalla, the counterpart of paradise for men killed in battle. The piece, with a growing sense of foreboding, anticipating something will happen, is ominous and powerful, and it is nothing if not dramatic. It sounds as though it's evil, but that depends on the listener's view of death and ascension. I found it beautiful—this transition—or is it terrifying? There are many differing opinions, and I always felt it was a bit of both.

I started again, picking up my pace, reaching West Chop lighthouse, and passing the railed fence as the trees parted, revealing a ferry coming into the harbor. The briny smell of the sea invigorated me just as the chorus started. I ran harder, sprinting, as I pursed my lips to control my breathing, feeling like I was headed for battle. Racing now, I turned onto Franklin Street and soared past the walkers and bikers, smiling as I passed. The radio host introduced the next piece, and I slowed to a jog, then a walk, feeling my chest heaving as I panted, lifting my chin to the sky for air. I continued walking, putting my hands on my hips and feeling the moisture dripping down my back.

Thinking I'd take in the sounds of the island on the way back, I pushed my headphones down my neck when I saw it—Dagget Avenue. The green and white street sign loomed over me as a reminder that it was not finished and might never be—there will always be reminders. It surprised me that I was already here, closer to town, when it seemed like I should be back at least a block or two. Dagget led to Herring Creek Road, a short dirt path with a few small cottages. At least, that was how it used to be. It was Cat and Summer's street, where their house had been. I hadn't come close to coming down this way since, but here I was. I wasn't sure Cat even lived there anymore, and Summer, last I knew, left—New York? That's what Coop had said. My mother never said anything about them, and I found it hard to believe that if they were here, she wouldn't have run into them, although they weren't in the same circles. Cat had always kept to herself. She worked and came home; that's all I'd ever remembered. I only thought Summer may have left because I didn't see her in the graduating class picture from the high school in the *Martha's Vineyard Times* when I came home after college.

I stepped off the curb, quickly pulled my foot back, and paced, looking at the sign and then down the street. The song came into my mind again, and I envisioned the Valkyries, brave and bold, riding their flying horses down the road and feeling their wind as they passed. I'd seen the opera in Chicago on spring break that same year. I had gone with Jennifer Thorn, not someone I was particularly interested in being friends with, but we had been in some of the same classes. I couldn't remember how that even happened, us together, but I wanted to see it and feel, as the song spoke to me at a time when nothing much did.

Richard Wagner composed the music, the infamous song, and three other operas that compromised The Ring of the Nibelungs. I leaned against the stone wall on the corner, remembering all this, thinking there was a connection. These operas are based on the Norse saga about a tumultuous family and a race of gods pursuing a magical golden ring. There was so much connected: flying horses, golden rings, sisters. So much except courage. *Where was mine then?* My heart pounded with anticipation as if the song was playing again and the Valkyries were coming. I stood tall and tough, and without thinking, I turned the corner down the street.

The song coming on was a sign; it must have been. Seeing the house might do something, good or bad. I wasn't sure, but I existed off instinct these last few days, and while I'd love to think it wasn't steering me wrong, I couldn't answer that yet. The aftermath of it all, my father's denial, the truth about my mother, and my truth hadn't fully surfaced. I hoped it brought forth what I was searching for—healing, a chance to live and find myself again or create a new me, and a better relationship between my mother and me. I didn't want to think it, but I knew I wanted something from my father and me: a label, maybe, or closure—boundaries. I wasn't sure. A way to be sickened by his actions without understanding them and never trying to, but to feel his love for me as a daughter and mine for him as a father was real, even if we couldn't live that in the present. To recognize the past was real and that one part may have nothing to do with the other, I could accept, even though they have everything to do with each other now.

Chapter 22

My walk changed to a slow jog as the anticipation was killing me, and I also wanted to get this over with. Tears had already formed at the corners of my eyes, and I wiped them back hard with my hand just as the small red house came into view from the road. We hadn't been here often, Summer and I, but I knew every detail about it: the white shutters with paint chipping and the squeaky screen door. Summer's bedroom was upstairs to the right, with a traditional Cape's low ceilings and built-in drawers. There was only one bathroom on the first floor, and Summer had always commented on how nice it was at my house to have a bathroom near our bedrooms, to not go down the cold steps in the frigid night to pee. The house was tiny inside, but Cat kept it immaculately clean. Summer had lots of chores that I sometimes helped her do after school so we could hurry to my house. A smile emerged on my face, thinking of our walks and talks from Vineyard Haven to Oak Bluffs, sometimes catching a ride from someone we knew.

The bushes were overgrown, and I stopped at the house before it, wondering who lived there and where they were—Cat and Summer—and what they were doing. I hadn't seen it at first, but a green car was in the back between the two houses, and I couldn't tell which one it belonged to. It was old and beat up with rust on the hood. Maybe it'd been there awhile—trapped in time like us, at least my mother and me. I hoped Summer came out unscathed, but I couldn't see how. I could only envision her worse off than any of us. She was the victim, and just as I wanted to know her fate and where she was now, I didn't want to. I wanted to pretend she was somewhere far away, happy and safe. I twisted my hair, tucked it in my sweatshirt, trying to tame it, and turned, heading back up the road, envisioning the Valkyries flying by, defeated with no souls. I'd offer mine, but I was no warrior, and I should have been for Summer.

"Have you seen my cat?" a child's voice called, startling me. I twisted, seeing a little girl through a haze of dirt road dust, wondering where she'd come from.

"A cat?" I asked, shielding my eyes, squinting in the sun. I looked at the houses, not seeing anyone else.

"Willy. My cat is lost. Have you seen him?" she asked again, taking a few steps closer. Her hair was pulled back neatly with two mismatched barrettes, one pink and one blue, and she held a small Ziploc bag of what I guessed to be dry cat food.

"I haven't, but I bet he'll come if you shake that bag of food you got." I pointed.

She looked at the bag and started shaking. Food flew everywhere, as it wasn't closed.

"Willy!" she called, still shaking the bag.

"What's he look like?"

"He's gray and has a half-gray and half-white nose," she answered, pointing at her nose.

I scanned the area, seeing nothing, then heard a door slam and a voice.

"Lila, who are you talking to?"

A woman appeared in the driveway of the red house, just in front of the green car, and walked toward us. The sun was bright, and I couldn't make her out, only seeing her yellow hair and shape. She passed by the bushes, and I noticed her walk—it was her. It was Summer.

"Lila," she started again, looking at the girl, about to say more, then stopped as she saw me. We both stood a few yards away from each other, silent and stunned.

"Maddie?" she said after a few moments, looking as if she'd seen a ghost.

A lifetime of words clung to my throat, and I swallowed hard and repeatedly blinked, trying to focus—trying to speak. I coughed and swallowed again, barely getting it out; then, it came, just her name: "Summer."

"She is helping find Willy," the little girl said, coming close.

"What are you doing here, down here, I mean?" Summer said, not taking her eyes off me.

My cheeks flushed, and I fidgeted my hands. Why hadn't I thought she could be here—or Cat? I couldn't tell how she felt: angry, happy, annoyed. It was all unreal, like we were characters in a movie, playing ourselves, like a dream, but a reoccurring, familiar one. Everything about her I recognized, except she was older; we both were. But she appeared hardened and as though life had toughened her some, which didn't surprise me, but at the same time, it did. It was Summer, exactly her, with lighter, longer hair, filled out in the places women do. Last I'd seen her, she was a teenage girl—the girl that had taken residence in my thoughts all these years. I'd never thought of her in any other way, and here she was, grown and a woman with life experiences and a life beyond us, and I was both glad and mad about it.

I gazed up to the sky, searching for something to say, trying to remember her question. "I-I went for a run . . . here visiting my mother," I stuttered, watching her study me. "I guess I just sort of ended up here as if my legs knew where to go."

"Your mom is still here, over on East Chop?" she asked. She was pleasant, and I hadn't noticed it before, but she was nervous too. She pulled at her lip, which meant nerves, or she was thinking. It was usually a combination of both. She was thinking of what to say, feeling unsure.

"She is." I moved the dirt around with my foot.

"You're in the city, right? Writing at that magazine? I've read some of your stuff. It's good."

"Yeah, I am. And thanks," I said awkwardly, not expecting her to compliment me, let alone speak to me. "I didn't think you guys still lived here. I mean, I hadn't heard or seen—"

"I didn't; I left in high school, and now I'm back—well, I've been back for a bit," she said abruptly, cutting me off and turning around, eyeing the little girl.

"Coop said you went to New York?" I took a step closer. I wanted this to end, the awkwardness. I wanted to run and wished the Valkyries would swoop me up, fly me away, and take me out of there, but I knew I wouldn't have this chance again. I also wanted to talk to her and know everything about her, but I didn't. For so long, I was unsure if she was even real or that we existed because I stopped existing. But we did, and that validated and pained me more than I thought possible. My heart sputtered. I inhaled deeply, trying hard for her not to notice.

"Coop?" she said, smiling. "How is he? Do you still talk?" she asked, tilting her head from the sun.

"No—no, I ran into him just yesterday, oddly. I don't get to the island much. He's a painter, I guess."

"I thought I saw him once or twice at Dippin' Donuts, but I wasn't sure he recognized me. Maybe next time, I'll say hi."

"Yeah, I mean, he asked about you," I said, seeing her perk up, wondering if something was still there.

"Wow, okay." She shrugged, seeming unsure of what to say.

"I saw Hank too. He's an Oak Bluffs cop." I attempted a smile, watching her reaction.

She smiled. "Really? I thought I heard that. I think my mother told me when I was in New York. That's pretty funny."

"Yeah, I thought so too."

"How is Cat?" I asked, looking at the house and then over at the little girl on her knees with her head under the bushes.

Summer's face lengthened, and she glanced down at the dirt.

"She's . . . she died six months ago. That's why I'm here."

"Oh, my God!" I gasped, touching my heart. "I'm so sorry, Summer."

I wanted to go to her, hug her, or touch her arm, anything besides standing in this spot, frozen, unsure of my place.

"Cancer. She had breast cancer. I came back to take care of her, Lila, and me." She turned to Lila, who was by the trees, kicking rocks.

"I didn't know. My mother never said," I blurted. I wanted to put the words back in my mouth as I said them. I wouldn't know, and my mother wouldn't either, but we would have if we asked, only because everyone knew everything on the island, especially if someone died, even if you didn't run in the same circles.

"Well, there was no announcement in the paper. She didn't want that. Just me, Lila, and a few hair salon ladies," she said, her tone becoming defensive.

A heaviness filled the air between us. We stood, quiet, not knowing what to say, and I could feel this was it. This was the end.

"Willy!" Lila shrieked, running toward the car.

"Lila!" Summer shouted, walking a few steps toward her, then stopped as she emerged with the cat slipping from her arms.

"Oh, Willy. You bad boy. Where have you been hiding?" Summer said, patting the cat's head as Lila passed her, heading straight for me.

"This is Willy, my cat."

"Hi, Willy." Lila was Summer's daughter, and I was dumbstruck that it took me so long to realize. She was just like Summer, the girl I knew, my friend.

"Glad you're back, Willy," I said, touching the cat's nose. "He looks tired."

"Yeah, he is." Lila shook her head.

"My name is Lila; what's your name? Did you know my grandmother?"

Summer smiled, shaking her head.

"Lila, I love your name. I'm Maddie." I stuck my hand out. She looked down at her hands, wrapped around the cat, then back at me and shrugged.

"It's Lilac after a horse. But they call me Lila. Do you know the horse? She's at the merry-go-round. She's the purple one."

My jaw firmed, and I tried with everything I had not to let the tears come. I wiped my face with my sleeve and blinked hurriedly. "I do know Lilac. In fact, I just saw her yesterday." I wiped my face again.

"Are you okay?" Lila asked, tightening her grip as the cat squirmed.

"Yeah, yes—yes," I stuttered, "I'm okay. I knew your grandmother too. She was wonderful."

"Yeah, she was, but she was sick."

"I'm sorry."

"Lila, go put Willy in the house, okay? I'll be right there," Summer said.

Her eyes softened, and she bit her lip, watching Lila go, taking her time, before turning back to me. "Bye, Maddie," Lila yelled as she hurried toward the house.

"Bye, Lila. It was nice to meet you," I called, watching her disappear up the steps. The screen door squeaked and closed behind her.

"She looks just like you," I said, meeting her eyes, wondering if I should go and if my being here was hard for her if she hated me. My thoughts took over. I felt myself leave where we were—although my feet were unable to follow. I couldn't leave us, as right here was exactly where I wanted to be.

"I know, acts like me too." She chuckled, and I did too.

She turned serious and rubbed her hand against her leg, appearing nervous. "Maddie, I thought you hated me." She cleared her throat, staring at the ground.

My heart shattered, and I suddenly felt sick.

I blew out a long breath. "I guess I did. I mean, at first, I thought I did. But I never did. I never could," I stuttered. "You should hate me." My eyes glazed over, and everything blurred as the tears formed and fell, one after the other. "I do," I finished.

"Are you okay?" she asked.

Am I okay? She asked if I was okay. I was in disbelief hearing the words come out of her mouth. I didn't know how to respond, but I didn't overthink it, and I couldn't.

I pulled at my hair ends, twisting and swaying back and forth.

"Summer," I stammered, wishing there was something to hold on to. "Am I okay?" I squinted, looking confused. "Forget about me. I'm just—I'm just so—" I chewed on my lips, knowing I couldn't control myself.

"I don't hate you," she said, looking at me sternly. "I never hated you, Maddie. Why?"

"I'm sorry, Summer," I interrupted her. "I'm so sorry," I whined, rubbing my eyes firmly with my sleeve.

She hugged herself as it became colder. We wouldn't last here for long.

"What are you sorry for? You didn't do anything?" she asked, contorting her face.

"Didn't do anything?" My ears hurt, and my heart ached. My legs weakened, and I needed to sit.

"I didn't believe you. We never talked again. I-I—" I flailed.

"Maddie," she said loudly, not letting me continue. "We were kids. He's your father. I guess it never dawned on me that we wouldn't be friends anymore. I mean, it did, but not really. I'm unsure how I didn't anticipate that fully, but I was a kid. Everything happened so fast, and I just wanted it to stop." She shook her head. "It had to stop," she whispered, lowering her eyes. "But I never wanted us to." She looked at me. "But of course that would happen." She sighed, tipping her head to the sky.

"Neither did I." I sighed too, feeling lost.

"This is all hard for me to talk about." She breathed. "Clearly, it is for you too." She sidestepped toward the house, and her eyes met mine again. "It screwed me up good for a while. I took off to New York and got involved in some bad stuff I'm not proud of, but I went to therapy. I'm not sure how I got there, really, but I had to do something after Lila came." She breathed, raising her shoulders. "What I'm trying to say is . . ." She rubbed her arms, shivering, and tucked her chin to her chest. Her blond hair blew behind her as a gust of wind came, just as the sun appeared from behind the clouds, hitting her eyes and making them glimmer. "I'm sorry too."

I shook my head in disbelief. "You're sorry? You have nothing to be sorry for. He did this to you. I should have believed you!" I said, raising my voice and then quickly lowering it, composing myself, unsure who could hear.

"Why? Because I was your best friend?" She stared through me. "He's your dad, and he was good to us." She shrugged. "Just the other stuff—it was just that other shit." She struggled to speak.

I said nothing, putting my head down and breaking into pieces. I was sure she held back, trying to spare me, and if I were anyone else, she'd say more about him and what he did, or at least how he was a monster. She could say that to me. I wanted to tell her, but what was the point? We were dust.

She moved close, reaching to touch my arm, and I averted her eyes. She pushed my hair from my neck back, and I noticed a tattoo on her hand and followed it, reading it as she moved her hand to her side, trying to make out the words.

"Live with no regrets," I said, delighted at the memory. "Your father." I tapped her hand, and she picked it up, holding it in front of her.

"Yup. He was good for one thing—a saying." She laughed, rolling her eyes. I saw moisture in them, and she pressed the corners with her fingers.

We were there, just the two of us alone in the stillness of another lifetime.

Then she spoke. "Well, I have to go in. Work at four o'clock. I'm cutting hair at Mom's salon," she said, stepping backward toward the house.

"Really? That's great." The clouds came and then passed again quickly, exposing the sun that captured us in two beams that fell on the road.

"It's a living." She smiled, smirking in her familiar way.

A tear rolled down my cheek, passing my lips, and I tasted salt. This was it. "Okay. Well, I don't know what to say," I said, hating that I couldn't think of anything.

"Nice seeing you, Maddie," she said, her lips quivering. She turned toward the house and walked, glancing back, waving when she was at a safe distance.

"You too," I called, feeling my eyes burn, filling the never-ending river of us again. I watched, seeing her wipe her eyes as she walked, trying to hide it.

I struggled up the road and was about at the corner when I heard her.

"Maddie!" Summer yelled.

I turned, seeing her standing at the edge of the driveway.

"Lemonade!" she shouted.

Tears spilled down my face, and I walked backward, nodding my head up and down, beaming from ear to ear, and crying uncontrollably.

"Lemonade," I said softly, unable to speak, hearing my voice crack. Reaching deep into my belly, I pulled the word loud and strong, trying to believe what it meant, that I'd be okay, and she was. "Lemonade!" I called, clearing my throat and throwing up my right hand. "Lemonade," I said again, this time just a whisper, turning around, then back to her again for one last look. She walked up the steps to the house and waved one last time. I waved back, hearing the screen door screech.

As I turned the corner slowly, I started to jog, pulling up my shirt and wiping the tears and snot with the collar. I could barely breathe but ran as fast as my legs could carry me, cutting through side streets to the bridge and the base of East Chop. Just as the lighthouse appeared on Telegraph Hill, I stopped, clutching my head and catching my breath. My heart throbbed, and I trembled uncontrollably, trudging up the hill. I turned, walking backward, watching a ferry head into the harbor. Right then, I never wanted to leave, but at that moment, I traveled to the what-ifs and the should-have-beens. Looking across the water to Vineyard Haven and seeing the ferry pull in, I knew I had to go.

Nothing had changed, and everything had, but nothing would return to what it was. It never could. We were dust, remnants of a time gone by, and right now, I was happy, for once upon a time.

Chapter 23

"My name is Madeline Plympton."

"Can you spell your last name, Madeline?" Gabe Heinz asked.

"P-L-Y-M-P-T-O-N," a younger me sounded through the truck's speakers. Somehow, I figured out how to connect my phone to the truck's Bluetooth.

"Have you ever testified before?"

"No," I said, traveling back in time, recalling the day and how nervous I was. My stomach hurt as it did then. I'd already lived this but was in a fog about what was asked and what I said. I could only remember the feelings; they were coming to life in me again as I drove Route 24 away from the Cape back to Boston.

"So, it is your first time in court?" Heinz asked, clearing his throat.

"Yes."

"Okay. When you testify, make sure to answer the questions and avoid nodding. Okay?" He spoke to me as if I were a child, and I technically was, just shy of eighteen, but no babies were in the room that day.

"Okay. Yes," I answered.

"Madeline, where do you live?"

"I live in Oak Bluffs with my mother and father," I answered softly.

"Can you speak up some?" Heinz asked, and I repeated the statement louder.

"I live in Oak Bluffs," I repeated. My voice shook nervously.

"Is your dad here today?"

"Yes."

"Could you point him out for us?"

"He's right there."

"I'm going to ask you a couple of questions about a friend you had, Summer Starr. You know her, right?"

"Yes."

"When was the first time you remember meeting Summer?"

There was a long pause. And I remembered, lifting my head, scanning the courtroom, wondering why Summer wasn't there, expecting her to walk in at any moment. Initially, I hoped for the chance to confront her and speak of my belief in my father, and I hoped her seeing me and hearing my words would provoke her to tell the truth and admit that she had lied. But that morning, I flatlined at the thought, locking myself in the bathroom at the courthouse, listening to my mother knock, pleading on the other side of the door until I finally came out when she said my testimony might be the only thing that would help him. I couldn't have that on my conscience. I wanted him home and things to go back to how they were, but I didn't want to see Summer. I couldn't, and I was thankful I didn't have to because she wasn't there, choosing not to be. I'd find out after. She couldn't see me either. At the time, I thought it was because of her guilt, but not long after, I knew differently. She didn't want to see me for the same reasons I didn't want to see her. I knew she'd never lie, and I loved and missed her, and she missed me and never wanted to hurt us even though he was hurting her.

"She was one of my first memories. I remember her there and always being there."

"And her mom's name is Cat?"

"Yes."

"And how old were you when you two met?"

"I believe I was around four or five."

"And Summer is the same age as you?"

"Yes, our birthdays are a few months apart."

"Did Cat and Summer come and stay with your family for a time?"

"Yes."

"Do you know how that came to happen?"

"I think they had money troubles, and my mom and dad helped, but I don't know much."

"And you became friends with Summer then. Tell us about that: your friendship."

"She was like my sister. She was my sister. We hung out and would spend our days together."

"What kind of things did you do?"

"We painted and watched movies and had snacks. Things like that."

"When she lived with you, did she have her own room?"

"The art room was her room."

"At one point, she moved into her own house, right?"

"Yes."

"Did she still come and sleep over?"

"Yes, all the time."

"Would your dad sometimes hang out with you and Summer or take you places?"

"Yes."

"Did he take you to the beach?"

"Yes."

"Madeline, did you ever see anything transpire between your dad and Summer at the beach or anywhere else that worried you?"

"No. Of course not," I protested loudly.

"Did you ever see your dad touching Summer inappropriately?"

"No!" my voice shouted through the speaker, causing me to jump in my seat. I could hear that I was on the verge of crying, which ruined me. I felt so much in that moment for the girl I had once been and, by all accounts, still was—stuck in the past and reliving it for all these years.

As I turned onto 93 North to the city, the traffic slowed to a crawl, and for the first time in my life, I was glad for it. There was no rush to get home. At the moment, I wasn't sure I knew where home was. The trial continued with mundane questions from Gabe Heinz about our friendship and a couple of objections from Sarah Martin for things I didn't quite get. The day was long, and I could hear myself growing tired, like the rest of us, destroyed. The police, psychologists, friends, teachers, nurses, etc., all sounded well-rested and professional, their voices never changing much except to emphasize a point. It was apparent who the involved parties were: Summer, Cat, me, and my mother. We all sounded broken, in tears, and exhausted not long into our testimonies because of the choices, sickness, and unnatural urges of a man we all cared for, a man my mother loved. I did too, as much as I was torn between love, loyalty, and anger about the truth.

"Madeline, would you say you knew Summer well? She was your best friend, right?"

"Yes."

"Sister, you said. She was like your sister, correct?"

"Yes."

"Do you ever remember her gossiping about anyone or getting involved in gossip?"

I knew where he was going. Because he had prepared me for the question, I was ready to answer it, seething with anger, trying to dig up any time Summer misspoke about anyone: a landslide starting with a pebble, speeding toward the ground, picking up rocks, dirt, and disaster, leading to today's destruction. But now it felt wrong. The pebbles seemed just as they were—pebbles that amounted to nothing against her character.

I looked into the courtroom again at the faces, scanning for Cat, not seeing her. The only ones on their side were the salon ladies and a few others I didn't recognize. My insides twisted as they did the day Heinz asked the question. I'd reached the city, seeing the sleek buildings of the financial district as I headed under the overpass through Chinatown and followed 93 to Storrow Drive. The evening sun sat low in the sky as I turned onto the Harvard Bridge to MIT, where Kevin worked, to drop the truck. Cars idled and inched, like a parade procession, just as I turned onto the bridge, coming as close as I could to the car in front of me so the truck bed wasn't sticking out in traffic as the light turned. Jay finally responded to my text, telling me to drop it in Kevin's parking space and that I could leave the keys in the glove box, which I thought was brave, but Cambridge around the college was a safer area. Who was I to argue? I was glad not to have to go in and talk to him. I didn't want to talk to him or anyone. I only wanted to disappear.

"She sometimes did gossip." I winced, hearing my words.

"Can you give me an example?" Attorney Heinz asked.

A static sound came through the speakers, and my voice trembled. It was the moment I caught my father's eyes, and I had forgotten about that until now. I began to cry, trying my best not to. He looked at me, stoic and unfeeling. Then, there was the tiniest hint of a smile, and all I could feel was that it was my job to save him.

"She-she sometimes would say things about friends." I sniffed. "Other friends in our group," I said.

"May I approach, Your Honor?" Heinz asked.

"You may," said Judge Stone.

"Your Honor, I would offer this page as an exhibit."

"I object," Sarah Martin's voice rang out.

They argued for a while about a text message Attorney Heinz wanted to present between Summer and me. I'd forgotten about that, and I knew it was about Summer's then-budding friendship with Kaia and mine with Shelby Smalls. Things were changing, and our friend group was evolving in junior high. We were both sort of mid-level, not extremely popular, but not dweebs. We were friends with everyone, really. But starting around the seventh grade, Summer wanted to be more popular and fit in with Kaia and her group, the cooler girls in school. I did too, but it bothered me that Summer might think I wasn't enough. It was then that I started becoming a little more friendly with Shelby. In hindsight, it was to make Summer jealous, but I was the jealous one.

Traffic hadn't moved an inch, and I rolled down my window, sticking my head out to see. A few orange cones and a cop were at the end of the bridge, so there had to be construction or an accident. I glanced at my phone on the passenger seat and pressed the screen to see the time.

"Five o'clock. Rush hour," I said, moaning.

The traffic moved some and stopped in the middle of the bridge. The rowers glided on the Charles, getting the last strokes in before dark and the coming winter. I looked at the trees, seeing the varying shades of brown and orange; most still clung to the branches while a few fell to the ground.

"Madeline, sorry to keep you waiting. Can you tell me if there was a time that you thought you and Miss Starr were drifting apart?"

"Well," I started. "There was a time I was invited to a party, and Summer wasn't," I said. I thought this was profound during trial preparation, but that was a long time ago. At the time of testimony, I was nearly eighteen and realized how ridiculous it was, but there was nothing else to say.

Heinz went on about this and tried to lay a foundation for Summer being jealous of my friendship with Shelby. It wasn't that way; if it was, it was for a moment, just like my moments with her about Kaia. We were two young girls going through young girl things, except for Summer; she wasn't. She was going through hell, and here I was, worried about Kaia and Shelby. Small things that didn't matter but were the only things that should have.

"Madeline, let's move on. You and Miss Starr mostly slept in the same room when she stayed over, is that right?"

"Yes."

"Would you say you're a heavy or light sleeper?"

"Objection, Your Honor. There was a ruling in this line of questioning earlier," Sarah Martin said confidently.

"I'll allow it," Judge Stone said. "But to the point quickly, Mr. Heinz," she finished.

"You can answer, Madeline," Heinz said, clearing his throat. I envisioned his crooked tie and bulbous nose that reddened every time he raised his voice.

"I am, well, both. A light sleeper and heavy sleeper, depending on how tired I am," I responded, lacking confidence in my answer.

"Madeline, did you ever see your father near Summer?" Heinz asked loudly and quickly.

"No. I mean, he was near her, yes, but—" I stammered.

"Was he ever near her at night? Did you see him in the room near Summer while you were right there across from her? Did you see anything at all?"

The dreams weren't there yet, or were they? Or the thoughts I perceived to be dreams but were real memories. Everything was a haze, and there hadn't been anything unshakable since any of this, except for Jay. But it wouldn't have mattered then if I had remembered it, seeing my father near her and feeling something wrong. Blinded then by my need for him and a belief that things like this didn't happen—not to us—is what made life bearable. He was good; therefore, he couldn't not be. He couldn't sicken me. There was no perversion in Bill Plympton. He was strong and steadfast, and my world, more at that time than ever. If he was innocent, then we all were, and life could return to normal, at least some form of it. I envisioned it more than once: everyone apologizing, and life on the island would be the same—better even. Summer would apologize and get the help she needed because she must need some, making things like this up.

I'd always been proud to be his daughter. Nothing would immediately change that, even if I had seen it with my own eyes. I'm not sure I'd have connected it to reality; it would still have been a dream. This had always made me feel weak. I was weak for my friend, myself, and my mother. But who was strong for me? Then there were the dreams from all this, the repeated nonsense of my father doing things to Summer in the same room as me, on the same beach. To me then, it was unfathomable and unimaginable; every sign or clue was a dream created by what she said, playing tricks on my mind until they weren't dreams. There were no dreams. If there had been, they came after, from the reality of it, enhancing the truth after it was exposed. It was real. I knew it because I saw and felt it. I felt it then and remembered. I remember now and know.

"I never saw anything," I said.

I cried for that girl, who I was, feeling my hands shake on the steering wheel as I turned right off the bridge when the cop waved me on. My breathing shallowed, and my stomach hurt from hunger and emptiness. I pulled into the parking lot, space thirty-six, and put the keys in the glove box as instructed. The sun lowered behind the buildings, and shadows fell over the street. Everything darkened, and I did with it. I grabbed my phone to call Jay for a ride but paused, feeling stuck. There wasn't any closure or relief. It felt empty. I felt empty and as if there were still secrets to uncover and searching to do, but there weren't. Just moments were left in the trial audio, and then nothing was left except me.

Chapter 24

I grabbed Kevin's work coat in the back and put it on, thinking I'd walk—at least for a bit. I'd never been so tired, but I wasn't ready to sleep. Dreams come with sleep or restlessness. And I didn't want any. The past few years, lying there with nothing but thoughts I tried to avoid and only sleeping when I'd reached exhaustion. My headphones dangled from my bag, and I grabbed them, plugging them into my phone and shoving them onto my head. I rubbed my stomach, feeling the air press on my diaphragm, making it difficult to breathe. I held my breath every time I heard my voice. Although I had lived that day already, it still seemed new, and hearing my fear and grief was something I'd not experienced, as I'm sure most people hadn't. It agonized me, and I hesitated to press play as I headed out of the lot to the bridge, but masochistically, I did.

"Cross, Ms. Martin?" Judge Stone asked as someone sneezed.

"Yes, Your Honor," she answered.

"Good afternoon, Madeline. It's nice to see you again."

"Hello," I said, sounding hesitant.

"Madeline, or can I call you Maddie? I believe that is what you told me everyone called you when we spoke at the deposition last year?" Sarah asked in her euphonious way.

"Maddie is okay," I answered.

"Great. So, Maddie. I will be brief. You have certainly been through a lot today. I don't want to add to that much. A lot of evidence has been presented for the jury to review, and I want them to get to it."

"Okay."

Sarah reviewed the house's layout again, my family's relationship with Summer and Cat, and how it came to be—all the same things they asked Summer. I figured she was just trying to ensure it was accurate or that no one was lying.

"Okay. So, there is the basement, the main floor, and then another floor?"

"Yes."

"On that floor, there is your room, the guest room, and an art room, right?"

"Yes."

"And when Summer spent the night, you guys would hang out up there, in the art room?"

"Yes."

"You'd spend a lot of time in the art room?"

"Yes."

"Often, you'd sleep up there?"

"Uh-huh."

"Please say yes or no, Maddie, okay?"

"I'm sorry, yes. We mostly slept there."

"Thank you. When Summer slept over, you would stay up late sometimes, right?"

"Yes."

"Really late?"

"Sometimes."

"Okay. And Summer slept over almost every weekend, right?"

"Yes.

"And you both had known each other your whole lives and called each other your best friends, sisters even, right?"

"Yes."

"You did things together, like go to the movies or the beach?"

"Yes."

"Sometimes it wasn't just you two. Your dad was there, right?"

"Sometimes." I sighed.

"And sometimes your dad and Summer were alone?"

"Objection!" Heinz shrieked.

The judge paused, pressing her finger to her lips. "I'll allow it. But hurry, Ms. Martin."

There was a long pause before I spoke. "Not really," I answered.

"So, Summer and your father, Bill, right there"—she pointed; I recalled her movements and him looking away. It was the only time I saw it; his eyes changed direction— "were never alone?"

I walked hurriedly and turned up my collar in the cold, feeling like I was holding my breath, and I blew out forcefully. The disconnected feeling came again. I'd had it many times and did what I could, what I learned to keep it at bay, although I was unsure I cared this time. I breathed out again, then took a deep breath in, inhaling the evening air and trying to control my anxiety, learning this from somewhere, McLean's or Doctor Harper, maybe a meditation group; I forgot. I crossed the street to the bridge.

"I mean, they were sometimes, I guess."

"So, sometimes they were alone?" Sarah continued her questions, and I wanted to travel back in time and save myself.

"Were they ever alone in the ocean?"

"I think so. I don't know."

"So, you were always in the water with them?"

"I think so—I mean, no. I don't know."

Tears filled my eyes. I tilted my head, blinking as I walked steadily in the light of the passing cars.

"Did you ever get out of the water, and they were still in it?"

"Objection, Your Honor," Heinz gruffed in the background. "Asked and answered."

"There hasn't been a clear answer, Your Honor," Sarah said. Her sweetness and lisp disappeared.

"Quickly, Ms. Martin, quickly," Judge Stone warned.

"Madeline," Sarah said songfully now. It was sure to draw me in.

"Yes."

"Did you ever get out of the ocean, maybe to dry off or get something out of the car? Maybe you weren't feeling well, and Summer and your dad stayed in?"

"Yes," I answered, and it was true. I looked at my dad, pleading; his face stayed unchanged.

I'd forgotten that moment and so many moments. I wished they had stayed that way. My heart raced, and my head seemed detached, or my mind did; I wasn't sure. People walked toward me, threatening and unmoving. I maneuvered through them, averting my eyes from the headlights to the towering city above me, glowing from the remnants of a setting autumn sun.

"You and Summer met when you were four or five years old. Is that right, Maddie?"

"Yes."

"You girls did everything together?"

"Pretty much, yes."

"She slept over and went on vacations with you?"

"Yes," I said, exhausted.

"She went to the Park Plaza Hotel in Boston every New Year's with you and your mom and dad, right?"

"Yes."

"And you told each other everything?"

"Yes."

"You saw each other nearly every day at school and after?"

"Yes."

"And Summer slept over almost every weekend and lived with you with her mom, Cat, when you were both young?"

"Yes."

"I have just a few more questions, Maddie."

"Okay."

"Being best friends, you trusted each other?"

"Yes," I said, hesitating.

"Did you know Summer to lie?"

"Umm—no. I mean, no."

"No?" Sarah asked.

"No."

"Did you and Summer have a falling out? Were you having problems as friends?"

"Well, no. Not that I think," I replied, my voice cracking.

"Maddie. Did Summer ever tell you about being assaulted by your dad?"

"Never," I said. My voice was breaking and firm.

"You cared about Summer, right?"

"She is like my sister. *Was* like my sister." I was on the verge of cracking.

"Maddie, your dad is on trial here, right?"

"Yes."

"You love your dad, right?"

"Yes." I cried softly at first.

"He's always been there for you, right?"

"He always has." I cried, becoming louder.

"And he loves your mother and takes care of you both?"

"No matter what."

"You don't want to believe what's happened here, is that right?"

"I can't believe it!" I wailed.

There was a long pause, and I heard nothing except myself crippled and crying.

"I have nothing further," Sarah said coolly.

I started to run as the closing arguments began, but my bag slowed me down. Gasping for air, I couldn't breathe again and tossed the bag in front of me, watching it slide across the sidewalk and stopping at the guard rail on the bridge. Feeling dizzy, I grabbed onto the railing, putting my head between my knees. I needed to keep running away from here, from where anyone could see me.

"Are you okay, miss?" a woman asked, slowing in front of me. I turned my face into her briefcase and looked up at her, waving her away.

"I'm fine. Just—go." I gasped, pushing the hair from my face and shoving it into my coat collar. I closed my eyes, listening to the cars, and stood facing the water, clutching the rail with both hands. Minutes passed that felt like hours as Heinz and Sarah made their closing arguments in my ear. I barely listened. An inner stillness washed over me, and I opened my eyes, seeing the river's ripples glow from the city night lights as far as I could see. It was eerily quiet except for the voices in my ear, and I turned, seeing no one else on the bridge. A sudden burst of relief overcame me.

I stood, silent and cold—stuck between my past and any chance I had for a future, but right now, there was nothing. It was like I didn't exist. The present wasn't here, and neither was I. My hands molded to the railing, waiting for the verdict as all the hope I had that day filled me, and I started to choke, not expecting it. Judge Stone read the jury's instructions; her detailed and thought-out words left nothing to chance. The verdict would be clear even if I didn't already know what it was. There was no smoking gun or eyewitness account, but there didn't have to be. The mountain of circumstantial evidence and expert witness testimony was compelling. That's all they needed, and I barely knew any of it.

I never heard it. I never knew everything—what they had said and what everyone would say. Just my father's words of it being a mistake—a misunderstanding. I based everything on one thing: because he was mine. This, alongside the testimony of a young girl, an innocent victim who never wavered for years and lost everything, and every action after that supported everything she said. The same could not be said for him. But even here alone on the bridge, I had the same hope as I did then before they read the verdict . . . as if my emotions had memory. Because if things could be different, I wouldn't be here now, alone, with just myself. There was nothing left but me, who I am now and who I'm expected to be. It was said and done. It was final. There was nothing more to know and nothing else to do except find or fix me; all that was left was me and a choice to live beyond it. To some, that may be freeing. I hoped it would be, but it was more than I could bear.

Just as the lead juror read the verdict, I tore my hands from the railing and picked up my bag, shuffling along the sidewalk, shivering and hopeless. I listened intensely, trying to drown out the traffic. The bustling city ahead of me was one I was unsure I could enter, fitting in and drifting along with everyone. They had a purpose and a destination. My soul had no home. There was some cosmic disconnect, and I no longer belonged in my shell.

"On count one of the indictments, aggravated felonious sexual assault without penetration. What say you, Madam Forelady and ladies and gentlemen of the jury?" Judge Stone asked.

"Guilty as charged, Your Honor," she said. I listened, hearing us burst into tears, my mother and me. A scream of "no" shot through me as I recalled my mother collapsing into my arms.

"On counts two and three of the indictments, aggravated felonious sexual assault with penetration. What say you, Madam Forelady and ladies and gentlemen of the jury?"

"Guilty, Your Honor."

My heart slowed to normal, and my breathing reset. Gently, I pulled my headphones off and disconnected them from my phone. I tossed them both over the railing, hearing a small splash between the noises of the city around me. There were no cars—no other people. It was only me, with thousands of others out there, but not here. A truck turned onto the bridge, speeding quickly on the open road. My eyes fixed on its lights, watching them flicker and dim with each bump. I set my bag down again and turned toward the road, moving onto the curb and feeling it shake below my feet. The city went silent, and so did I. I closed my eyes, and there was nothing.

Chapter 25

"Hey, you," a voice said, and I turned from the mirror. "Jennifer, is that you?" I smiled, drying my hands and tossing the paper napkin in the barrel.

"It's been so long." She came close, giving me a polite hug. "Look at you, all fancy."

"I know, right?" I turned to face the mirror again, hardly recognizing myself in the crisp white strapless gown and diamonds around my neck. The necklace was borrowed from my mother's jeweler on Newbury Street, and I was terrified of losing it. "I haven't dressed this fancy since New Year's Eve here as a kid. I hated it then, but tonight I'm sort of—"

"It suits you," Jennifer interrupted, reaching into her purse and pulling out lipstick.

"How are things at *North Shore News*?" I asked.

Jennifer Charles was the editor there. It was a well-crafted magazine she started that took off in the north of the Massachusetts area. I'd interviewed with her before taking a permanent position at *Boston Living*. I declined, feeling I was betraying Jerry to even speak to another magazine after he offered me a job at the end of my internship, but I needed to see what was out there.

"We're good. Wish you had come aboard way back when?" she asked, applying the crimson color, and I wondered if my mother was here yet.

"Jerry and I are a thing." I laughed. "I couldn't break his heart." I put my hand to my chest, ensuring the necklace felt secure.

"You certainly make a good team, Madeline. Congratulations." She touched my arm.

"Thanks, Jen. See you out there."

I walked out of the restroom into the lobby, feeling the energy in the room. Servers passed trays of champagne, and a trio of classical musicians played in the corner where the gingerbread house usually was. I scanned the room for Jay, annoyed he had moved from where we'd been. I looked again, finally spotting him near a cluster of gold balloons, and headed over.

"I'm honored, absolutely honored," Bruce beamed as I approached, grabbing my hands and stretching my arms.

"Thank you, Bruce. It's me who's honored—really. Here at the Plaza. I'm just glad the award committee asked for suggestions." I leaned in and kissed his cheek.

"Well, thank you, Madeline. It's a prestigious and incredible event," he said proudly.

"The Park Plaza is quintessential Boston and a New England landmark. I'm glad they decided to have it here and not that new place in the seaport district."

"Northeast Regional Writer of the Year, Madeline," he said, resting his hand on my shoulders. "I'm sure they listened a little," he finished, nodding to Jay.

"Plus, you know the city, and the subject matter fits," Jay interjected. "You just did a piece about the Plaza before," he went on, grabbing a mini crab cake off a tray as a server passed, tossing it in his mouth.

Bruce put his arms around Jay and me, pulling us in. "Well, I am just glad to see you both, and you give me a shout if you need anything," he said, his bright white teeth glowing against his tan. "I am off to do a sound check," he said, being silly, raising one arm and twirling as he headed toward the ballroom.

"He's a nice guy," said Jay, kissing my cheek.

"He is." I smiled, looking at everyone dressed in tuxedos and gowns. It felt special, just like New Year's.

"I'm proud of you, Madeline Plympton. Have I told you that?" Jay asked, grabbing another hors d'oeuvre as a waiter passed.

"You have, sir." I tossed my hair and sidled up to him.

"Come closer, why don't you?" He grabbed my waist, pulling me in front of him.

I grabbed his lapels. "You in this monkey suit, I think I just might." I laughed, feeling for his hand.

"And you look stunning, I might add." He squeezed my hand, smiling, showing his dimple. I'd never seen him look so handsome.

"There she is!" a boisterous voice said, and Jerry appeared, standing out in the crowd.

"Look at you," I said, widening my eyes.

"I know. I know. It's a rental," he said, shaking Jay's hand and adjusting his bow tie.

"Like me, you don't usually go to these things, Jerry, I gather?" Jay said.

"That's a loser's statement, Jay, that I've said many times." He slapped his back. "We're winners now!" he shouted, grabbing my hand, and I pulled away to wipe something from his sleeve.

"Powdered donuts?" I winked.

"You caught me, Maddie. You always do."

"Nothing gives her more pleasure," Jay quipped.

"Okay, okay. Let's not form alliances, boys," I said.

"But why?" Jerry asked just as a voice came over the intercom.

"Ladies and gentlemen, please make your way into the ballroom."

"Shall we?" Jay said, bending his arm.

"We shall," I replied, putting my arm through his.

"Let's roll, folks." Jerry barreled ahead of us, grabbing a handful of food from a tray on the bar. I rolled my eyes at Jay, and he smiled.

"Madeline," a voice called, and I turned, seeing Doctor Harper. He was in his usual suit, choosing the blue one today over the brown.

"Doctor Harper, hi." I faced him. "What's this?" I said, clutching his tie.

"Tonight is a big deal," he said.

He appeared odd and uncomfortable outside his office, and I wasn't sure if it was him or me.

"It must be. In all our sessions, I've never seen a tie on you." I let go, reintroducing Jay as they had only met briefly at McLean's but knew all about each other. Jerry was long gone, and I was sure already eating at our table as I'd seen them passing plates through the entranceway.

"I didn't think you'd come," I said as the people walked past, narrowing into the room. "You know the whole patient-doctor thing you explained when I invited you." I nudged him, being cheeky, which did nothing to change his rigidity.

"Tonight, I can just be Robert." He stood straight, smoothing out his jacket. "And Robert and Doctor Harper, well—" He paused. "We are both proud of you."

Moisture filled my eyes, and Jay caught it. "No-no-no. Not now, Maddie." He rubbed my back. "Save it for later."

"Okay. I know, Jay." I waved my hands in front of my eyes to dry them.

"Sorry," Doctor Harper said.

I lifted my dress over my shoes, grabbed Doctor Harper's arm, and started walking. "And no. There is no Robert. I mean, there is." I looked at him, confused, nodding my head. "Doctor Harper is my doctor and the man who's helped me. So, this award and this article and—let's be honest—my life, I owe a lot of that to you. There's no shame in it," I said, pulling him with me.

"Thank you, Madeline. But you did and continue to do the work."

"There's no hiding you, Harper; you're a huge part of the piece," I went on.

"I know. I know." He nodded, walking alongside us.

"You're a celebrity now, Robert." Jay patted him on the back, raising his eyebrow at me as he sensed the doctor's discomfort, knowing he was skeptical about letting me mention him in the work.

Jerry confirmed that our table had a few extra seats as Gayle, the fashion editor, and her husband were ill. I pulled out Doctor Harper's chair on the other side of me and nodded, reassuring him it was fine, looking at him firmly, letting him know that I wouldn't take no for an answer. He was a big part of it all, one of the largest parts, and without him, I wouldn't have had the courage to live, let alone write about it.

They cleared the plates, and dessert and coffee were delivered just as the lights dimmed and the music faded. Nina Brown walked to the podium, modestly dressed as she always was in a black pantsuit, except this evening, she wore heels, and her platinum hair had a shape to it, framing her heart-shaped face just so. I'd only met her in person once when I came to the awards four years ago when the magazine had been nominated for an article about the best coffee shops in the city by the longtime food writer Maria Guzman. But I'd seen Nina on magazine cover after magazine cover and in the *Globe* at least a few times a year. She was always in the spotlight, making significant gains for magazines and implementing new marketing strategies. She kept abreast of the changes in the publishing world and saw the future well before it arrived. Her look was always the same—a dark-colored power suit and no smile—which I'd heard was purposeful so she would be taken seriously as a woman in a man's world, which, without a doubt, publishing was.

I felt a flurry of activity behind me, and I turned, seeing my mother handing her wrap to a server and hurrying toward me with Marta trailing behind. She'd pinned up her hair, except one red curl fell out of place in front. I enjoyed the imperfection. She looked classic and effortless as usual: a sleeveless burgundy top paired with a long gold chiffon skirt. The whole look was designer, no doubt. It was unlike her not to have her arms covered. She'd said it was a faux pas many times for women of a certain age, and I never knew why because her arms were better than most thirty-year-olds. But it was summer in the city and a humid ninety degrees. Everyone was hot; even in the air-conditioning, it lingered for a while once you came in.

"Madeline," she whispered, leaning in and air-kissing each of my cheeks. "I'm so sorry we were late," she said, flustered, and headed to the empty seats on the other side of Doctor Harper. "The pilot was late," she went on. "It was an awful situation."

Marta moved behind her, taking a chair and nodding at me. I could tell she'd had enough of Missy Plympton. She had a distinct look when she did and became quiet, and here it was.

"It's okay, Mother. I'm glad you're here." I smiled as Jay waved to them.

"I'm so proud of you," she said, beaming, leaning across Doctor Harper. I'd never seen her beam.

"You remember Doctor Harper, right, Mother?"

He sat unmoving, only smiling uncomfortably.

"Why yes, yes, of course, Doctor Harper," she said, seeming confused about why he was here.

"Hello, Mrs. Plympton," he said, turning quickly toward her and then away again.

Nina finished her opening monologue about the writers of our great area and the emergence and calling for more marginalized people in the arts. We listened to all the awards given to some excellent writers and colleagues with whom Jay and I were familiar, along with the publications they belonged to.

Every day for years, I have awakened with nervous trepidation about the coming day. I'd get through it, only trying to survive until I didn't care about that anymore. I wanted to live but didn't know how. Tonight, I felt the same nervousness, but it was different. Physically, the same feelings emerged; my stomach flipped, and I felt heat move up my neck, but for a living experience and one that excited me. A feeling that I wasn't sure I would ever conjure again.

I scanned the table, studying the faces of these people who cared about me. It was my life that they were in, and I in theirs, which was meaningful and had a purpose. Our relationships led me to find myself and the freedom to think again about more than what happened, and I gave myself permission to love and be loved and to feel each moment. Right now was a big one.

Bruce walked the aisle by our table and stopped standing against the wall, watching, his hands folded. Just as Nina announced the Writer of the Year award, I glanced at him, and he winked.

"Here we go," Jerry squealed, bouncing in his seat and pulling at his beard.

"Northeast Regional's Writer of the Year is given to risk-takers and dream-makers. People who capture the spirit of living and compel us to feel more, live better, reflect, and see things through different lenses or sharpen an idea that has dulled. Writers who turn things on their heads." She smiled, tucking her hair behind her ear. "This year, we have a writer who did just that and more, recounting the art and artifacts in her life that have linked her to her existence when she felt, at times, she didn't exist. The courage this young writer exemplified to discuss her own battle with depression, threaded with the brilliant examples of art in and around New England, such as the carved wooden horses on the historical Flying Horse's carousel on Martha's Vineyard and the exceptional pieces that hang here in the Plaza. Linking her life and searching for its meaning, gathering proof of her existence in these pieces and the many that she states have given testimony to her life; the testimony she needed moved us all," she said and then paused.

Jay grabbed my hand and squeezed, and Jerry's eyes were transfixed on the stage and moist with tears.

"Who would have thought the industrial design of our very own Citgo sign would have so much power?" She laughed. The crowd joined her, and Jerry stood, putting his fingers in his mouth, whistling.

"Power beyond the hundreds of thousands of dollars it takes to light it," someone shouted, and everyone laughed again.

"I am thrilled to announce that this year's award for Northeast Regional's Writer of the Year goes to Madeline Plympton of *Boston Living Magazine* for her three-part series titled 'Art Is Life and Life Is

Art.' The editor is Jerry Wentzel," Nina shouted and clapped, moving away from the podium.

Jerry jumped up and down, and the crowd applauded, watching our table. Jerry grabbed my hand and pulled as I attempted to kiss Jay but missed as he dragged me. I waved, seeing my mother clapping, and headed for the stage.

I hugged Nina and shook her hand as she handed me the plaque, which I gave to Jerry. He kissed it and held it up in the air, and everyone laughed and applauded some more. I smoothed my dress, looking into the sea of writers, editors, and all walks of life in the publishing world. Jerry stood behind me, and I unfolded my paper, seeing the blurry words on the page as the lights blinded me, making it difficult to read.

"This certainly is a surreal moment that I never expected," I said, my heart beating fast. I felt my hand shaking and glanced over at Jerry. "I'd first like to thank my editor, friend, and mentor, this very mundane man over here, Jerry Wentzel," I said, grinning and reaching out my hand to him. He took it, holding it tightly. The crowd applauded again, unable to resist Jerry's palpable excitement. "I presented him with an idea that was unlike anything I'd written, and it was not in the magazine's usual wheelhouse." I folded the paper and spoke from the heart. I knew what to say. I'd lived it so many times, it came easily once I'd pressed my fingers together—the trick Doctor Harper taught me to calm myself. "He was hesitant. But he trusted me." I took my hand back from him and looked at him, smiling. "He always has. Depression is difficult to discuss, and I know this all too well." I breathed. "There is a stigma attached to it, which almost killed me." I paused, pushing back my hair. "Secrets can destroy you. And while we all have pain and a past, and some of us have experienced more trauma than others, each and every one is okay to discuss. The people in our lives and our life experiences define us, both the good and the bad. I didn't get into specifics about my life in my piece; there is no need because the topic applies to us all. And if I do, it may be for another publication."

Jerry laughed, tapping me.

"But certain events led me on a downward spiral. I'd lost myself. The feeling of hopelessness in the disease and thinking that there is nowhere to turn crushes the soul. In my darkest hours, I searched for meaning and needed proof that I existed somewhere before this took over because I'd forgotten what living was and wasn't sure I had lived." I looked at the clock and moved closer to the microphone. "In that journey, the art proved my existence and linked my relationships: classical music, hand-carved horses, paintings, buildings, bridges, trinkets, fabrics, and last, the fabulous 1960s pop art signage that looms over our beloved Fenway Park." I chuckled, and the crowd laughed. "These were my proof of life and reminders that I'd lived before my pain. I'd wandered for so long, but all along, I'd had a home; it just wasn't what I'd envisioned or known. It was art that anchored me. It always had. I just lost my way, and with the help of a wonderful doctor, a supportive partner, a mother, and a backdrop of essential characters, I've found it again. Art is life, everybody. Thank you," I finished. Jerry came over and scooped me into his arms, kissing me on the cheek, his beard scratching my face.

The crowd cheered, and Nina clapped at the side of the stage. We headed out into the lobby. I spent the next hour shaking hands and talking to all kinds of familiar and unfamiliar faces making introductions and applauding me on my work. I'd noticed my mother speaking to Bruce and wondered how she was feeling being here.

"I'm heading home," Dr. Harper said, stretching out his hand for me to shake. I grabbed and hugged him. He didn't reciprocate initially, then patted my back with one hand. "See you Thursday," I said, and he smiled, turning to the door. Jerry was at the bar with a group of people amid a story. His hands flailed all over as he had everyone's attention. I could see his red nose sticking out through his beard and knew he was feeling tipsy, and I was happy for him.

"We have to get going, sweets," Jay said, looking at his phone. I glanced over his shoulder. "Oh, crap," I shouted, seeing the time.

"Jeesh," he said, pulling away.

"I'm sorry." I laughed, realizing I'd yelled in his ear. "Let me go say goodbye to my mother."

"Say goodnight for me. I'll call for the car," he said as I hurried away, wincing from my aching feet.

"Sorry to interrupt," I said, touching Bruce's back.

"Here is the star," Bruce said.

"Jay and I have to go. Mom, are you flying back tonight?" I asked.

"Actually, Bruce said we should stay here for the night," she said, glancing at Marta and taking a sip of champagne.

"Oh, that's great," I said, surprised.

"It will be nice to see the new décor and design. Bruce was telling me all about how they chose it and—"

"That's wonderful," I interrupted, knowing I had to hurry. I wanted to ask if she'd stay in the penthouse but figured it best to leave it alone. We were both making efforts, and her being here tonight was a valiant one—*one step at a time.*

"Okay, thank you so much for everything, Bruce." I hugged him and Marta. "And thank you for coming."

Her glasses slid down her nose as she said, "I wouldn't have missed it."

"Madeline, can I speak to you for a moment? Privately," my mother asked, and I followed her to the couch in the corner, wondering what I was in for. We'd come so far, and I was happy where we were. We were different and had evolved into a relationship beyond before; as much as it was different, it was ours.

She sat, patting the seat next to her, crossing her legs. More of her hair had fallen out of the gold ornament she had it pinned to. I took my hand, moving it behind her ear. Her lips were darker than usual, a pale burgundy matching her shirt. I liked it, thinking of the picture of her free and alive.

She took my hands. "Your father wanted me to tell you how proud he is of you," she said nervously and seriously.

I became quiet, unsure of what to say. After a few moments, I spoke.

"I know that he is. He wrote me a letter," I said, clasping her hands.

"You read it?"

"I did." I breathed. "This one. I did."

"Well then. Okay," she said, standing and smoothing her skirt.

"I love you, Mother." I kissed her cheek. "Thank you for coming."

"Of course, Madeline," she said, our eyes meeting.

"See you in two weeks. Oh, and have my crab cakes from Larson's ready. Don't forget," I called out, waving as I rushed to the exit.

"I will, and while I love my granddog, I'd like grandchildren," she shouted, unlike her.

I laughed, following behind some people to the sidewalk, and walked to the car as the valet opened the door.

"Thank you," I said, reaching into my purse and handing him a twenty.

◆ ◆ ◆

"The Sox must have gone into extra innings," Jay said as we passed Fenway. I rolled down my window, seeing the spotlights and feeling the baseball energy, listening to the noise from the crowd. The Citgo sign towered over the field with its flashing lights and the soft neon glow of the letters against its illuminated background. You could see it for miles, lighting up Boston's clear night sky every night, and the predictability in that was rhythmic and beautiful. That night on the bridge, I'd had no hope. Seeing Summer and that she survived, had a daughter, and was living on the island, back where it happened, should have inspired me. It should have brought the smallest amount of peace, enough to go forward, but it crushed me. All that was left was me without her, without the island and what was, and without the shame of my father. There was a different version blooming between my mother and me, but it wasn't enough for me to cling to. The thought that I had to create a life from scratch, with the foundation being the poisoned dust of another, was more than I could take. The feat seemed too much, and I had no strength left at even the thought. They had the island, she and my mother. I'd never have it as I had then, and I accepted that I wouldn't and couldn't. It comforted me that she did. I hoped she'd be happy there.

When I turned to the truck, I felt free but different. Different from I'd felt that day on the bathroom floor. I felt free that it was over and chained to the possibility that it would never be unless I cut my chains. At the moment, after hearing my pain at the trial and experiencing it again, I thought that it meant dying and ending it all. But it was different, and I was confused. I didn't want to die. I wanted someone to show me how to live. I wanted a home and longed for my heart to have a place as it once did.

I froze as the truck passed, feeling the blowback from its wind. I opened my eyes just as it passed, seeing the Citgo sign. Then something clicked, and that night, like so many before and so many after, its light guided me home. I'd had this home for a long time with Jay, in our apartment, in the city, and at the magazine with Jerry. Boston University and McGinty's: this was all mine. I had created a life; I just wasn't present in it. I was stuck, but it was there, and my life was more than dust; it was full. It once was with Summer and the island, and it is now. I had a life if I wanted to live it, and Doctor Harper helped show me how.

"He is going to be so mad," I said, following Jay up the steps.

"I know. We're bad parents." I heard rumblings in the apartment and a yelp as Jay put the key in the door.

"Blue!" I said, passing Jay, pulling up my dress, and kneeling before him. "Blue. I'm so sorry." I hugged him, watching the little Boston terrier wag his tail wildly, yelping and barking, darting between Jay and me.

"Let's go, Blue boy," Jay said, grabbing the leash from the coat hook. He jumped, becoming airborne, circling in front of him. "I'll be right back, winner," he said, clipping on Blue's leash and heading out the door.

"I'll be here," I said, wincing again as I unstrapped my heels, tossing them on the floor. I walked over to my desk, put the plaque on the shelf above it, and stood back, admiring it, thinking of her, Summer. I thought of her and me and let go of my father's shame and the Summer before—us before. I let go of what we could have been.

Summer and I would never be friends again, and I wasn't sure I'd ever fully get over that, but I accepted it. Our friendship and life together had been stolen, hers more than anyone's, along with our innocence. It didn't surprise me that once again, she showed me her resilience and kindness, and that day in front of her house, our sisterhood was there. If we never saw each other again for the rest of our lives, it still existed in both of us. I was sure of this now more than ever.

I leaned back on the couch, putting my feet on the coffee table just as the door burst open. Blue ran in, jumping on me, dirtying my dress.

"Oh no, Blue, get down!" Jay yelled, shooing him with his arms.

"It's fine." I laughed. "When am I wearing this again?" I said, patting Blue's head as he licked my face.

"Hey, I think there's a big future for you around here, writer girl," Jay said, hanging up the leash and his tuxedo jacket.

"Oh, yeah?" I said, smiling and watching him pick up my shoes. "I guess you may have some competition."

"I look forward to the challenge," he said, disappearing with the shoes and bringing them into the bedroom. He opened a window as he always did during the Red Sox season, listening to the sounds. The fresh air revived me, although it was humid and stagnant, but tolerable, with the air-conditioning that hummed from the other window. I sat back, thinking of the night.

"Do you want something to drink?" he asked, opening the fridge. Just then, cheers erupted from outside in the distance.

"Lemonade," I said, peering out into the night.

"Did you say lemonade?" he asked. "We don't have any lemonade, I don't think," he said, rummaging through the fridge.

"I know," I said and kissed Blue on the head.

Acknowledgments

Writing this book was anything but easy. Darker topics never are. For those who've experienced trauma, writing can be a way of reliving it; for those who haven't, it's an attempt to capture emotions that are both elusive and profound. Terrible things live among us—and for some, within us. It's a reality we cannot ignore, and we never truly know how we'll respond when confronted with darkness.

First and foremost, my deepest thanks go to my husband, Jason. Your unwavering support and love, even through the most challenging moments, carried me through this journey. Despite the hardships we faced as a family, you stood by me every step of the way, and I couldn't have done this without you.

To my friends and family, I am endlessly grateful. This past year has been filled with difficulty, and losing my mother—my biggest fan—made me question whether I could keep going. Yet here I am, still writing, still moving forward, finding peace in the love and authenticity that surround me, and feeling her presence by my side.

My heartfelt thanks to Koehler Books and the entire Koehler team for believing in this project. A special thank-you to Abbey Remer, my first-round editor and brilliant writer, and to the incredible publicity team at CP Media Management. A huge thank-you to my media marketers, beta readers, reviewers, and the incredible members of my launch squad. Your collective efforts have been invaluable in bringing this book to life.

To the professionals who work tirelessly to support victims of sexual assault—law enforcement, first responders, medical personnel, attorneys, and advocates—you are true heroes. Your strength, compassion, and dedication give survivors hope. The courage I witnessed during my research has left a lasting impression on me.

To the families and friends of both victims and perpetrators: You too bear the weight of these traumas. It's time to break the silence, shame, and stigma surrounding these crimes. The more light we shine on these dark corners, the less space there is for darkness to grow.

And to the voiceless victims: You are not broken. I hope this book offers you some solace and helps you find the healing and support you need.

If you or someone you know is a victim of sexual assault, please don't hesitate to reach out. Call 1-800-656-HOPE (4673) or visit the RAINN (Rape, Abuse & Incest National Network) website. On Martha's Vineyard, you can contact the Martha's Vineyard Community Services' CONNECT to End Violence program, where part of the proceeds from this book will be donated. Their twenty-four seven crisis hotline is 508-696-7233 (SAFE).

CONNECT's mission is to reduce domestic and sexual violence on Martha's Vineyard through education, advocacy, and community mobilization, as well as providing crisis intervention, counseling, and support services for victims.

Printed in the USA
CPSIA information can be obtained
at www.ICGtesting.com
LVHW042103170924
791345LV00023B/120/J